C
R
O
S
S

Also by Austin Duffy

The Night Interns

Ten Days

This Living and Immortal Thing

CROSS

AUSTIN DUFFY

MELVILLE HOUSE
BROOKLYN • LONDON

CROSS : A NOVEL

First published in Great Britain by Granta Books, 2024

First Melville House Printing: September 2024

Melville House Publishing
46 John Street
Brooklyn, NY 11201
and
Melville House UK
Suite 2000
16/18 Woodford Road
London E7 0HA

mhpbooks.com
@melvillehouse

ISBN: 978-1-68589-177-0
ISBN: 978-1-68589-178-7 (eBook)

Library of Congress Control Number: 2024939448

Printed in the United States of America
1 3 5 7 9 10 8 6 4 2

A catalog record for this book is available from the Library of Congress

For my mother, Pauline Duffy

'It is very important to know why the senses exist. What are the eyes for? For not seeing. There's what cannot be seen, cannot be heard, cannot be said . . . What about the mouth? The mouth is for keeping quiet.'

Mariscal, from *All Is Silence* by Manuel Rivas

I

IT WAS HIS job to know things and boy did Our Francie know things, flying around in that Datsun Cherry of his. Francie knows, we'd say, Francie knows. Sure he'd practically know your business before you knew it yourself. He'd know who was back in town before anyone had seen them hanging around The Square. He knew who was on the up or who was lying low and thinking of going on the run down the South. He knew who'd had a good night at the dogs the previous Thursday or who'd been giving jip to who at Lacey's on the Saturday. And he knew who was marked and who was seething and who was out for blood. Sure, he'd know all about your uncle before your cousins told you. Francie just knew things, mundane as they come, what no one in their right mind would consider worth knowing. The make and colour of a man's car for example, or the varied routes he might drive it on any given day of the week. He would know what a man's soft edges were, the habits and indulgences that made up his life, such as his fondness for the pastry buns sold across the street from his place of employment. He would know the man's family, the names and birthdates of his children, what ailed his aged parents and which outpatients' they attended for it. He'd know the hobbies of the man's wife, which afternoons you'd find her at the tennis club and when she'd get together with the girls. Francie kept track of all of it, more perhaps than was advisable, far more than was strictly necessary. He would follow the man to the barbershop, to his weekend four-ball, to his church on the sabbath, where he'd sit and watch him worship from the side aisles. He would know that he sang in a choir, and that the choir met every fortnight in the town hall in Dungannon. That it was hard for a man of habit to break his habits, especially if they were nature's habits, and Francie even knew the man had prostate trouble. Meaning that the very first thing he would do upon arrival at the town hall of a Tuesday evening was beeline to the gents to empty his bladder, full from the long journey. And obviously Our Francie knew the building had an alleyway running out the back of it. And obviously he knew that halfway down this alleyway the one light in the whole entire area to be illuminated would be none other than the gents whose basement windows reached just above ground level, meaning that the head of a urinating man would be framed like a picture, the brightest, most visible thing for a hundred and fifty yards in both directions. That a urinating man might look up upon hearing a low whistle coming from outside the window, and that the moment of reckoning for a man would be manifest in the smallest of gestures – a stiffening of the shoulders, a groan of realization, a widening of the eyes – just before he got his brains blown out.

That last part Our Francie would not in fact know, or at least not before hearing all about it at the debrief he would organize afterwards with his two volunteers. Until then he would have nothing but his pure imagination to go by, maintaining the everyday façade at his customs job on the border before rushing home to park himself rigid by the radio, ears pricked in his darkening kitchen as he eagerly waited for the local Ulster bulletin to come on and give first public mention of this, his hard-earned achievement. Of an off-duty police officer having been shot dead in Dungannon, a married man, a father of four. Our Francie could relax only then, or as much as he ever did, the relief coursing right through him for a few blessed moments that the thing was done now, and seemingly without any of the many, many things going wrong that could go wrong in an operation of its kind, meticulously planned though it may have been and marked as it was by the obsessive attention to detail for which Our Francie was so renowned, with his prior weeks or even months spent in near-constant clandestine surveillance of this urinating man of his who by this stage Francie felt like he had come to know a bit, almost to the point of developing a fondness for the man, affection even. Not that Our Francie would ever use that type of terminology of course, no, no, no, not in relation to an officer of The Crown, one of Her Majesty's many representatives in this blessed and cursed nation of ours and an instrument of our oppression lasting these eight hundred years and counting.

But at the same time it's hard not to feel like you know a man when you get to know his habits, his little concessions to the precautions he was supposed to be taking. The pastry, for example, was a chester bun, and it was as Our Francie stood behind the man in the bakery line that he heard first about the choir in Dungannon, the exact type of detail he'd been on the lookout for, and around which he could now circle with intent. What song yiz workin on these days Paul? asked the lass behind the counter, and boy did the pair of them have a good chuckle to themselves when he joked back to her, Ave Maria. Our Francie chuckled too, silently into himself, his face a mask of the pure nondescript, blent grey into the background. But then even on the final day when all had come together, his volunteers Dungannon-bound to their predetermined positions – Mickey on the motorcycle, Kaja in the alley – there was Our Francie in the pastry shop to hear the chit-chat and the banter, and to order for himself the self-same chester bun despite the lack of strict need for any of this operationally speaking, after which he stood and watched his urinating man as he dawdled out the door with not a care in the whole wide world, sauntering across the street to the barracks, to no doubt a waiting cup of cha followed by permission to knock off at a slightly different time so as to go a slightly different route to the fortnightly singalong, arriving nonetheless bang on half past six to be greeted by his waiting choir mates, *there's Paul, howya chaps*, the quick trip down the steps, the light, the cold, the piss-reeking urinal, the dark window now lit up to frame his head all the better, the click, the whistle, the sudden flash of insight and the deep crimson of his brain fluid spattered all across the tiles.

– He did what?

– I'm telling ya.

– You're having me on.

– I swear to fuck Francie.

Francie liked to debrief his two volunteers in The Gullion Arms, halfway up the mountain and not far from the town of Cross. But as usual the boys were late and for the longest while it was just Our Francie sitting on his lonesome over there in the far corner of the red lounge, as antisocial as they come with a bottle of non-alcoholic Beck's planted down in front of him and getting more irritated by the minute. When he said eight he meant eight, and frankly he was of a mind to leave if these two pups didn't show up soon. The Arms was mostly empty apart from Nailer's crew in their regular spot at the small inner bar, the odd eruption of laughter out of them but otherwise generally quiet for the most part. Handy Byrne was over there as well in the inner bar, his arm in a sling, standing at the counter with The Young Goss, flicking a lighter on and off. No one had seen Handy since the Warrenpoint job went south a month back and word was he was lucky to get away with just the arm. Jarlath Heneghan, Nailer's main man, raised a fist to Francie in what presumably was some type of joke salute though Francie himself was unsure and not of a mind to interrogate it. He barely nodded back at Jarlath, taking out another Benson and Hedges, and it must have been another ten minutes before the side door to the inner bar opened and, to cheers all round, Mickey and Kaja entered like heroes. Francie stayed where he was. Triumphalism was simply not his thing, but nothing was holding Nailer's crew back, that's for sure, and they engulfed the two boys, Jarlath with his arm around Kaja's neck before putting him into a headlock, running his knuckles across the top of his skull. Mickey laughed and shouted, delighted with himself, but, perhaps seeing the stony glower on Francie's face, grabbed Kaja and pulled him off Jarlath, and here now, finally, finally, the two of them came over to where Francie was sitting in the corner, both bearing pints like gifts, not an ounce of circumspection about either of them, pure glowing they were, hair slicked back, electric from the adrenaline that was still buzzing through them, their skin gleaming. O, they'd score tonight, that was for sure, they were elected now so they were, it was pure heyday all the way. Francie could barely stomach to say hello to them as they sat down around him and started telling him their story.

– He did up his fly?

– I swear to god Francie.

– His fly?

– I'm telling you. He hears, you know, that low wee whistle I like to do and then the click of the glock, and I swear to fuck down goes the hand. I thought he was going for his piece. But then I hear it.

– What?

– Zip.

A pause and both Mickey and Kaja fell about laughing. Despite it only being a few hours it was obvious they had told their story a few times already. And it would only get better in the telling, there was no doubt about that. Francie closed his eyes tightly for Christ and patience' sake, irritated more than the average by his two boy soldiers, interacting with each other like children, giddy as kippers, nudging each other and smirking. Mickey in particular ought to know better. The big galoot, he was Francie's nephew, his depressed sister's young fella, her in the John of Gods this years. A decent enough lad, Mickey, he cared mainly for his muscles, sure he barely drank except for those protein shakes he'd carry around with him, a slab of them he'd keep in the back of his Vauxhall, handing one to Pat Behind The Bar and asking him to throw it into a pint glass there Pat with a bit of diluted orange in her and a few cubes of ice. And as for his sidekick Kaja, well, he was a total nut job so he was, Francie was under no illusions there. Kaja would cut you, use the full range of blade on you, what he kept about his person, well hidden up his ankles or round the small of his back, sellotaped to his pale skin even. Every gauge of thinness possible, the whole span of flick, to get into a man's subcutis or in under his nails, slice the ball sac or make a quick mess of the face. Nothing gave Our Kaja more pleasure. A bona fide psychopath in other words. One hundred per cent headbanger. Yes indeed, Our Francie could pick'em.

– I'd like to think I'd do the same myself. Under the circumstances I mean.

– What's that Francie? grab your mickey said Mickey, one last stroke said Kaja, one for the road said Mickey!

– You boys may laugh but I respect that. You're about to get your brains blown out and your first instinct is to maintain your dignity.

– O we respected him all right Francie. Orange cunt. With a glock to the face.

Francie glared at his nephew.

– The man was a legitimate military target Mickey. There's no need to personalize the situation.

Kaja and Mickey were smirking away to each other.

– We're sorry for your loss Francie. Here, are you

going to the funeral are you? Bring some flowers from us will you?

– Aye, pay our respects. Tell his wife we're very sorry.

Francie closed his eyes again and kept them like that for a moment, waiting for the laughter of his youthful companions to die down.

– Mickey. You are my wee sister's wee beloved, my own flesh and blood technically speaking. But shower me with your shite again and I'll set Kaja here on you, do you hear me?

– Ah don't be getting thick Francie. I'm only slagging you.

– Them anabolics has gone to your head so they have. Listen. Religion has nothing to do with it all right? We simply do not need that superstitious mumbo jumbo for right to be on our side. We have our political ideals and that's more than enough for us to be getting on with. Have you got that son?

Finding his lighter spent, Francie was glad to have an excuse to go up to the bar. After that, home. He was tired, and admittedly ratty, nothing a good night of sleep wouldn't fix, if that wasn't too much wishful thinking. As he was waiting to be served a young girl came in the main door and stood beside him. From the other side of the bar The Young Goss started making loud pig noises at her. Based on that alone, Francie guessed it was Cathy Murphy, The Tout Murphy's fourteen-year-old daughter, though he hadn't seen the young one in a while. Pat Behind The

Bar put a naggin of whiskey into a paper bag and quickly went over to her, passing it to her and taking her ten-pound note from her. The Young Goss continued with the pig noises, making ever more of a racket, while beside him Handy Byrne just glared over at the girl. It was pathetic really, but for her part the young Murphy one just stood where she was, waiting for Pat to return. But he was back over on the other side now, pulling a pint, so she had to shout over to him.

– You forgot my change.

Pat ignored her and after finishing the pint turned and went over to Francie to see what he wanted.

– I think you forgot this young girl's change Patrick.

Pat gave a loud sigh and went over to the till, then slapped a couple of coins on the counter. The young Murphy girl glared at him as she took up the coins, before turning and leaving with the whiskey. Pat came over to Francie again.

– The sins of the father Patrick, the sins of the father. Not the daughter.

– It's a disgrace Francie is what it is, you have no idea. The mother goes through one of those a night. More if she had the money.

– Hardly any of it's the girl's fault Patrick. Here, give us a box of matches there will you.

When he got back to the table, Kaja and Mickey were clearly talking about earlier, practically shouting about it, laughing about it, you could have heard them out in the car park, certainly you wouldn't need any hi-tech surveillance equipment, that's for sure, but it was indecipherable gibberish they were mouthing, both of them speaking over each other, jittery still from the rush. Francie interrupted them. He wanted to go over everything in detail, make sure it had all gone as planned. That they'd got in and out and not been seen, that they'd stashed the gun like they were supposed to, and burned their clothes like they were supposed to, and what about the bike, had they wiped it down before torching it? And were they sure no one else had been in the jacks? What about the chipper across the street? Was it full or empty at the time? And the security cameras, they hadn't been repaired from the previous week, had they? And what about that old fuck behind the desk of the office building opposite, was he still hanging around? The two boys found the questions increasingly hilarious, telling Francie that all was right with the world, chill hi, relax the cacks Uncle, it was smooth as, smooth as a baby's bum, but Francie was not amused, O it wasn't just the adrenaline that had them buzzing, that was for sure, they'd clearly taken something, pills or powder. Mickey and Kaja looked at each other and nodded, then took themselves off to the toilets. Powder, then. Our Francie watched them go. They had no clue these young pups, no clue and no idea. A man's life had been taken. True, an enemy combatant who had made his choices in life, but still. Not all that far from here was, right this minute, a grieving house with crying children and a hysterical wife. It was either a strength or a weakness that Francie could picture all of it. And he wasn't being sentimental either. There was also the matter of the all-too-predictable police response. At this very minute the RUC thugs would have already started to turn the place upside down with their vengeful and indiscriminate search raids, kicking in doors and hauling innocents off to Castlereagh, giving pure violent vent in other words to their innate tendencies, barely bothering to even hide them now under the procedural guise of supposed investigative police work. Francie felt angry just to think about them, thugs with truncheons is what they were, with an attitude on their faces that one hundred per cent belied the true nature of things vis-à-vis the unionist partitionist state, apartheid to its bones and discriminatory since the day of its inception and of which people in this community were only nominally a part, putting up with since the day they were born the disparaging mentality of the Orangeman, his pomposity and haughty disregard, his snide high-handed manner and the all-permeating institutionalized bias manifest in manifold ways, but always, alas, always to the detriment of one particular subsection of the population, that's for sure.

Francie took up his Beck's. When he looked over at the small back bar, Handy Byrne was in behind the counter stealing money from the register. His arm was out of the sling and seemed to be moving fine. Handy looked up and made eye contact with Francie, winking at him as he put the money in his back pocket and his finger over his lips, before returning the arm into the sling. Francie rested back in his chair and closed his eyes. God he was tired. Pubs were no longer his type of place, in truth they never had been. Give him the inside of a car any day and a long stretch just sitting there waiting. He could wait forever as long as there was a purpose to it, some act that would bring us all closer to deliverance, incremental though it may be, O, he could sit as still as a statue then, as relentless as they come. He sensed a figure had appeared in front of the table and, opening his eyes, saw that it was Jarlath

Heneghan, carrying two pints which he set down where Mickey and Kaja were sitting. A mischievous, devilish man with a red beard and an actor's instinct, Jarlath didn't take his eyes off Francie before producing out of his back pocket as if by magic a bottle of non-alcoholic Beck's and with some ceremony placing it down in front of Francie. He gave a little bow before walking off without saying a word. Mickey and Kaja came out of the toilets, laughing and shoving each other. Seeing the pints and Jarlath walking away, Mickey shouted his thanks after him before sitting and drinking.

– By the way, what does Nailer want with you Uncle?

– Fuck if I know.

– The boys there were saying that he's been expecting you every night this week out at the complex.

– Well as you know I've been busy of late.

– Is it to do with Donners do you think?

– Like I say I am agnostic Nephew.

– His oul one is creating an awful fuss.

– Well what do you expect her to do? The lad is her flesh and blood.

– He's a wee toerag Uncle. Take it from me. A fuckwit and a brat. Not sure about the toutin' now to be fair, but a pain in the hole generally speaking.

Francie gave a shrug to let the matter drop. It was nothing to do with him. Informer or not, that young Donnelly lad was a waste of space if ever there was one and his disappearance was of no relevance to Francie. Plus the mother was mad, hanging out at The Square like that, she should be ashamed, making a holy show of herself on her so-called hunger strike. Brit propaganda could not have planned the whole thing any better. But none of it was his concern. In this business you kept your head down and did your own part. Nothing more, nothing less. Besides, to the groans of his two accomplices, he wanted to go over everything again. Were they sure about the chipper, and that nosy office fuck? And, again, what about the cameras? He might take a drive by tomorrow just to make sure. The music came on louder and both Mickey and Kaja nodded their heads to it, sure they were barely listening to Francie now at this stage. Francie stood, putting on his coat. Mickey looked up at him, and practically shouted at Francie over the music.

– When's the next job Uncle?

Francie stared at him in total disbelief. He sat down again.

– Jesus Christ keep your voice down will you?

– Relax the cacks Francie. Are we not in The Arms?

Francie glared at him, shaking his head slowly, more disappointed than angry.

– Never. Relax. Do youse hear me? Never. Have I taught you nothing? How do you think The Brits nipped in the bud all manner of rebellions down the years? Red Hugh O'Donnell. The O'Neill boys. Wolfe Tone. Christ, the long and sorry list goes on. Go all the way back to Silken Thomas if you want. Then you can explain to me why we should be any different.

– This is 1994 Francie.

– Thank you Mickey, I am aware of that fact.

There was silence then. Francie stood up again, angrily zipping up his coat. He may or may not have noticed that, seeing him, Nailer's men were putting on their coats as well. Mickey raised his glass in the air.

– To Francie and his pissing man.

Francie took up his non-alcoholic Beck's, not taking his eyes off his nephew, the big, earnest face looking back at him. Sure they were still children practically and maybe he'd been too harsh on them. Let them have their night. In fairness they had earned it.

– Now, now, bit of respect boys, he said. Urinating man.

The two boys cheered and Francie clinked his bottle off their glasses then put it on the table and walked to the door, noting as he did that Nailer's men were also on their feet and heading for the car park.

2

BY THIS STAGE the Donnelly woman had been at it for weeks. Some sort of protest, supposedly a hunger strike, ever since that pup of hers had gone on the run after the shitshow in Warrenpoint. Nailer and his crew were still angry over it. Handy Byrne was lucky not to have lost an arm and obviously the whole thing was a stitch-up from the get-go. The police were sitting there waiting for them to come round the corner. Probably bored out of their minds waiting for them they were, wondering what was keeping them. Handy said it was fish-in-a-barrel territory, a pure miracle no one was killed. Darren Donnelly was supposed to drive the car, but he never showed, nor did he make it to the meet-up point afterwards. Pick your excuse. He'd slept in. No, he was off his head on drugs. No, he forgot so he did. Actually, come to think of it, no, he was sick as a dog that day, his asthma had flared up, and anyway, he never really knew about it in the first place. Handy Byrne had only mentioned it once to him in passing, but other than that nothing, not a word, and suddenly he's to blame, but sure how was he to know? He'd done nothing so he hadn't! Well, none of it stopped him hightailing it to Amsterdam, that's for sure. Guilty as sin in other words, the dogs in the street knew it. But then didn't the little so-and-so get homesick and want home? Rang his mother telling her he had only left out of fright. Leave it with me, she said, and from morning to night the woman began to plant herself on The Square, demanding that her little wretch be allowed return, perched right by the Monument to the Martyrs and directly across from the constituency office of Mairtin O'Cuilleanáin, rising star in national republican politics and main man representing Cross and its environs on the Newry and Mourne District Council. The woman knew full well the heat the whole thing would put on M.O.C., with the assembly elections upcoming. Every time he looked out his window he would have seen her bawling and crying on her pathetic protest, wailing and gnashing, putting on her best performance to draw sympathy and attention. Well, that wasn't going to work, not around here, people weren't born yesterday you know, hunger strike my hole being the general view. Sure at night wasn't the woman only too happy to take herself away off home to the comfort of her own bed where no doubt she nibbled away, and tippled away too by the looks of things, partial as she was known to be to the vino rosso, the brandy and the schnapps? The state of her then when she'd reappear first thing, puffy-eyed and bleary, making sure to be in situ for the school run and the shops opening, shouting and roaring at the good people of Cross passing by and merely going about their business. The roars and screeching out of her. Saying that she wouldn't move until her little pup was allowed home unharmed. That her Darren had done nothing, he was a good boy so he was, not an angel by any means but a decent lad, and all he wanted anyway was a chance to prove himself, to keep his head down and work hard, he'd applied for an apprenticeship so he had, he wanted to be an electrician, and this, *this*, is what happens to any young lad around here who steps out of line with a bit of teenage mischief. Lifted and disappeared like all the other ones, and all on the word of that psychopath Handy Byrne, who wouldn't know the goodness of a young lad like that, no, no, the likes of

Handy Byrne couldn't hold a candle up to him, her poor wee Darren.

O everyone knew all about her poor wee Darren all right. An antisocial menace is what he was right from the get-go, a bad article, pure lowlife scum. Physically nothing but a scrawny weasel of a thing, and an unmerciful whiner, stretching right back to the moment he first emerged into the world when even then there would have been a sneer across the little pup's face. Maurice Dolan's sister was a midwife in Daisy Hill around then and she swears he was an ill-tempered needy little bastard right from day one, the constant whingeing out of him, no mere colic, that's for sure. And it was no immaculate conception either. Marie Maguire, as The Widow Donnelly was then, was a well-known commodity in and around Cross. Piggy Brady had her behind Hynes' auctioneers after one of the cattle marts. Manus Matthews had her the Good Friday the post office was robbed. Oo-ah Mickey McGrath said sure half the GAA team had her, they used to pass her around like the O'Neills' pug between them (more so than they did with the actual ball, alas), from corner back to corner forward and back to midfield. Even Big Dessie Gaffney the goalie had her after some do, and him that never had anyone. Maurice Quigley piped up to say that he could have had her if he'd wanted to but decided against it at the last minute. Right you are Maurice, we said, whatever you're having yourself, sure the woman had to draw the line somewhere. She had the artistic temperament did Marie, heading off to England for a spell before coming back with the wild red hair and a bandana, you'd see her outside the cattle mart flogging her paintings which she'd hang from the railings like they do down in Dublin, the farmers looking at them, bemused, mad abstract colourful things that your dog would do. Eventually Jim Donnelly the bachelor took her on, as gentle and taciturn a man as ever walked God's earth. A suspicious six months later the sprog was born, his tumultuous boyhood precipitating an early cardiac grave for old Jim and in the process making Marie The Widow Donnelly. And then when the young muck comes of age he is nothing but pure trouble about the place. The joyriding and the robbing were one thing. But selling junk was another altogether, pills, grassweed, the acid, and lately powder, whatever he could get from a contact in Coolock. Nailer flipping out about it. Plenty warnings given, we can't be having that shite around here, if he said it once he must have said it a hundred times. A pure stain on The Cause the pup was, we're not Colombians so we're not. Kneecapping was mooted but, of all people, Handy intervened by getting him in on the Warrenpoint job. They needed a driver and it was the one bit of skill everyone in Cross agreed the Donnelly lad possessed. Nailer gave him one last chance, which only goes to show where good deeds will get you, because do you think The Widow Donnelly appreciated any of it? Not at all, of course she didn't. Even after M.O.C. promised the little brat safe passage back to Ireland you'd still find her a daily presence on The Square carrying on with this so-called hunger strike of hers, making all sorts of threats and dark promises. O, she would show them some symbolism so she would, she would give them an oblation, offering up her entire being as a pure howl of protest at what she maintained was the hypocrisy of the republican movement and the supposed noble cause of Irish separatism in general. She would turn herself to rags, skin and bones right in front of our faces, yes indeed, O she would show us what a hunger strike was, but not hidden in an H block this time, rather right in front of the world's cameras, how slow and deforming its sculptural processes were, with the worm of hunger gnawing away from the inside. See here, she proclaimed, this, *this* is the true face of Irish republicanism, its so-called righteous cause and high moral struggle, yes, let the world watch, let her watch and let her learn.

And everyone did watch, disgusted by the sight of her and this little performance of hers, people passing by ignoring her with their heads down, nobody speaking a word to her or even acknowledging her, except to mutter under their breath that she was making a holy show of herself, would you ever cop yourself on woman and grow up, get a life for fuck sake, sure you're nothing but a clueless bitch, an oul wench and slag, yes indeed a filthy whore is what she was and always had been, a slut from the very beginning, bringing shame on herself and shame on the people of Cross, and while she was at it bringing shame on the entire republican movement as well as our pantheon of martyrs, sure wasn't she only doing The Brits own sly dirty work for them, with their sneaky devious propaganda? The days went by and the weeks, there was no sign of her young pup and what about it anyway? what loss? a good riddance was the general view, wasn't he nothing but a nasty waste of space from day one, a layabout with a mouth on him, a get, a nuisance, and most likely a tout to boot, yes, that's what he was, you might as well call a spade a spade, he was an informer of the highest order, sure you only had to look at him, the sly face on him, the snarkey jib, there's no smoke without fire, that's for sure. And let's not forget, a druggie too, introducing that sort of thing into the community, corrupting the local youth, trying to bring them down to his level, no, he was a skanger from the get-go that Donnelly lad, a rotten apple, pure trouble to have about the place, go on, away off to Coolock with you, you little shit. Sure no doubt he was right this minute strung out in some hostel in Amsterdam or in a squat in Brighton or Bradford, and The Brits who planted all these rumours were laughing their holes off at the strife they could seemingly cause at will among the nationalist community, the seeds of division they could so easily sow. Well not around here they can't, or not as easily as they might think anyway, and all the time the stupid woman remained where she was, and as far as anyone cared she could bloody well rot there, ignored and shunned by the community at large, a demented fixture was what she was, a decaying decomposing hag of a thing that over the weeks everyone got used to stepping over or around, sure they barely noticed her now at this stage, not even bothering to avoid her gaze or pretend that they couldn't see her, until truthfully nobody could recall the way she used to be, the looker she was at one time, a fine thing perhaps, a bit of a ride actually, but this was now impossible to imagine, the disgusting current state of her, the skin blotchy with red patches on her neck and arms, little pustules of malnutrition dotting her face, yellowed and scabrous, the skeletal starving look which settled in on her, her dirty rags hanging loosely off her bony frame, the uniform of poverty that everyone agreed she had created for herself out of thin air and which she wore wrapped like a veil around her.

3

NAILER USED NAILS once on a man lying flat on the floor. Not a religious man – it was the brother who was the priest in the family – but Christ that was some crucifix. Nailer was an introspective man who didn't say a whole pile, but when he spoke they listened. Nailer was a decent, upstanding member of the community. Didn't he look in on his nosy old neighbours, keeping them in peat briquettes through the winter and their mouths shut the rest of the time? Nailer owed the taxman what he said he owed him and not a penny more. Nailer was something of an autodidact on account of having left school at fourteen. Nailer was a bachelor with a big farm complex straddling the un-ancient and illegitimate border between north and south, meaning that when they came for him from one jurisdiction he could scoot across into the other one. Nailer kept prize pigs that won rosettes in competitions and whenever one of them died he was inconsolable. Nailer held what could be termed board meetings in his kitchen given that Nailer was the head of a corporation of sorts, the COO and the CEO and the CFO and the what's it to you anyway?

Nailer was out in the field with Rehab, The Tout Murphy's son, when the boys pulled up to the farm. Just standing there, the pair of them surveying like gentry the sodden night in silence. The Murphy lad must have been about nineteen or twenty now at this stage, he was young

Cathy's older brother. But unlike her, he wasn't all there in the head, whatever way they had repaired him up in The Royal. Regardless, there they were, the old farmer and the tout's son, seemingly oblivious to the convoy of cars pulling up around the front, standing there like equals just down from the farmhouse, at that crest point where the field takes a sudden dive as if to burrow under the invisible but all-too-present border starting at the old hawthorn tree. No one could ever fully comprehend why Nailer tolerated Rehab Murphy's presence on the farm given his pedigree, but he was like the trusted hound of the place. He was hardly fit for any other line of work, the lad, and apparently Nailer gave him a modest stipend. He was more or less mute as far as anyone could tell, you'd be uncomfortable in his presence, the way he'd just stand there gawking at you, the big brain-injury head on him, there was no fixing that so there wasn't, no we were well past that stage, prone as he was to twitching and jerking, every now and then lying down in the rigid embrace of the full tonic clonic, the eyes wide open to the skies, the stump of tongue chewed right off him, fists knuckled white as solid bone. Not that he was exactly presentable the rest of the time given the general oddness of his appearance, O, no doubt about it there was strange blood running through that Murphy lad, green blood, yellow blood, a black admixture, whatever it was that had acid-corroded his bossed forehead, the jutted lumpy structure of the skull bone, making it an odd blunted shape of a thing, clumps missing out of it, perched atop the scaffold of a bona fide giant's bodice.

Up pulled the van and the few cars to the front of the complex and there was the commotion of the doors opening and closing, the voices spilling out disrupting the night's silence. Nailer winced, irritated at the interruption. Christ in heaven why was it so hard to get a moment's peace? Taking deep, slow breaths just as he'd been advised to do, he stayed where he was, trying as best he could to ignore the wholly unnecessary stir his crew were making as they barged into the house, getting the dogs all agitated, ignorantly slamming doors and roaring his name, Christ broadcast it why don't you? A minute of this and the back porch door whined open and sprang shut and, he could already tell without turning, two of them had emerged on to the back yard, their voices quietened to whispers, one laughing at whatever mimicry the other was up to, the crunch of their approaching feet on the gravel. Nailer looked over his shoulder and saw, just as he would have guessed, the figure of Handy Byrne, accompanied as usual by The Young Goss, before turning back to contemplate the dregs of the evening from this elevated vantage, this fine view he had of the silver-backed sea not too far off, the lights of Forkhill and beyond them the Cooley peninsula, it was some sight, and it would be good for the soul to just linger for a while longer looking at it, but chance would be a fine fucking thing around here. Surrounding Nailer's complex on all sides, the thick hedgerow was like a rampart and, to his left, volcanic black against the still-light sky, the sulking loin of Gullion absolutely towered out of the earth. It had been raining solid for a week and this was the first bit of let-up in it, the sky and the mist with the failing light manufacturing some serious bit of drama up there, and he wouldn't have minded savouring it a bit more. Chance indeed. There were moments when Nailer was more aware than usual that there was no let-up with this thing and no rest, but anyway, such was the way he'd chosen and there was sure as hell no going back on it now. Before him the muddy ground swept steep away from him, all the way to the bottom of the field where the surface water collected above the table, forming an impromptu moat that the pigs would absolutely revel in in the morning when the Murphy lad let them out into it. Nailer could practically hear their squeals of ecstasy already, the animals crowding around the Murphy lad's knees, nuzzling up against him, Christ the thought of it would put a smile on your face no matter what. The gravel crunch got closer and closer before coming to a stop behind him. He took another deep, slow breath and let it out before speaking.

– The Newry man?

There was no reply, which forced Nailer to turn around. Handy Byrne was looking not at him but at the Murphy lad. Handy spat on to the ground, not taking his eyes off Rehab for an instant. Nailer noticed it, just as he was meant to.

– Ah Christ will you leave him alone will you? He's grand so he is.

For his part Rehab didn't dare look up from the ground, his eyes fixed downward on his big mucky boots. Though he carried a pickaxe he seemed embarrassed by this fact. Handy eventually looked away from him and back at Nailer.

– Aye, the Newry man.

– Youse took your time anyway.

– Well we're here now aren't we?

The Young Goss stared at the ground, scandalized by his companion's words, trying not to smirk too much. Handy was perhaps the only person in Cross who could be short like this with Nailer, who just looked at him, somewhat hurt it must be said. He would simply never understand why people took it upon themselves to be needlessly discourteous. For one thing it was rarely necessary. Frequently counterproductive too. Regardless, he let the comment pass, and instead addressed Rehab.

– You'll shift the rest of these stones Thomas.

Rehab, with his head lowered, mumbled some form of speech that only Nailer could decipher.

– Good lad.

Nailer turned to Handy and The Young Goss.

– Well, come on then.

– I'll follow you in boss man, said Handy. I just want to have a wee word with Rehab here about something.

The Young Goss started laughing into himself but stopped when Nailer glared at him.

– Will youse ever leave him alone? Christ Jesus youse have the lad plagued so youse do.

Nevertheless he continued on, his massive farmer's frame churning the gravel as he strode across it with his big limp, the unbent leg curving in an arc after him. He disappeared around the side of the farmhouse and there was the sound of his feet stamping loudly on the mat to kick the muck off his wellingtons, then the tired effort of removing them, the jarring squeak of the porch door opening against his shoulder as he struggled with them, and the release of the door springing shut behind him as he entered the house in his damp socks. The whole time Rehab Murphy remained standing in place with his eyes looking down at the ground, the odd twitch running through him like electricity, Handy glaring at him with disgust, The Young Goss expectant, eyes lit, keeping a close watch on Handy, ready as ever to take his cue and imitate his mannerisms, shriek at his every utterance. That was the way it was with those boys, the gang that went around with Handy, it was nothing but hero worship from one end of the day to the other, idolatry didn't even begin to cut it. The way they talked the way he talked, laughed at what he laughed at, and generally did whatever Handy told them to do. Nobody thought it was a healthy situation, whatever else was said, and there was plenty said regarding Handy Byrne of the Byrnes, that's for sure. That Handy dropped the hand. Certainly that was one thing said about him. Boys o boys did he what? Handy dropped the hand, whether they liked it or not. And in fairness most of them did. What was there not to like about the famous trigger finger's finger burrowing away out the back of The Arms teenage disco of a Saturday night? He'd have them practically lined up waiting for him. He had the good raven looks, though for a man's man he was a somewhat slight-of-build specimen. It was his crackshot gift which explained his indispensability to The Cause. He could shoot reliably from 300 metres, one famous shot taking the head off a young Brit from over 500 metres and it a windy day. That was Handy's number one job, to lie flat in the bevelled-out back of a vehicle stolen and repurposed, the rear seat taken clean away, with two drilled holes for the butt of a long-range rifle and its telescopic sight. What he did the rest of the time was his own business, and everyone else's of course. And weren't his revolutionary credentials otherwise impeccable, genetically speaking? Wasn't his oul fella none other than Mossy Byrne, killed by The Brits in '74? A cousin was a hunger striker, and two brothers also gave up their lives for The Cause. One ambushed by the SAS in Germany and another cut to ribbons by loyalists up in Lisburn. Even Ma Byrne was a bombmaker before cancer took her. It was just Handy left and the older brother Gerry who did time in the Maze and now didn't drink. Pure Fenian in other words, from the purest, greenest stock, young pup and all though he was.

– All right Rehab? Hi, do you have what I gave you the other week still? Do you Rehab?

Handy turned around to The Young Goss, smiling like a demon, The Young Goss grinning away back at him, his dental braces gleaming at him.

– You haven't lost it now, have you Rehab?

The Murphy lad fished in his pocket and pulled out something plastic and shiny. A Durex, still in its wrapper.

– Ah there it is! Good man Rehab, good man! Don't lose it now. They're hard to get them things. Tell me, have you worked out what it's for yet, have you Rehab?

The Murphy lad stared at the ground, saying nothing, still holding out the Durex in the palm of his enormous hand.

– Why don't you show it to your ma Rehab? Ask her to show you how to put it on.

The Young Goss meanwhile was cracking up. Though just as quickly there came now the change of tone that you could easily get with Handy, more devil than devilish, and everyone around here knew what this was like. He took a quick step towards the Murphy lad and a flash of panic spread across Rehab's face. His bad arm released from the sling, Handy had both hands up and out in front of him, as if to say Easy now, Easy, but in the next instant they were down by his sides, not visible anymore, up to whatever they were up to, like adders lurking there, coiling and uncoiling in the dark, capable of inflicting a quick hurt. Closer and closer he came, to well within stabbing distance. It was like something you'd see in the zoo, the keeper approaching the beast, baiting it, full of threat, despite the monster having all the natural advantages, the brute and latent force contained within him, the pure size of him towering over Handy, sure wasn't he twice the beak of him at least in terms of body weight? But none of that mattered and Rehab leaned back, it was all he dared do, as if his weight and mass were the very things set against him, keeping him rooted to the spot.

– Or even better than that Rehab. Show it to that little bitch sister of yours. She'll know all about it all right. Take it from me, she's an expert at it so she is.

The Young Goss shrieked like a chimp. Later he swore blind to The Old Goss that at the mention of the young sister there was an instant of eye contact between Rehab and Handy and some flicker of possibility that the giant was about to erupt, after all these years of God knows what submerged rage and buried depth of fury, years of stewing in whatever was swishing around in that black and yellow strange blood of his, that it had come now to the boil, the memories simmering in his bruised and battered brain causing him to finally deploy his brute untapped power and slap Handy into the middle of next week. But there must have been a bit of sense in the giant freak because the instant was as quickly gone and Rehab went back to looking at the ground, his shoulders slumped again, the pickaxe limp against his hip. Handy took a step even closer to the Murphy lad, his head only reaching the top of Rehab's chest as he looked up into his face.

– And while you're at it you can tell her she shouldn't be sniffing around Calmor's Rock late at night. It's not for little girls that place. She'll only come to harm up there so she will. Will you tell her that for me Rehab, will you?

Handy stared at him for a moment before stepping back. He took out another Durex from his pocket and threw it at him.

– Here, you can give her that. But from now on tell her she's to bring her own one OK?

With that the two boys turned and went on their way, The Young Goss shrieking and laughing, skipping and hopping alongside Handy, nudging into him with his shoulder, rubbing up against him, slapping him and elbowing him on his arm, saying that was gas Handy did you see it Handy did you, pure gas so it was, Jesus did you see the state of him Handy did you, the face on the big ugly freak, the bubble of snot coming down out of him, God it was disgusting so it was, the sick spa, God he was even swallowing it so he was Handy, did you see it did you, the snot coming down out of his nose and the drool leaking down out of his mouth, he was like a bullock Handy wasn't he, did you see him did you, a bullock with a shovel stuck up its hole, did you see him Handy, did you, the rotten stuck cunt, the filthy freak, did you see him Handy, did you? And alongside him, cool as you like, Handy Byrne of The Byrnes, hardcore local republican legend, gleeful yes, triumphant yes, but at the same time somewhat circumspect, perhaps even perturbed about something, not saying a whole pile as they made their way back up the path to Nailer's house.

4

WHEN NAILER CAME in through his back door from being out in the field Francie was sitting at the kitchen table waiting for him. Nailer's men were spread about the room but nobody was talking. Pat Mitchell, 'Lee Trevino' Murphy, Jarlath Heneghan obviously, Maurice McCabe (aka Taxi) and a few of the younger lads. Nailer took his time putting on his house slippers, then stood for a few more seconds just staring at the sitting Francie. Truthfully, both men were in bad form and the tension in the room was no joke. Nailer moved over to the sink. There were engine parts in it and he lifted one of them, a heavy metal pipe that would do some shape of damage to the side of a man's skull. He placed it to one side on the draining board.

– Cup of tea Francie?

– That would hit the spot nicely thanks.

Nailer grabbed the kettle and started filling it under the tap. Then he flicked it on and leant back against the counter, not taking his eyes off Francie the whole time, his gaze going up and down him. The two men hadn't seen each other in a while, and no doubt Nailer owed the other man an apology for hauling him out here more or less against his will, but what about it? He was either in charge around here or he wasn't. For his part, Francie didn't bat an eyelid. To him Nailer looked older, he'd put on weight, living the good life closeted away up here in his castle like a king. Still with his eyes locked on Francie, Nailer cupped a handful of seeds into his mouth and immediately started to spit flecks of them out. Then he rubbed his hands together to clean them.

– Shocking weather we're having, Francie.

– It is.

– That poor flamingo must think he died and is in the seventh or the eighth circle of hell. Whichever one of them causes the most in terms of desolation. Truthfully I can't recall my Dante.

Francie looked back at Nailer, not quite following.

– You didn't hear about that, Francie?

Nailer turned to switch the kettle off even though it had hardly boiled. He put a teabag in each of two cups and filled them.

– I have to say that comes as a disappointment. There's me thinking you knew everything. *Francie knows. Francie knows.* Isn't that what they say?

– I don't know anything about birds.

– Aye, they say that too.

There were a few sniggers from the boys standing about the kitchen.

– It's a flamingo Francie. It arrived down the docks of The Town the other day. Can you believe that? Appeared out of nowhere like The Virgin Mother. And in that harbour too of all places, with its acreage of sludge and mud, where no self-respecting ship has passed through in decades. She must have had a stroke in the head, the poor wee bird, for her sense of navigation to be so banjaxxed.

– I wasn't aware. I'm sure the relevant authorities have been notified.

– They let me know about it that very evening.

– I was more thinking of the zoo.

– You should see it Francie. A thing of rare beauty so it is. Whatever the thinking is behind it.

– I wouldn't be one for omens.

– Me neither Francie, me neither. But nonetheless, a bucken *flamingo*! In The Town! There was an expert there on the radio, he reckons she must have gone askew on her migration path. Got separated from the pack the poor thing. And in serious shock as well I'd say, expecting as she was no doubt the Gobi Desert.

Nailer approached the table with both cups of tea in his hands, placing them down on the table and squeezing around Francie to take the seat against the back wall.

– Phoenicopterus *chilensis*. From the Americas, Francie. Or so I'd say anyway, judging from the newspaper snaps. On account of the more pinkish hue, which is what distinguishes it from the African flamingo. Also they tend to be a tad shorter than the African lads.

– I'm impressed.

– Sure why wouldn't you want to find out about a thing like that? Good to trade in harmless knowledge for a change, wouldn't you say? Fine precious creatures. There's the whiff of paradise about them, from the crest of the Andes Francie. Southwest Bolivia to be exact. The salt lakes, which I don't know if you're familiar with at all, Salar de Uyuni?

– Can't claim to be.

– Now there's a spectacle for you. The world's largest salt flat, pure prehistory, from a lake that ran dry they reckon forty thousand years ago, leaving behind nothing but the starkest whitest desert. Brine Francie. Pure salt of the earth.

– Like I say, I am suitably impressed.

– It's the most stunning thing you'll ever see Francie. It'd burn the back of your eyeballs to look at it. You'd go snow blind so you would. And then when it rains it gets covered in the thinnest layer of water which takes weeks to find its way into the earth. Turning it into you'd never guess what?

– What?

– A bucken mirror Francie. Eighty miles across. Eight miles of sky and cloud right there implanted into the ground. God himself could look deep into His own eyes.

– Must be some sight.

– Must be.

– O you've not seen it yourself then?

– Not at all. Sure do you think they'd let me go anywhere? The Yanks have me banned from going next nor near an aeroplane. Never mind the southern Americas where plenty of our comrades in arms reside, doing God's own work. The FARC, the Sandinistas, I don't need to be telling you about that.

– It's a pleasing thought all right, what could have happened there. Might pan out yet of course.

– No, it's all from pictures I've seen this type of thing Francie. Books. The Encyclopaedia Britannica in particular, the one unadulterated bit of goodness The Brits did for the world. I'm working my way through it Francie. It would be an ambition of mine to get to the end of it if I'm spared.

– Is that so? The oul lad used to have them in the house growing up. Not that he ever opened them. Too busy drinking himself into the ground. What volume are you up to?

– Not even halfway, I have to admit. You see I came to books late in life Francie. It would be a regret of mine. Trying to make up for it now. If they're ever looking for me, all they need do is go to the library here in Cross any day of the week and they'll find my nose buried there. They got the fresh edition of the Britannica in a while back. Proud to say it was at my behest. Remarkable to think that the world's knowledge is contained in it. You could just about wrap your arms around it. Or throw it in a wheelbarrow. Set a flame to it if you were of a mind. But that's thug's talk. And contrary to perception, we're learned around these parts. It's good for a man to keep his perspective open to things like that. The world as it is Francie, the world as it is. And how it was and how we found it. How we should leave it too.

– I couldn't agree more.

Both men paused to drink from their cups of tea. Nailer cut something of a jaded figure. He inserted his thick farm fingers into his eyes and gave them a good long rub. There was a Trócaire box on the table and he leant over and reached for it, turning the photo of the starving black child on the front outwards to face Francie. The two men looked at each other and Francie fished in his pocket and took out a tenner and put it into the box.

– I was beginning to think you were ignoring me Francie.

– You know me. When I'm on the job I've time for nothing else.

– I do, in fairness. Sound bit of work by the way.

– Thanks.

– We had our own bit of business there. A bank job which we'll have to put on ice for now. Was going to be a big 'un Francie. Twenty mill we reckon. Like the Brink's-Mat, only bigger. But anyway, it's on ice for now. Your thing put a bit of extra light and heat on the area shall we say.

– Sorry.

– Now, now, no need to apologize Francie. Just speaks to a need for a bit more, shall we say, coordination.

– I've no problem with that. In principle.

Nailer laughed.

– Well, you were always a man of principle, that's for sure. Anyway, it seems those two new lads are working out for you. Your nephew and the young Kerrigan.

– We'll see. For now I would give them a passing grade.

– O you're a hard man Francie, a hard man. Always were and always will be.

It was at this point that the back door opened and Handy and The Young Goss came into the kitchen. Handy had his arm back in the sling and had the door held open for him by The Young Goss. He flashed a grin at Francie, who nodded back at him. Nailer looked back too before turning his attention to Francie again.

– I presume you heard about this Donnelly lad?

– Aye. Sure you can't cross The Square without tripping over his oul doll.

– It's a sorry sight all right.

– She's beginning to smell now so she is.

– Really? That's interesting. Seemingly that's when the hunger strike turns into the home stretch. On account of the body starting to eat itself.

– Hunger strike? I'd say it's more a question of hygiene.

– O you couldn't power hose the stench of that away Francie. I believe the term they use for it is catabolism.

Nailer looked around the kitchen at his men.

– Now, never say I don't teach youse anything.

– I suppose the body has to feed itself somehow, said Francie, taking up his tea.

Nailer turned back to him and sat forward, putting both elbows on the table.

– But I'll tell you something for nothing Francie, our political friend is not one iota happy.

– M.O.C.?

– On account of all the press attention she's getting. He says it's putting a spanner into his whole thing, all the backchannelling et cetera, what with the Yanks now involved.

– Good.

– Easy for you to say Francie, but it's not as simple as that.

– It's as simple as them trying to surrender, Nailer, and them with no mandate. Sure they're two a penny them political hacks. They're just trying to get on in the world, M.O.C. and the rest of his pencil pushers. They'll sell the likes of you and me down the Swanee in a jiffy, that's for sure. Jobs for the boys in suits is what they're after. In Stormont God forbid. After that, the UN possibly.

– Even so, it's them fellas who controls all the dumps, not to mention the cashflow. I'm but one vote on the council. One vote Francie! And the others are all with them. Lock, stock. The clever cunts have it engineered that way. I admit that I was slow to see it.

– What does he want?

– M.O.C.? He wants what any politician wants with problems like that.

Nailer made a little motion with his hands and said 'Poof'.

– That they simply go away.

Francie took a moment to think about things.

– Where is he?

– The Donnelly kid? He's getting the Sealink over from Zeebrugge as we speak. Arrives into Larne at midnight. M.O.C. has granted him safe passage.

Both men looked at each other and laughed.

– That was nice of him.

– It's the only thing that will shut the mother up.

– Well it's not working. She was still in The Square this morning.

– Wisely she doesn't trust the cunt.

– Why do I get the feeling I'm not just being told all this by way of mere chit-chat?

Nailer turned to his men, smiling.

– See, what did I tell you boys? *Francie knows.*

There was a murmur of laughter from the men. Nailer turned back to Francie, again putting both elbows on the table.

– Ah I'm only slagging you Francie, don't mind me. But seriously, I was hoping you might go and meet them when they're situated. Our Italian friend is meeting the lad off the ferry.

– Casio? Sure there's only going to be one outcome there.

– He'll do nothing until he gets the nod.

– From who though?

Nailer grinned.

– Just go and meet them Francie. Once they're settled. See what you think. That's all. I'd value your input. The rest of it is not your problem.

– I take it M.O.C. knows nothing of this.

– Francie, Francie, Francie. Don't overthink it. Just go and suss the situation out a bit, that's all I ask. As I said, I'd value your opinion. Given that it's, shall we say, politically sensitive, I want to make sure it's done right whatever happens. Go on your holidays then. I hear they got a few new rides into Mosney. Get the sea breeze into them lungs of yours.

Francie finished his tea and stood up, saying he'd better hit the road. Nailer waited a moment before standing also, saying he'd walk him out. The two men went alone through the front of the house, Francie looking around the bare hallway that had bits and pieces of carpet strewn on the cement floor, completely unchanged since the last time he was out here. Behind them he could hear a commotion as there was a rush to the snooker table in the adjoining room. They went out through the front door and Nailer pulled it after him but left it ajar. They stood out on the front driveway. It seemed colder now, the exhalations of both men thick on the air. There was a squeaking noise coming from somewhere and it took a second for both men to attribute it to the Murphy lad, who was walking up the driveway pushing an empty wheelbarrow. Francie watched after him until he had gone around the corner and was out of sight.

– Still sentimental in your old age Nailer I see.

– Ah he's harmless so he is. A good worker too I tell you. . . . But I do admit to having conflicting feelings about this oul lad. Don't get me wrong now. A tout's a tout, and a grumpy fuck as you well remember. But Christ he could field a high ball like no one I've ever seen, before or since. Would absolutely soar through the air. We wouldn't have won any of those county cups without him.

Francie took out a cigarette and lit it.

– So Nailer. This Donnelly lad, what's going on really? Seems like a whole song and dance about not very much.

– He's a toerag Francie.

– So?

– And he knows more than he should.

– So?

– Christ Jesus Francie, it's been one shitshow after another recently in case you haven't noticed. Not a single op has gone to plan. And Handy was lucky to get away with just the arm. The others all lifted, looking at serious time so they are. Sure the police were sitting there waiting for them.

Francie said nothing but kept looking at Nailer. After a moment Nailer broke into a smile and finally looked back at Francie and put his hands up.

– OK, OK you got me. Truthfully I'm indifferent as to the pup's fate. And I do admit to a perverse enjoyment watching our political friend in heat over it. Christ they're piling into him from all sides on the radio. But, safe passage? I mean, talk about getting out of your box. And how does that make me look? Am I or am I not supposed to be in charge around here?

– Is he an informer Nailer? A tout, yes or no?

– I couldn't say. But going on the run like that wasn't a good look.

– Understandable though.

Francie took a drag of his cigarette and both men admired the thick swirl of it as he exhaled.

– I presume you've considered the other possibility?

Nailer looked at Francie, curious at first, then in disbelief.

He went to speak but stopped and went over to pull the front door completely closed before returning to Francie.

– Jesus Francie. I'd go easy there now. Handy is from serious lineage in case you haven't realized. The Byrnes is the closest you get to royalty around here. Christ, if his brother even heard you think about Handy in those terms. And I've seen Gerry in action – missing fingers or not, he'd tear you limb from limb so he would.

– Which is to say you've considered the possibility.

– I have.

Both men stood in silence. They could see the lights of The Town in the distance, a thick covering of fog over the brewery. Francie threw his cigarette on to the ground and stood on it, then leaned down to pick up the butt. He was slow to stand up straight before facing Nailer. He let out a big sigh.

– Don't we all, by the way? Know more than we should.

Nailer laughed.

– Ah Francie. Are you depressed?

Even Francie had to laugh at that. He put the butt in his pocket and walked down to his car. Nailer waited for him to open the door before calling after him.

– Just suss it out for me Francie. That's all I'm asking. Suss the situation out. Then go to Mosney or wherever the fuck. I'm telling you. Get some sea breeze into them lungs of yours. From the sounds coming out of them they could do with it.

– You're the boss Nailer. You're the boss.

5

THE YOUNG MURPHY one circled The Square. As usual she was on her own, ignored by the groups of other girls from her secondary school dotted about the place. Her bus for home had left ages ago, but something must have been keeping her, because now the second one was pulling out as well. Round and round she walked, almost as if she was afraid to go up on to The Square itself. Ahead of her on the path were some girls from her class. She knew right well they'd all be looking at her when she walked past, and someone would say something snide that she wouldn't hear properly, making the others laugh, and then O but she'd glare right back at the little bitches then because she could be fierce herself as well. But still, best to avoid all that, so she did finally go up the steps on to The Square. The Widow Donnelly was there. Maybe that's what was causing young Cathy to linger. She looked in a bad way, The Widow, perched as always these days on her upturned mineral crate, a soggy cardboard box sticking out from under her. Young Cathy knew her well to see. The Widow Donnelly lived down the road from the Murphys a couple of miles outside Cross on the other side of Silverbridge, though they'd never spoken. No one spoke to the Murphys, and now no one spoke to The Widow, so there. She walked towards The Widow, but slowly, reluctant to get too close, until she was standing about ten yards from her. The Widow was fast asleep or maybe in some type of hunger-induced trance. Young Cathy had an apple in her pocket and gripped it tightly. Would it be a good, noble thing or a horrible, cruel thing to go over and leave the apple in front of her? On the ground beside her was a framed picture of her son Darren as a young boy, and God the photograph was something else so it was. Angelic wouldn't even begin to cut it. The blond curls on him, the puffy cheeks, it was hilarious really because everyone knew he was nothing like that in reality. Darren Donnelly was the same age as Cathy's brother Thomas, and part of that group that hung around with that bastard Handy Byrne. They absolutely terrorized her Thomas, those boys, making his life a complete misery right from the get-go, from the minute he transferred over from the protestant primary school. *Murphy the mouth son of a tout.* Chasing him with sticks, using hurleys to fling dog shit at him, stealing his coat off the rack to put it in the urinal, and all of them pissing on it, they'd spit on his back as he walked home from school, and then finally there was that day when they cornered him at the railway bridge, causing him to leap over the wall to get away from them, straight into a deep bed of nettles, Handy Byrne, Darren Donnelly, the rest of them all spitting down on him, a shower of phlegm of all colours raining down on him, yellow phlegm, green phlegm, frothy pinky bloody phlegm, laughing their heads off at the strangled whimpers out of him as the nettles stung him like it was a nest of vipers nipping at him, engulfing him from all angles, and him completely stuck, wedged in by the base of the bridge wall and the thick bristly hawthorn behind him up to his neck he was, whining like a puppy being boiled alive, railing around getting stung continuously, his hands up to his throat, swelling up like the Michelin Man, his whole face and neck becoming engorged, his eyelids puffed out, the eyeballs looking like they might pop in their sockets, his skin red and blotchy, his voice gone completely by now, as mute as a cat as his throat closed over, choking him from the inside. Naturally the boys ran away, and that would have and should have been the end of it had it not been for Alan Magee – Scrawny's brother – who heard the commotion and saw the boys running off and, looking down from the bridge, saw the unconscious Murphy lad lying in among the nettles and called the ambulance, which took him to Daisy Hill before transferring him up to the intensive care in The Royal. They say the lad was barely alive when they got to work on him, seemingly there was hardly any oxygen getting into his brain, they put him on a ventilator but debated taking him straight off it, but in the end left him there for weeks, grudgingly, sure seemingly he barely scraped the tests for brain death, then more weeks apparently of weaning him off the machine and more after that then of so-called rehab. The next time anybody saw him around here he had a permanent hole in his throat that rasped as the air whistled in and out of it, he had grown in bulk, but was oddly shaped, his skin pockmarked with acne and scabs from all the tubes, and a skull scar from a bore hole for a brain bleed, the steroids bloating out his hide like a tent, pinkish stretch marks rippling across his enormous girth, he had tits like an old woman and a thick mound of a neck and a buffalo hump and that empty moony spacer vacant look behind the eyes. He was barely human now at this stage, no, subhuman is what he was, sure you only had to look at him to realize it, the state of him, a big fat lump of a thing, people couldn't stand to set their eyes on him for very long, he was a freak so he was, a helmet and plastic fork job, an imbecile, no, a spa, yes, that was the name for him, a spa. Well he was still her brother so he was, he was still her Thomas, even with all of that, and it brought young Cathy to tears just thinking of him standing there surrounded by those little fuckers who he could have should have pummelled into the middle of next week so he should. But you see that was the problem with her Thomas, he had a whale's heart in him and that hadn't changed, despite everything, and again it made her cry to think of the whole thing as she stood gripping the apple and looking at The Widow Donnelly. God she'd never forgive those bastards so she wouldn't. Handy Byrne, Kaja Kerrigan, The Young Goss and yes Darren fucking Donnelly, this widow's little knacker scumbag of a son. She was tempted to throw the fucking apple at her but instead took a big bite of it. What was it to her if they disappeared her little shit? And the pathetic state of The Widow Donnelly now, the clothes on her like rags, soaked right through from the recent rain, the thin windcheater covering her of absolutely zero use or protection whatsoever, sure it was practically plastered to her skin now at this stage, practically see-through, gleaming, covering her head like a veil, her eyes closed like they'd gone up the back of her head. She must have been frozen stiff, the woman. The sun was out but it was Baltic, a sharp wind whipping right through The Square. Cathy went a bit closer. The thing was though that she knew he wasn't a tout, The Widow's son, because it was Handy Byrne who was one. Young Cathy had seen him herself with her own eyes, out at Calmor's Rock meeting that man she'd swear blind on her mother and brother's life was with The Branch, he had that look about him. Handy and him talking away intensely to each other, Handy freaking out about something. Young Cathy was only there because she'd got a note under her desk from Dean Rafferty saying he wanted to meet her which of course turned out to be a cruel joke played on her by some of the bitches in her class, Suzie Breen and Lorraine Hammill especially who she fucking hated to the point of absolute tears they were such cruel wenches. So instead of nice quiet oblivious Dean out at The Rock it was Handy and his Branch man, and God didn't they shift pretty sharpish when they saw young Cathy coming, that's for sure, the Branch man disappearing and Handy going pure white in the face. Then he came over to her a few days later furious as fuck demanding to know what the fuck was she doing nosing around up there, you little bitch you, he was only buying drugs so he was, and if she said anything to anybody he'd get her so he would, he'd get her and he'd rape her and kill her and while he was at it he'd kill that retard brother of hers who should be dead anyway, just like her tout fucking father. She walked away from him stunned, tears in her eyes. Who was she going to tell anyway? Not this widow anyway, sure the woman wasn't even moving, she might not even be breathing now at this stage by the looks of things, she was like a statue, as rigid as rock, like the pietà Cathy saw in that picture at school recently, yes, a granite stone pietà, that's what she was, the eyes closed, grieving but empty-armed, no Jesus in them, that's for sure. Young Cathy stared hard at her, staring so hard she seemed to be drawing closer and closer to her, staring so hard that she didn't at first notice that The Widow's green eyes were now open and maybe had been for a whole minute, open and fixed on her, causing young Cathy Murphy, with a fright, to drop the apple on the ground and hurry away to get the next bus home before it too pulled off.

6

THE CHURCH WAS packed to the rafters. Out front the hearse was laden with wreaths which Francie lingered by, reading the messages. Always worth checking, though nothing jumped out at him, so he went inside and sat in the side aisle near the back. Scrubbed up and in his finest, the three-piece on, clean shaven, shoes gleaming, he had the heavy funeral overcoat on as well. The service was longer than it needed to be, not all that different from a Catholic ceremony actually, the usual palaver, sure it was all hocus-pocus to him. But looking around the church he did, he had to say, appreciate the minimalist presbyterian décor, they had plaques up instead of paintings, no cross or baby Jesus or any of the other nonsense, but rather fifty, maybe a hundred of these plaques, all bearing simply the names of dead congregants, a nice touch, probably more meaningful to the people down in the pews. Very long-dead congregants some of them, going back two, even three hundred years and always a surprise to be reminded of it. He didn't begrudge them it, no, Francie wasn't as extreme as some people. At this stage they had their own claims to be here. And in his opinion they'd be welcome to stay as well, and be part of the whole thing, as long as it was all upended first of course, right down to the roots, no, that would be his caveat so it would, it was non-negotiable, and anyway it was the only thing that would work in practice, no, it would have to be a total rehash job so it would, there could be no mere tinkering around the edges, the entire apartheid system would have to be dismantled and then put back together again from first principles. If that was done he wouldn't give a shite who lived here. They could be Sikhs from The Madras for all he cared. Midway through the ceremony he went outside and stood on the little kerb running alongside the well-cut lawn. A man came out and walked over to him.

– Can I borrow one of those?

Francie gave him a cigarette and lit it for him. The man leaned back in relief and exhaled, saying Jesus that's good, Jesus that's good. They stood in silence then before Francie chanced conversation.

– Did you know Paul well?

– No, said the man.

They smoked some more in silence. The man's obvious reticence told Francie all he needed to know about him. And from the cut of him he might even be a detective. Hard to know though, everyone looked like a detective at a Protestant funeral. He let the silence build, giving the man the room to think he'd been rude.

– And yourself?

– Not really. I know for a fact we had a shared love of music.

– Ah, you're in the choir then?

– No. No, I'm not.

He glanced at the man, who he could tell was mulling things. Francie gave it a moment before speaking again.

– To be honest, I shoot with the other foot. I barely knew the man at all. You see I'm from Newry, but I used to take the dog to Warrenpoint. A stroll by the sea does wonders for the emphysema, or such was the advice I was given, whether it's true or not. He had been given the same advice seemingly, though it was the prostate that was his main bugbear. No dog either. After a while we started to nod at each other. One time we ended up sheltering under the butcher's awning, and it lashing hail. Spoke about music. Jazz actually. Coleman Hawkins. Lester Young. He was for Hawk and I was for Pres. That was about the height of it. I didn't know he was in a choir until the minister mentioned it just now.

The man didn't look at him. If it all sounded plausible it was because some of it was true. The man put out his hand and Francie shook it.

– Well, we're all Christians here.

– I appreciate that.

They stood smoking in silence. Francie closed his eyes and let out a deep breath.

– You're not in the choir yourself then? he said.

– No. No I'm not.

Again the man's reticence confirmed all Francie needed to

know. They finished their cigarettes and the man stooped to pick up both their butts. Giving Francie a nod he said he'd better get back inside or it would be his funeral next. Francie laughed in sympathy, then stood there watching after him. He gave it a minute and then went back into the church just in time to see which row of pews the man entered. For the rest of the service Francie kept his eyes on him, getting familiar with how he looked, likewise the woman in the burgundy coat sitting beside him, guessing their height and weight, committing their images to memory, and at the end he kept his eyes on them as they walked out, sympathizing with the widow and the others standing beside her, the family of the dead man, the elderly mother it looked like, and four children, ruffling the black curly hair of the older boy and then going off into the grey Cortina with the number plate which Francie wrote down before following it out to the graveyard, lingering not too far behind them and then parking down the street, which allowed him to be first out behind them as they drove off, taking the coast road for seventeen minutes and going over the roundabout on the outskirts of Warrenpoint, then the second exit on to the Belfast road and after three and a half miles turning into Cherrywood Heights, a spruce development of about a hundred houses that Francie was not familiar with, making specifically for the middle cul-de-sac, parking outside the end house with the red front door. It wasn't as easy as that of course, there was going to be more to it than that, much more, but it was a start at least, possibly even a good start.

By the time Francie got back to the office the day was nearly half over. He changed into his uniform in the car before going into the glorified prefab that was situated just inside the border on the northern side and the location of

Our Francie's day job, that of diligent and conscientious – almost to a fault – officer in Her Majesty's Customs and Excise service. Samantha the receptionist gave him some jip about where he had been all day before telling him someone had rung looking for him, an old friend from school. She was already starting to answer another call as they spoke and, muting it, told him it was for him again and that it sounded like the same person. Francie told her he'd take it in the back office, which was empty given that the Blockhead twins were out on inspections. Closing the door, he headed to Blockhead Number 1's desk, where he saw the light on the phone blinking. Francie got these calls from time to time. Most likely it was just someone planning on bringing a lorry through and wanting to make sure Francie was there to wave it on. Well, they better not be in a hurry. Francie had worked hard at establishing himself as the pedant in the office, liking the fact that the Blockhead twins laughed at him behind his back, calling him Mr Jobsworth. And then every now and again there was the thrill of hitting gold. An off-duty policemen who might be stupid enough to pass him his police ID instead of his driver's licence, and which he could later cross-reference on the database to find out where he lived. So it was a surprise indeed when he picked up the phone to find the politician Mairtín O'Cuilleanáin on the other end. Francie only knew him from the television, they had never exchanged a single word, but here now was M.O.C. inviting him to meet up later in The Town.

As he came out of the office he went to say something to Samantha but she was on the phone, talking – he knew instantly – to her fiancé Stuart. A few months back one of the Blockhead twins let it slip that the chap was a UDR reservist. Since then Francie had been getting to know her a bit to see if he could get any more information about him. But there was nothing of note in what Samantha was saying now, only telling the chap she'd see him later and then putting the phone down.

– Hot date, Sam? I hope he's taking you somewhere nice.

– Chance would be a fine thing so it would.

– Let me know if you ever get sick of him. I'd be happy to take you to the pictures.

– And I'll let you know when you're the last man on the face of the earth. Or if hell freezes over, whichever happens first.

– Denial is a terrible thing so it is.

– How's your friend from school?

– Fuck knows. I have no friends.

– Tell me something I don't know.

– Certainly none from that religious asylum, that's for sure. It was, as I'm sure you guessed, a tip-off. Probably a load of bull, but I suppose I'd better check it out.

– My hero.

– Here, can you tell the two fuckwit twins that I'm away off to look into it?

– Right you are, Clint Eastwood. I'll have your medal shined and ready for you when you get back.

– I've always been more of a Charles Bronson type in my own mind.

– Was he the one in those dirty films? The one with the wee willy?

– Nice to know you think of me in those terms. I'll leave the van so as not to draw attention, in case the fuckwits are asking.

– I'll tell them where you've gone. Anything else is not part of my job description.

Francie went out and around the side to the car park and got into his own vehicle. From there he could see his two colleagues standing on the side of the road laughing to each other. Not that it mattered hugely, but he was relieved that they didn't notice him pull out and on to the slip road and then on to the Dublin Road and southwards across the border. The line of cars on the other side told him his two colleagues were taking the piss as usual. They got a kick out of having a build-up of traffic stretched out before them like a line of penitents approaching the altar for communion. Francie headed townward, making excellent time until he ran into a funeral cortège coming up Dowdall's Hill. Keeping an eye on the clock, he slowed down and had a good look but didn't recognize anyone of note among the mourners. He didn't linger too long though, and was in fact on time as he pulled into the car park behind The Imperial. M.O.C.'s white Fiesta was already there ahead of him, with hardly any other cars around.

With an excess of caution Francie drove through without stopping and then did a lap of the block before eventually parking on The Ramparts, making sure to point the car in the direction of the bypass. He walked back to the car park, coming at M.O.C.'s car from the rear. But when he rapped on the window, M.O.C. didn't bat an eyelid, simply beckoning Francie in with a wave of the hand without even looking up. He was at the wheel eating a sandwich fresh from the delicatessen. There was a smell of warm food, and on the radio sentimental pop music playing quite loudly. The politician raised both his palms, apologizing that they weren't in a fit state for shaking. He had some napkins tucked into his shirt collar and looked a bit ridiculous. Francie sat in beside him and pulled the door closed.

– Ah the famous Francie! Good to finally meet you boy.

– Don't know about that.

– Now, now, don't be modest, I hear great things.

– Modesty's got nothing to do with it.

– You don't mind if I eat.

– Not at all.

– Do you want a crisp or something?

– I'm fine thanks.

M.O.C. took a big bite out of his sandwich and then spoke with his mouth full.

– Carroll's delicatessen. They do some chicken breast roll so they do.

– So I've heard.

– Could you not find a parking spot?

Francie smiled, a tad embarrassed.

– Aye, back of the church.

– Ah I'm only slagging you Francie. This is just a chat. So hopefully the manoeuvres is unnecessary. But I respect the caution. I do.

– It's second nature now at this stage.

His sandwich finished, M.O.C. meticulously gathered the debris of his little picnic into a paper bag and then crunched it into a tight ball.

– I thought we should meet.

– Sure. Anything that might help.

– That's the spirit Francie, that's the spirit.

He reached over to turn off the radio but stopped when the opening strains of a new song could be heard.

– Are you a Wet Wet Wet fan at all Francie?

– Can't claim to be.

– Here, listen to this . . . This fella's got some voice on him.

After a few seconds of listening to the song he pressed the button to turn off the radio.

– Anyway, to business.

M.O.C. turned and looked at Francie.

– It's been noted up in Belfast the fine job you seem to be doing Francie.

– Is that so?

– I wouldn't lie to you.

– Well it's good to hear.

– Those small ops you're running. Not earth-shattering but it speaks to an all-round capability that is not as common as you might think.

– Thank you.

– You seem to have a nose for the intelligence work in particular. Don't take that the wrong way now. I'm sure you're fearless and all, I'm not saying that you're not. But there's other skills that are even more scarce. They say, I'm told, that Francie knows. *Francie knows*. And a man with knowledge is a beautiful thing.

– It can be, certainly.

– Because, Francie, we especially need to know what's going on round these parts. These lands here are our fortress. The Gap of the North and all that. Has been that way since the time of Cú Chulainn and the Red Branch knights. The Táin and all that rigmarole, Queen Medb et cetera. Even Oliver Plunkett sought refuge up in this bastion of ours, hiding out from The Brits on the slopes of Slieve Gullion. A fat lot of good it did him, mind. Sure, a quick trip up to Drogheda cathedral would show you that!

– True. The Christian Brothers brought us up there on our school tour every year to see his head. The zoo must never have occurred to them.

– Indeed. Anyway, you get my drift regarding the strategic importance of having a protected area like that.

– I do.

– You're a man of the left Francie?

– I am. Why do you ask?

– No, no reason, it's just that I can picture you bent over your Marx and your Engels.

– Aye. Back in the day perhaps. No time for that these days.

– Well then, this is our Iron Triangle Francie, to use

a more relevant reference for you, given that I know you'd be up on your Ho Chi Minh.

– One of the greats all right. No doubt about that.

– Which makes it all the more important that if there's any threats to the integrity of this jewel in the crown of our resistance we have to be wise to it Francie, I'm sure you would agree.

– I would.

– Can I speak frankly to you Francie?

– You can.

– We have a situation with this young lad who's gone missing. The mother is creating an unmerciful ruckus.

– So I hear.

– And it couldn't be happening at a worse time for us Francie. Things are . . . delicate. On the political level. The Yanks are involved now and you know how sensitive they can be about these matters. We can't afford to look like goons. It only weakens us so it does.

– I don't disagree, but not sure how I can help . . .

M.O.C. looked at Francie for a second. He was very serious, even angry looking, but then broke into a smile.

– Well, a little bird told me you've got yourself involved somewhat in the situation. At the behest of our mutual friend. Now, now, you don't have to tell me anything. In fact, it's better if you don't. But I just wanted to inform you Francie, semi-officially, that it's in everyone's interests that this lad gets reunited with his mother, and sooner rather than later. The word is he's clean Francie. Bit of a little shit right enough but that's all.

– Even if what you're saying is true I'd imagine that there'll have to be due process.

– Absolutely Francie, absolutely! I wouldn't have it any other way!

M.O.C. stared at Francie in that severe manner again.

– But at the same time the process has to end a particular way. Trust me Francie, you'll be doing Nailer a favour here in the long run. He's out on a limb here so he is.

Francie said nothing and both men sat looking at an old woman putting her shopping in the boot of a car. Her disabled son stood beside her doing nothing. It started to rain.

– It's a cruel world isn't it?

The politician then turned to face Francie. He was relaxed again, smiling.

– You're in a good position here Francie. Not sure if you realize it, but it's to your advantage that you'd be seen as your own man. Neither here nor there if you don't mind me saying so, there's the bit of the ghost about you. And if you play your cards right, it's all upside from here on in. I mean, don't get me wrong. Nailer's a great man so he is and I know you and him go way back. A legend. Practically a one-man Cause and Struggle all by himself. An historic figure really. But the thing is he's knocking on a bit Francie. And time waits for no man. You can see that he's not the rule of iron he used to be. There's a few of the young ones giving him jip, starting to talk back to him and such, getting a bit uppity, which would never have happened back in the day. And I don't mind telling you Francie that it makes us nervous. Because you know as well as I do that one notch below Nailer and you're into pure headbanger territory.

– A tad harsh but I think I catch your drift.

– Again, don't get me wrong Francie. Fine lads. Soldiers. Patriotic out the wazoo. But we need to be able to control them, even if it's only for their own sakes.

– Well good luck with that.

– O there's ways Francie, there's ways so there is. Don't you worry about that. But the concern always, *always*, is that tightness be maintained. Especially *here* of all places.

– I agree with that all right.

– Because there can't be any splintering Francie. No schisms. It can't be like it was with The Stickies back in the day. That's utmost so it is. Absolutely paramount. Given where we're headed.

– And where might that be?

M.O.C. looked at Francie but didn't speak for a moment. Again he looked almost angry but again he broke quickly into one of his broad smiles.

– The promised land Francie. The promised land.

7

MICKEY, SURROUNDED BY a world of madness, sat like the lord of it, on a throne of concrete, insulated by his total concentration on what he held out in front of him. Around him was the wild hour, but it could have been the end of days, a rent having appeared in civilization to let nature roam, and off it went loping yellow eyed about the place, jaws open, rabid, venereal, the screams and the gutturals of abuse and slagging, siren calls for the blood and the blade. The square of The Town, Saturday night. Mickey was in the corner where the old phone box was, sitting up on the wall next to it, his feet planted on the bench. The buses had returned not long ago, emptying their drunken cargo of teenagers from the nightclubs in Carrick and Newry. The weaponry of choice was glass, fingernails and hair. A new fight had just broken out at Malocca's on the other side of The Square, and for some reason this one in particular attracted a crowd that spilled out on to the road around it. But Mickey's attention didn't stray, focused as it was on what he held out in front of him, fascinated by it, studying it, a fistful of someone's hair, the clump of bloody scalp still attached to it.

– That's disgusting so it is. Absolutely. Dee. Skusting.

He brought the clump of hair closer to him, staring intently at the roots.

– They're fucking moving so they are! Look at this Kaja! Look at this! They're like little maggots. Swarming over it.

Kaja, urinating in the telephone box next to him, looked through the broken glass.

– I could have told you that scumbag would have nits.

Mickey threw away the clump of hair, but it caught the air and drifted down in front of him on the bench. He kicked it on to the ground and gave a shudder, wiping his hands on the sides of his leather jacket. He took out a cigarette and lit it, stretching out the back of his hand to reassure himself that it probably wasn't broken, the knuckles scraped and bloody, a bit puffy, certainly sore as he clenched and unclenched.

– Where the fuck is Handy anyway? He's been gone for ages so he has.

Kaja finished urinating and emerged from the phone box. Then he reached back and picked up the receiver that wasn't even connected to the vandalized phone but rather lay on top of it.

– Hello, hello, Handy? Come in Handy, Earth to Handy, hi. Your bum chum Mickey wants to know where you are.

Cupping the receiver, he put his head around the side of the phone box again.

– He says he's riding the hole of some young one up at The Rock. But he'll have to go in a minute before she wakes up.

– Some boy, said Mickey.

Kaja let the receiver fall then climbed up on to the bench and sat next to Mickey on the concrete ledge. Mickey offered him a cigarette and then handed him his own one to light the other off it. Both of them sat looking out at the mayhem. The Square was a packed purgatory. Big queues at the taxi rank meant there was no hope of escape. Several people were vomiting nearby. Couples stood around eating each other's faces, their hands down each other's outfits, rooting and pulling at each other. Someone staggered by, barely able to put one foot in front of the other. It was balmy enough though, continental, a nice breeze on the face. The crowd outside Malocca's chipper was getting bigger, it was their cheers that were the loudest. Kaja stood up to get a better look.

– Hey Mickey, look it, it's your girlfriend.

Mickey had to laugh at that. He looked over to the crowd.

– Yep. That's my Wheelie Bin all right.

Even from here they could see that it was Sandra Magee, Bin Man's daughter, who was fighting. The circle had formed around her and whoever she was fighting. It was no one they recognized, but from the looks of him he was probably one of the students from the regional college. Long hair, glasses, lumberjack shirt, bad acne that you could appreciate or at least guess at even from all the way over here. The guy had his hands up to say that he didn't want to fight, but Sandra wasn't interested, no way Jose, sure the girl lived for this hour. She was only fifteen but already well over that in stone weight, the image and shape of her father in that regard. The student was pleading with her, but Sandra wasn't having it. She slapped him in the face a few times and the crowd cheered her on. Each time the slaps got harder, more of the punch about them. It was annoying to her how easy it was, the student wasn't even defending himself for fuck sake, Jesus he was starting to cry now, you could hear it in his voice, pleading with her, the pimply fuck. It made her mad so it did. She was going to stamp the fucker's face in completely now. Her own face lit like a warrior's, hurt, triumphant. This was the way to feel love all right, fame delivered in spades, she'd bask in it so she would, these very moments of pure glory, destined to be the high point of her entire existence.

– It was the same deal last Saturday, said Mickey.

– She's some unit all right. This is her Anfield so it is.

– I mean Handy you spa. It was the same last Saturday. Disappearing off on us. Wherever the fuck he gets to.

– Well at least he won't want to go down the docks now at this stage.

– For the pink bird? I thought he was only joking about that. God, that would be pure batshit so it would.

– Pure.

The crowd's cheering got louder. Sandra was properly punching the student now. He tried to get away but the circle of drunken screaming mouths wouldn't let him out and anonymous hands kept pushing him back towards the big figure of Sandra, who didn't need to move around much.

– Some fucking unit all right, Kaja repeated. I wonder has she considered turning pro?

He seemed genuine, even thoughtful.

– Fair fucks to you man, he said then, that's all I can say. Fair fucks to you. Respect.

– A mouth's a mouth, Kaj. Close your eyes and it could be Claudia Schiffer down on her knees in front of you.

The student was now begging Sandra. She was laughing as she hit him. But in a rage as well. She hated him. Blood was coming from the student's nose and a thin stream of it from one of his ears. His glasses had fallen off and he staggered around after them saying please please my glasses please they're new lenses, but Sandra walked over and stamped on them and the crowd cheered at that as well. The student shouted and got down on his knees crying openly now, trying to pick up the ruins of his glasses. Mr Malocca had come out of his chip shop and was trying to get the crowd to disperse. They were losing interest anyway, starting to thin out.

Handy finally surfaced, coming from behind Mickey and Kaja, grabbing both of them by the mouths from behind.

– Here, smell, he said.

That gave them a fright and they shouted at him, and he walked around the concrete wall, still laughing, to stand in front of them. They rubbed their moist faces with their sleeves and cursed him. Handy looked over at the thinning crowd at Malocca's and saw the young Magee laughing and joking. Someone had gone to her and raised her arm in the air.

– I see your woman's scrapping again Kaj. All that rage. Are you not satisfying her?

– She's Mickey's now. He was just telling me how much he loves her.

– Where the fuck were you? Mickey shouted.

Handy stared back at him. He didn't appreciate the question, but it was the tone which really annoyed him. He stared at Mickey, cold with anger.

– What's it to you Newry boy?

– We've been waiting ages so we have.

– So?

– I'm just saying. It was the same last Saturday when we went down the docks. Who was that fella in the car?

Handy stared hard at Mickey. He hadn't realized they had seen the car, much less who he was meeting. He leant over with his hands in his pockets, glaring at Mickey the whole time.

– What fucking car? You're fucking dreaming so you are. Seeing cars everywhere, just like your paedo uncle.

Kaja laughed. Handy stood up straight, relaxed and jovial again.

– I was off with the young McGrory one if you must know.

He held out two fingers and brought them under his own nose, and made a big sniffing sound.

– Hmm . . . nineteen-ninety-four Louis Girls' convent. Inter Cert year. Pure vintage. Wait till she matures a bit.

Kaja laughed but Mickey was still sore. He came down from sitting up on the wall. Handy hadn't moved and as Mickey walked past him Handy swung his leg and kicked him as hard as he could on the upper leg. Mickey turned and, towering over Handy, squared up to him, furious. But Kaja reacted quickly and instantly had a blade out and up under Mickey's chin.

– Down boy, down.

Handy laughed as Mickey backed away and then turned and started to walk. Handy shouted after him.

– Walk on Marky Mark, he said. Walk on. And mind your own fucking business in future. Do you hear me

Newry boy, do you? You'll be back working for Uncle Francie again so you will.

Kaja noticed something coming their way and, acting the peacemaker, called after Mickey.

– Hey, look at this Mickey. Here's the bollocks that was fighting your girlfriend.

Then he looked over at the student as he made his way towards them and shouted at him.

– Hey you, you shouldn't be hitting women!

The greasy-haired student didn't hear him. He was coming closer to them, unsteady on his feet and crying, cradling his broken glasses as he limped, hunched over and cold, blood patches on his shirt, which was ripped all the way down the front, an Iron Maiden T-shirt visible underneath it. Both Mickey and Handy watched as Kaja moved towards the student in a zigzag, talking to himself as he went, bent over, compact like a boxer.

– Stevie Nicol has the ball. He passes it to Ronnie Whelan. Whelan back to Hansen. Hansen passes it to Jan Mølby. Mølby turns, crosses the ball . . . curves it in nicely towards Ian Rush lurking at the back post.

As Kaja was saying all this he was weaving and bobbing, getting closer and closer to the student, who only now looked up, just in time to see Kaja ducking low then launching up at him from a crouching position with a firm upward headbutt pushing on to his nose that could clearly be heard to snap.

> – GOAL!!!!!! Kaja roared, wheeling away with his arms in the air and shouting. Ian Rush scores!! With an absolute bullet of a header right up into the roof of the net leaving Neville Southall in the Everton goal absolutely and completely stone dead.

The student collapsed unconscious on to his back, blood pouring freely out of his nose and over his face as if a tap had been turned on. Meanwhile Kaja was dancing around shouting to the sky, his arms aloft, receiving the adulation of Anfield.

> – The ball came in from Mølby, and Ian Rush with an absolute darting bullet of a header puts it into the top corner of the net. The Kop are in absolute raptures so they are. What. An. Absolute. Beauty.

But Handy and Mickey barely noticed what had happened. Mickey was looking at his hands and thought again about that clump of scalp, riddled with nits. Ordinarily he might have mentioned it to Handy, but he didn't feel like it and, despite the noise – from Kaja, from The Square, from the whole world – both of them walked on silent and resentful, in the direction of Malocca's.

8

IT WAS FRANCIE'S suggestion that Handy tag along for this one. As he explained to Nailer, he didn't really know the young man all that well and it would allow him to rectify that, while also giving him a chance to talk to him about the Warrenpoint job, maybe find out why it went south, no big deal, just suss things out a bit. Besides, with Kaja away in Tenerife with his mother it would be handy having Handy there. An extra pair of eyes and an extra mouth too because he was straight into The Arms afterwards to tell everyone all about it. Nailer was uneasy but relented, telling Francie to go easy on the lad now, he might be a bit of a hothead but he wasn't as stupid as he looked either.

On the morning in question Francie picked Handy up from the side of the road. At the crack of dawn, Handy later complained, and not only that, but wasn't Francie full of the joys for once, in fine fettle altogether. Evidently he regarded this little outing of theirs as an opportunity to cast himself in the role of mentor to his young companion, a fount of knowledge and purveyor of wise counsel, someone the callow lad could lean on going forward. So he was in full-on didactic mode practically the whole way there, expounding to the hung-over Handy on matters not only relating to his general tactical and strategic philosophy as regards this type of operation – the scouting, planning and execution thereof – but, Christ Jesus, Handy told us all later, didn't the old fart then start banging on about the Marxist principles underpinning the whole shebang, setting out his own particular credo vis-à-vis the materialist interpretation of history, and his (admittedly not entirely unoriginal) ideas defining the parameters within which modern industrialist-based societies were anchored (rather than existing independently thereof), and which, in Francie's humble opinion, represented not only a tragedy in and of itself, but also a fantastic opportunity, because it was exactly this materialist interpretation of history which mandated (no, practically guaranteed!) that if the working class could only make itself the ruling class and destroy the basis for a class-based society – eliminating in the process the prima facie case for private property in the first place and the existence, no, the entire *raison d'être*, of the bourgeoisie – then the inevitable result would *have* to be a classless Marxist society with no conflict and no wars nor any manner or multiplicity of the various social ills that currently afflict western civilizations and capitalist economic systems in general with their emergent so-called liberal democracies. And, obviously, *obviously*, Francie went on, it went without saying that there would be no need even for a system of centralized government, whose inherently oppressive nature was practically inbuilt from the get-go, going right down to the marrow of its bones, and was at the end of the day as irrevocable as it was entirely predictable. Well, people could only laugh at the idea of Handy having to sit through that nonsense, getting the head bored off him with all this leftist cant. Everyone could relate to that one all right, having heard that particular spiel many a time down the years from the likes of not just Francie but all the other lefties who used to be far more common about the place. Always banging on about Marx and Lenin those boys were, advocating for the prosaic poetry inherent in their ideas, the hidden beauty that was contained within them, the sheer underlying simplicity of the world as it should be, and the absolute and utter tragedy that it wasn't at all that way in reality. Utopianism didn't even begin to cut it with those lads, the thought of Trotsky in particular would bring them to tears. Needless to say, they barely dwelt on the subsequent and entirely predictable betrayal of the movement by the forces of Stalinism, mainly Stalin himself of course, but tended to skip over that bit, focusing on the triumphant rebirth which followed, the brief blooming and glorious resurgence of revolutionary animism as it took the shape (alas only illusory) of a wild and seemingly rampant gospel promising the remediation if not outright perfection of society and her ills and spreading as it did through the jungles of South East Asia and the central Americas in particular, propagated by their brothers and sisters in the Viet Cong, the Sandinistas and lately the FARC, not to mention of course their more proximate cousins in the Baader–Meinhof, the Red Brigades, and of course ETA. Basically any and all of your nationalist separatist movements, which tended to have a Marxist–Leninist bent to them almost by definition. Francie, like all the old lefties who preceded him, would practically wet himself at the potential prospects of it all adding up to Utopia herself, an unheard music stirring in his soul as he stared misty-eyed into the middle distance with a big loopy grin on his face, his core vibrating like a tuning fork to the strains of The Internationale. Handy though, needless to say, was the exact wrong audience for this type of talk, given his short attention span and general disinterest in historical matters, not to mention the splitting hangover he was suffering from. Christ it was like being back at school, he told us later in The Arms. But on and on and on Our Francie continued, on a pure roll he was, the man simply could not contain the enormous didactic bore that was bursting out of him at the seams, as he proceeded to explain to his young companion how the ultimate aim of The Cause was, lest it be forgotten (and before it was hijacked by the likes of Pearse and his narrow priest-ridden brand of rosary-bead republicanism), to establish on this island of Ireland a *socialist* republic in accordance with the original aims of the Irish *Socialist* Republican Party whose intent was to muster *all* the forces of labour for the radical, if not outrightly anarchic, revolutionary reconstruction of the modern industrialist anti-agrarian society and – this is the key bit, Francie said, nudging Handy – the *incidental* destruction of the British Empire. It was, he maintained, this type of approach, and *solely* this type of approach, that was necessary *not only* for the purposes of getting rid of The Brits but for *establishing in their place* the structures of a truly just and lasting socialistic society that would cater to *all* the proletariat thereby liberated in the process, allowing them to cast off the capitalist materialist yoke that went hand in hand with the colonial one, to say nothing of the suffocating merchant mindset of the petit bourgeoisie that was a legacy of both, and thus achieving once and for all the overthrow of the colonial-based hierarchical system of the elites, of which the modern British state was merely one of many examples. Because, my young friend, Francie said to Handy, smiling, don't you know well that the governments of a capitalist society are but committees of the rich to manage the affairs of the merchant class?

Here he couldn't resist nudging Handy once again on the elbow and giving him a wink.

– James Connolly.

At this point Handy, who had been fierce quiet in the front passenger seat of the car the whole time, a baseball cap pulled down over his eyes, said that he simply could not take it any more.

– Fuck me Francie, will you ever shut up. Me head is hanging off me so it is. Here, stop. I need to go for a slash.

– What?! Are you mad in the head? There are no doubt squaddies hiding in them there bushes.

– Well in that case, they better keep their mouths closed because I am bursting so I am.

Handy reached for the door handle, forcing Francie to pull to a sharp stop, cursing.

– Christ Handy, what are you up to lad?!

But he had no choice other than to hit the hazards and pull in. Handy jumped out and scampered off the verge and into the bushes while, casual as you like, Francie emerged from the vehicle and stood there in plain view, stretching his poor oul back, taking a cigarette out as if it was the most natural thing in the world to be having a bit of a break from the rigours of the road slap bang in the most militarized square kilometre in all of Europe. He put the bonnet up and pretended to be examining underneath it, all the time shouting out to Handy to hurry the utter and absolute fuck up. Handy meanwhile was finding the whole thing hilarious as he waded further and further into the long grass shouting back at Francie to relax the cacks and, as he found relief for himself, breaking into snatches of rebel song which he bellowed loudly into the hillside around him, in absolute knots at the sight of pure agitation evident in the figure of Francie bent over the engine with the bonnet up, until Handy eventually, eventually, climbed back up on to the verge of the road and into the car so that they could resume their journey northward through Newry and along the loughside inlet. As they passed Narrow Water, Handy rolled down the window and before Francie could stop him stuck a fist out it.

– Thirteen gone but not forgotten we got eighteen and Mountbatten. Woohoo, tiocfaidh ár lá hi!

– Christ son, Francie shouted at him, will you shut up! It's less attention you want to be attracting on these jobs.

Francie checked his rear mirror, before continuing the drive into Warrenpoint until they had to slow down once more in traffic. Handy calmed down a bit and not much conversation passed between them until Francie, taking up where he had left off earlier, started pointing out the rich array of economic targets in that middle-class oasis. There was the Ulster Bank for starters, where the police no doubt lodged their wages, and the Bank of Scotland across the street, not to mention numerous commercial enterprises, butchers, the bakery, the supermarket, the cash and carry, a men's suit shop and several small women's boutiques and hairdressers, things which were the very economic engine of the locality, capitalism with a small c, allowing it to motor on in all obliviousness to the structural injustice, the iniquity and rank oppression that was de rigueur in other parts of the Unionist sectarian state. Handy grunted but didn't say anything.

– You see, said Francie, here even the Catholics have grown fat and comfortable, their middle-class petit bourgeois concerns regarding their social progression and material attainment nullifying any nationalistic instinct or socialistic concern that they might have had at one time for their fellow man. Self-interest has taken over and right there is the problem with your crony capitalism, how it has only led to the commodification of us all, with its rampant consumerism and greed, to say nothing of its market-centred approach to social policy, it makes me sick to the stomach so it does to even think about it.

Again Handy just grunted.

– Nothing a few firebombs wouldn't put right, Francie added then, laughing, and giving Handy another elbow nudge. Give them a taste of the war-torn eh? Sure, you wouldn't even need to kill anyone.

Handy looked at him in disbelief.

– What would be the point of that? Isn't that half the craic?

They stopped at a traffic light just across the way from the post office. It was open, with people coming in and out, but the front window was still boarded over from the attempted robbery the previous month. Francie saw the alleyway where Handy and the others would have hoped to get away. He knew the area well. The alleyway led to a narrow one-way, easily blocked. It was madness. If anyone had bothered to ask him in advance he would have told them that the whole thing was a shitshow waiting to happen.

– Bring back any bad memories for you?

Handy opened his eyes and looked over. He was quiet for a moment, but then closed his eyes again, nonplussed.

– Ask the stupid cunts who were caught. I got away didn't I?

– You were lucky all right.

– Lucky? I nearly lost an arm.

Francie gave it another minute before speaking again.

– I heard you getting delayed is what might have saved you.

– The door jammed on that banger. A bloody miracle I was able to get away in it at all.

– That's what I mean. Tell me, how far in advance was the Donnelly lad looped in on the whole thing?

Handy didn't respond. Francie looked at him.

– It would be helpful for me to get the timeline right in my own head. Presumably you heard I'm heading up next week to have a chat with him?

Handy was sitting up now with his eyes open. He was staring hard at Francie, who could feel the gaze of the younger man burning the side of his face as he looked ahead at the car in front of him.

– What the fuck is this, Newry man? A debrief?

– Not at all. I'm just looking for as much detail as possible.

Handy was still looking at him.

– Was that little pig talking to you? The Murphy bitch? I saw you standing next to her in The Arms the other week. What did the little toutspawn say to you?

Francie was taken aback by the sudden fury that had come into his companion. He was like some manner of cat hissing at him, his green eyes wide open.

– And you can tell Donners when you meet him that I said he's a lying cunt so he is. And I hope Casio draws it out before putting him out of his misery. Be sure to tell him that for me, Newry man, OK?

Handy sat back in the seat and after a while leant his head back and closed his eyes. But from the rapid movement of his chest it was obvious that he was still agitated. Neither of them said anything else and it was probably good that the traffic was brutal and the roadworks kept them stalled on the main street. Francie changed the radio channel a few times and then put on a Bob Dylan cassette. By the time they got through to the other side of the town centre the tension had eased and Handy may even have been sleeping. Francie followed the sign out for the golf links road and when they got to the golf club he nudged Handy awake before circling the car park twice and finally locating the grey Cortina from the funeral the other week. Francie stopped to double-check the number plate against the one he'd written in his small notebook.

– The nearly retired ones is the easiest so they are. Habit does not even come close to describing them. And they have the added sense of relaxation in their subconscious, as if they're practically there already. They can't help it. It's only human nature I suppose.

Handy sat forward and gave a vigorous stretch before rolling down the window and hocking some deep phlegm out it. Francie pulled out of the car park and indicated to go right.

– Why not do the fucker here?

– Are you mad in the head my young foolish friend? Half the peelers in the state are here on their annual coppers' outing.

– Even better.

– We have to be cautious around these parts. You're not in South Armagh now. This is not friendly terrain. As I was saying earlier, even the Catholic citizenry are not well disposed towards us. They have become inured to the status quo. Which is to say son, to put it another way, we wouldn't get very far.

Handy laughed again, and the way he told the story later in the inner bar of The Arms, everyone there laughed as well. There was no doubt he could do a killer impression of Francie. Close your eyes and the voice you heard was Francie's, open them and you'd expect to find the fucker right there in front of you, the facial tics, the bad teeth, those rodent eyes of his darting right and left, the pasty yellowy skin, the big mock serious head on him – it was all Francie, Handy had him down absolutely pat. They went along the road two hundred yards and waited. A good hour and a half passed before Francie shook Handy awake.

– See, what did I tell you? Like clockwork.

Ahead of them the grey Cortina was pulling out. They followed the car back out on to the main road and in the direction of the town. At the big sign advising Belfast (via the scenic route) and the Magnificent Mountains of Mourne they took the second exit on to the Belfast road and after three and a half miles turned into Cherrywood Heights. They caught sight of Mickey standing beside his recently hijacked motorcycle. Francie flashed the lights at him and Mickey disappeared, running into the undergrowth and away off on the pre-identified shortcut through the back of the estate. Francie drove after the Cortina as it meandered around the middle cul-de-sac, parking outside the end house with the red front door. By the time they got there the car was already parked and the detective was at the boot taking out his clubs. Mickey, bally on, came up alongside him and when the man put the boot down, there was Mickey confronting him with his Glock to the face, the pair of them frozen in position, for what seemed like an eternity. Nothing happened.

Mickey took his gun up close to his own face and looked at it.

– His fucken gun's gone and stuck! Handy said.

The man made a move to run but fell to the ground. Mickey froze, not knowing what to do. He aimed the gun again at the man on the ground but again nothing happened. Then behind him out of nowhere a woman appeared in her dressing gown. It was the man's wife, Francie recognized her from the church, and she started belting Mickey on the back with an umbrella, screaming at him. Handy found the whole thing hilarious.

– Fuck me, he said, the old bat's clobbering him!

Francie put the foot down and they pulled up beside the scene. Get in, he shouted over to Mickey, but out jumped Handy. Cool as you like he walked over to Mickey and the woman, pulling the baseball cap down over his face. He took out his pistol. Bang bang, shooting the man on the ground dead, causing his wife to let out a scream and run to him. Handy pointed the gun at her too. Leave her alone Handy, Mickey said. Handy stared at him. Doesn't she know my name now? Bang bang. Husband and wife dead, sprawled out on the ground, blood leaking out of them forming a puddle down to the gutter. In The Arms that evening, Handy mimed these actions with his finger, then blew on the tip of it like they do in the westerns. There was silence around the small inner bar as everyone sat looking at him. Some boy. No doubt about it and there was something like reverence as everyone watched him take up his second Fürstenberg and glug a good bit of it. Some boy all right. What he left out of the telling was the part where, afterwards, he had climbed back into the car beside Francie, the eyes wild on him, breathing heavily through the nose, alert as an animal, and went right up so close to Francie's face that Francie could feel flecks of moisture on his skin.

– Do you still think I'm a tout, Newry man, do you?

9

IT WAS ABOUT a mile of a walk from her house first into Silverbridge then up the side of the mountain to get to The Arms. She kept to the other side of the narrow road to avoid the frequent cars coming from behind her who would think absolutely nothing of clipping her, sure half of them would be half-cut already behind the wheel. All day she'd been in two minds about whether to go or not. She'd heard the bitches in her class talking about it, what they would wear et cetera, what boys would be there et cetera, making sure of course that Cathy overheard them. But why shouldn't she go? She was as entitled as anybody. And it was *her* Spanish teacher who was organizing it. And even though Ms Gonzalez had said to the whole class that she hoped to see them there she was *specifically* looking at her when she said it, no doubt because Cathy was the only one to bother asking a question or to show the slightest bit of interest in what Ms Gonzalez was telling them about flamenco, which she said was her native dance, even showing them a video of dancers in their wild, colourful costumes that of course the little bitches only smirked at while saying snide things to each other under their breath. Cathy thought the costumes were stunning and the dancers were fierce and magical but she felt stunted by the inarticulacy of her own stupid questions afterwards when she went up to Ms Gonzalez and started mumbling and rambling to her, the words spilling out of her and making absolutely no sense to her smiling, indulgent teacher. All she really wanted to say was that it was all amazing so it was, just amazing and how do you even get started with doing something beautiful like that in the world? But then right up until the last minute she wasn't sure about going, deciding that no she wasn't going to go before quickly throwing on her one half-decent top and jumper and denim skirt and the puffy but at least dark green jacket that used to be Thomas's and off she went, taking the dinner up to her mother in the bed first of course. Anyway Thomas would be in from his work soon from that thug of a mafia boss, and what else was she going to do for the night? And, again, for the thousand millionth time, why shouldn't she go? So off she hurried out the drive under the awning of massive sycamores and sessile oaks swaying to a breeze she couldn't feel and up the dark country lane and then left across the small bridge and up the snaky incline and then down and up again until after a while she saw the bright lights of The Arms in the distance, the car park sunken down a bit off the road already nearly full with cars pulling in, the voices of the people carrying all the way down to her on the evening sky as they shouted out their crude greetings to one another. She walked on, her pace admittedly slowing down a good bit and at this stage she was really having to force her legs to go one in front of the other. She wondered if that man Francie would be there. She'd heard he was *involved* somehow and maybe she might try and talk to him. She'd have to see. Maybe if she happened to find herself standing next to him again, just like in The Arms recently, when he was the only one in that dump of a place who even acknowledged her. Yes if that happened again she might say something to him all right. He didn't seem as bad as the others. And at least that way her conscience would be completely one hundred per cent in the clear no matter what they did to Darren

Donnelly. She could forget all about the whole thing then with zero guilt whatsoever. But the closer she got she started to dawdle even more, admittedly. God it would be great if Suzie Monaghan was still here and her and her family hadn't had to move to Australia after what Handy did to her at the Lark in the Park. Big mistake that turned out to be, them going to the police over it. You only had to look at their house to see that, or what used to be their house rather, burnt to the ground as it was, nothing but a big charred wreck now, Suzie and her family were lucky to get out alive so they were. Now Cathy had no friends at all, but sure she was nearly used to it at this stage. She would have been only about four or five when they came for her father, obviously none of it was her fault, and the girl could barely even remember him now at this stage, but God that was some night so it was, some night, the crowd of local men, people around these parts still talked about it, all pinted up we were, it was some craic, everyone clambering into the back of Taxi McCabe's Hiace to call round like trick-or-treaters like ghouls to the Murphy household. It was actually the mother who answered the door, anxious yes but none too plussed probably, only to get the shock of her life when she saw the gang of us, admittedly hooded, like goons backlit by the hall light gathered there at the front door which the woman only opened to see why anyone was calling at this ungodly hour, calling out to her husband as she went up the hallway that whoever it was they must be in a bad way altogether, it must be anyone in trouble, one of the neighbours needing help perhaps, was it the power out? Or their car needing pushing again? Or maybe only wanting to borrow a drop of milk for morning, the husband coming out from the living room then, the newspaper tucked under his arm, and behind them the young Thomas lad, who was a normal enough boy then, possibly even intelligent, holding hands with his sister, both children in their pyjamas, and remarkable how young Cathy still to this very day vividly recalls the puzzlement and guiltily stupidly the almost sense of excitement that she felt on seeing the group of men surrounding the porch, shapes in the darkness, spectres, ghouls, like from a fairy tale that she would always remember hazily as in a dream, a dream containing men like monsters who came one night like Rumpelstiltskin to take away her father and never brought him back.

But that was all years ago now at this stage, and at some point you have to get on with things. And anyway wasn't it a good riddance? That Tom Murphy fella was nothing but a bad-tempered sour bastard right from the get-go, so there was no loss there so there wasn't, ask anyone, a sour prick from day one was what he was, that's right, a bad-humoured bad-tempered unpopular oul miser, narky as fuck who always just kept himself to himself, never making any secret whatsoever of his general disapproval of The Cause, or so much as darkening the door of The Arms, not even on one occasion that anyone could remember, to have the chat or the bit of craic. No, he would have been too good for the likes of that so he would, which would have been fine were it not for the fact that wasn't he also only too happy to make a big and constant holy perennial show of it, parading around with that absolutely inbuilt superiority of his, like a big holy Joe he was, O the bastard absolutely loved nothing more than to lord it over people, shoving it down their throats and up their holes, arrogance didn't even begin to cut it with that fecker, which needless to say only got worse when he went away off to Leeds and married the Protestant woman. His face became even more set rigid then against the local ways, the prejudice that he seemingly now felt everywhere on account of her and their two half-Prod children when they returned, and he kept well away from it so he did, he had no interest in any of it, sure everyone was a bigot in his view, the whole pile and shower of them, we were nothing but muck savages and ignorant culchies, close-minded prejudiced border peasants basically, with our primitive senses of humour and crude alcoholic ways of going about the place. Certainly he wouldn't have had any qualms about betraying The Cause, that's for sure, no, no, of course he wouldn't, sure he would have been practically wetting himself getting down off his tractor that day and scurrying back like a rat to the house to put in the warning phone call to that new RUC hotline The Brits had set up. Seemingly he'd spotted a unit of local boys hiding in among the hedgerow, their blood up, a patrol of paras half a mile away and wandering towards them in bliss ignorance. Well, someone certainly let the cat out of the bag because didn't the paras come to an abrupt and sudden stop then, spreading out into battle formation, the local boys beating it pronto from the hedges, lucky to escape with their intact heads still on their shoulders. But then didn't the bastard only deny everything? It wasn't him he said, he had, he claimed, zero involvement, nada, zip, prove it, and it took Casio and his crew from Internal Security to have to come down from Belfast to get it out of him, a full and frank confession, signed and dated, it was pinned to the fucker's clothes when they found him down that laneway out near Cullaville, his hands and feet bound together, an oil rag shoved all the way down his throat with various other signs of shall we say discomfort on him after the prolonged interrogation, the word TOUT for instance carved into the wall of his chest, and a big gaping hole at the back of the skull. That was young Cathy

Murphy's stock, the nature of the black blood that was running through her and that retarded brother of hers who for some totally unknown mysterious reason Nailer tolerated out at his complex, a good worker though seemingly, worth two or three in terms of pure muscle to have about the place, doing odd jobs, whatever it was he did for Nailer exactly, no one knew for sure, shifting stones and the like, slopping out the animals, the prize pigs and the few cows and hens that he kept for working-farmer taxation purposes, spreading fertilizer, turning sod, shovelling manure, hammering stakes into the ground, fencing poles or sinking slurry pits, always grinding lifting grunting, plodding like a beast of burden on the slow go the lad was, dumb and persistent from one end of the day to the other. So it was mainly young Cathy you'd see about the town, doing the messages and out and about around the shops, collecting the mother's widow's pension at the post office because obviously the woman herself was never seen about the place. Seemingly she had gone completely loo-la in the months and years afterwards, her nerves were at her apparently, people said the woman wasn't right in the head, not that she ever had been in the first place, certainly she had never been given much to socializing, the haughty bitch, of course not, nor deigning at all to mix with any of the local women, she was said to be dissatisfied with the local shops, not a patch on Leeds seemingly, and nowadays she never left the house, she'd gone mad in the head completely, confirmed clinically skitzo, riven with the manic panic, and a mixture of mystique and gossip and legend grew up around her, the mad Murphy woman, The Tout Murphy's lunatic Prod wife who more or less required long-term care now, or so it was said, even the public health nurse refused to deal with her she was that bad, the woman seemingly never leaving the bed from morning to night and the whole place reeking of her shit and piss because she was content to sit in it all day, it stuck to her skin that was ulcered through, becoming badly infected, rats had free run of the place, they had the rafters completely eaten away, the wood of the structure of the place dissolving, the stairs in danger of collapsing, the whole house basically rotting away from the inside, and it was all her own fault anyway, her and that ignorant lump of a husband of hers, the high almighty big ignorant head on him, if he had only kept his mouth shut none of this would have happened, and now look at her, she should have been put in a home that one, wasn't it her own Orange state that had failed her? And those children should have been taken from her (but sure who would have wanted them?), she was good for nothing now so she wasn't and never had been anyway, look at her, the state of her, it was a disgrace so it was, the tongue hanging out of her, drooling down her bib, the nightdress on her sopping wet, clinging to her skin till it glistened, she'd stare at the moon, the wall, the ceiling, the swaying sycamores out the window that densely encased the house, their deep impenetrable shadows and the wind that whistled like herds of banshees racing and dancing and running wild through the dark forest. When the doorbell went she cowered and cried out and it might only be the meter reader or the milk man, but at midnight it was a different story altogether so it was. It was said that she would come alive then, wandering about her garden not a bother on her, straying into the forest, the lower slopes of Gullion, O she could cover some ground then so she could, when she wanted to that is, so obviously she was faking the whole thing for the social benefits, and to make the people around here look bad, many swore they had seen her with their own eyes at these odd hours, muttering and whispering and laughing to herself like some manner of ghost, a witch is what she was, no, a banshee who messed with Ouija boards, communed with the Devil, the Protestant one, and she knew the spells to get him on her side, praying hard the whole day long wishing ill upon her neighbours, the good and decent people of Cross, urging them to be visited upon by a vicious vengeance of the fates, cancers, strokes, heart disease, any manner of blights to descend upon them and their families, and in return everyone hated her and what was left of The Tout Murphy's cursed family, the Prod mother and the retarded son and now look at this young Cathy one snaking up the dark country road in the shadows, on whatever sly errand, whatever her motives, uninvited, unwanted, alone and disowned, completely friendless, and looking for nothing else other than to cause pure trouble that one, that's right, looking to cause nothing but pure trouble.

10

THE PLACE WAS crowded more than the average, steadily from about sevenish, the mood buoyant, the men shouldered in at the bar, crowing greetings and cawing as the door opened, raucous cheers, the slagging out of them, leaning in then whispering, laughing, gripping each other by the elbow, rubbing hips and backs up against one another, the air above them stinging with Paco Rabanne or Lynx Oriental and cigarettes that couldn't wait to get lit. They wore ironed Wranglers with big buckled brown belts, beige or silver Bobby Ewing blazers, denim jackets, checked shirts, maybe one or two flashy short-sleeved ones in among them as well, all tucked but unbuttoned, some of them well down their sternums, the hair showing, out and proud, half of them had on low-cut cowboy boots, there was the odd Stetson even. The women had removed their thick grey outer layers to reveal colourful puffy frocks and neck scarves, capri pants and shiny cardigans, brocades like body armour like suckling spiders splayed across their chests and looped earrings and thick heels and lipstick, many-hued in crimson, verdure or violet. They were largely excluded from the rump of men who as a body had their backs to them, leaving them to coalesce in the red lounge waiting for their gin and tonics to be sent over to them, doubles all round, then the same again.

Francie sat off to the side watching the whole parade, lighting one Benson off another. He was in his usual spot, somewhat jittery, annoyed at himself that he had completely forgotten about this event, a bloody flamenco of all things, organized by The Spaniard. Seemingly the foreign woman had popped her head in the previous week to propose this venture to Pat Behind The Bar. She wanted, she said, to put on a show for the people of Cross, what she called a flamenco puro, in praise of this flamingo and its recent apparition in this unlikely corner of the world. It was a miracle, she told Pat, a miracle that such an exotic creature should appear among them, whatever the tragic reasons behind it, however it got separated from its kin and was now so bereft and in despair, it broke her heart, she said, to think of it bedraggled there like something divine finding itself out of favour and in exile among the mortals. She wanted to perform her native dance in its honour, to celebrate the stunning sight, just like the original gypsies of her native Sacromonte did when they first saw one and in the presence of beauty considered themselves to have arrived finally at home. Pat hadn't a notion what the foreign woman was on about but it didn't matter, the man was smitten to his bones, apt to throw his shoulder into it and here now the whole of Cross appeared to have turned up. Even Nailer was due in with his crew and before long it was only their reserved corner of the red lounge that was unoccupied. Francie's eyes darted to the door every time it opened. As a rule he didn't like crowds, especially in the context of a public house, their fake excessive cheer annoyed him, their loose-tongued laxity, to say nothing of their raucous unpredictability, and as he watched them gather and form their mob his face twitched like he was in thrall to St Vitus' dance. When Mickey and Kaja eventually arrived Francie's glare told them they were as usual late and they squeezed into their customary nook, hunching on low stools around their Officer Commanding. Francie hadn't seen Mickey since Handy shot the detective and his wife the previous week and in fairness, both boys looked sharp, gelled up, slick and spiked, Mickey in his Chuck Norris vest and Kaja, back and tanned from Tenerife, wearing his other bomber jacket, the good one, the pair of them looking eagerly around the packed lounge, surveying for possibility, nudging each other at the effort some of the older women had gone to in particular. As Francie guessed from their giddiness, the two boys were well fuelled up ahead of time. Seeing the irritated look on Francie and still somewhat abashed by the stuck-gun incident, Mickey nudged Kaja and straightened up. Come to think of it, neither had he had the chance to congratulate his uncle properly since word had got around about Francie's promotion up the ranks, seconded seemingly by M.O.C. Internal Security, or what people around these parts knew as The Squad, that was massive so it was, nobody in their family had been such a big shot before. Mickey hoisted his pint glass of protein shake in the air.

– To Francie. Fair fucks to you Uncle. You're in with the big boys now so you are.

– Christ keep it down.

– Relax the cacks Francie. You of all people are safe now.

– Aye, said Kaja. You don't mess with Casio's crew, that's for sure.

– Internal Security, said Mickey. It's them that does the messing. Sure they can do what they like, those boys.

– Aye, no one asks them any questions, that's for sure.

– I'm just helping them out for a while, said Francie, that's all. It'll be back to normal then.

There was an appreciable chilling of the crowd's murmur, and when Francie looked over at the door he saw that Nailer and his crew had appeared in the lounge. Handy was stood at the head of the posse, a gargoyle grinning outwards on the ledge. The last time Francie had seen him was immediately after the shooting when he dropped Handy off at the safe house urging him to get inside and lie low, Handy sitting on the low window ledge smoking in the afternoon sun, grinning back at the older man.

– Besides, nephew, he continued to Mickey, if I wanted to be in with the big boys I would have done so years ago. In my experience the only difference between big boys and little boys is that big boys can hold it a bit longer.

Nailer and his crew were stood in full view by the door, looking around themselves, surveying the scene like lords. A few people went over to shake hands with Nailer. Francie took up his drink.

– Until they can't that is.

But now he looked at his two companions, trying to appear as stern as possible.

– In any case, there's no need to advertise it. I'm blue in the face saying this to youse.

– Sure the whole county knows at this stage Francie. Possibly beyond.

– Really? Is that so Nephew?

– You can't keep news like that from growing legs and haring about the place.

– Well there's one thing knowing it but it's another matter entirely to be going around shouting it to the heavens like a stuck pig.

– I said nothing so I didn't!

– Well someone's happy to be putting it about, that's for sure. Everyone on the street looking at me twice. Christ, it's like I'm Lord Diplock himself coming to deliberate on this wretched matter. The whole thing makes me queasy to my stomach so it does.

– When's your first meet Uncle?

– I'm on the road in the morning. Which is why I wanted to meet.

– How so?

– If anything should happen to me I wanted youse to know a bit of detail.

– Jesus Francie. Even for you that's a bit OTT by way of the paranoia. The word is you're elected.

– That's what has me worried Nephew. I've been on

the edge of things for years and now all of a sudden they want to let me in. Fascinated to find out what my thoughts are on certain matters.

– Nailer's nothing if not clever all right. Strategic.

– Him and M.O.C., Nephew. They're two sides of the one coin so they are.

– What's in your mind, I mean about the possibilities?

– M.O.C. has me on the hook boys. Such is my strong feeling, though I don't know what it is exactly, or where, that is to say its exact specific location, therefore I cannot see the damn thing to have it removed. All I know is the blasted thing is sharp and I can feel it digging into the back of my neck.

– He's a pro right enough.

– Stone cold Mickey.

– Never trust a political man. That's what my old boy used to say.

– Well even the lame cow squawks the Lord's truth in context.

– He was right as much as he was wrong you know Francie. Looking back like.

– Debatable Mickey, but I'll grant you it out of pure nostalgia. He was your *pater familias* at the end of the day.

– And he hated the Shinners.

– That he did. One of the few things he and I could agree on. He thought, as do I, that they would only lead us up the garden path and back down the other side.

– The way they keep coming at you, he used to say. Always looking for extra. They're like the knackers in many respects.

– Perhaps a tad unfair on our itinerant brethren but I get the drift regarding the political class in general. Especially when they're in need of an insurance policy like our M.O.C. is. I'm not entirely daft you know. It's just that I have the distinct impression this particular one might have been taken out in my name.

– To do with Donners?

– Such is my assumption.

– Like I said before, he's a toerag Uncle, a fuckwit and a brat. Again, I wouldn't be sure about the toutin' now, to be fair, but a pain in the hole generally speaking.

Francie saw that Young Cathy Murphy had come into the pub. As usual she was on her own. This time she was dressed up like she intended to stay, rather than just getting the naggin in for the mother. Kaja, who as usual had been saying very little, was also looking in that direction, squinting at her over his pint.

– Speaking of touts, he said.

All three of them were now looking at the Murphy girl. Francie looked at her properly this time, she'd certainly grown up, the girl, but it was a stunted effort, Christ, almost funny if it wasn't so sad, the pathetic attempt at dressing up, the misfitting clothes, a blouse that her mother might have worn thirty years ago, and was that just the lighting or was it some sort of effort at applying make-up on the girl's face? He was seeing what the crowd of girls on the other side were also now noticing, and laughing at, the whole thing was just tragic so it was.

– Possibly being a tad harsh there Kaj. Sins of the father and all that.

– If it's in the blood it's in the blood.

– Not sure if I go in for that local superstition myself Kaja, touting not being to my knowledge in the genes. Perhaps you've been hanging around with Handy too much.

The young Murphy joined the scrum of people queuing at the bar, but you could tell she did that just to have something to do. She felt the eyes of the room on her though in reality it was only a few that were looking at her, the nervous fidgeting out of her, each of them taking a closer look at her slightly bizarre outfit, nudging the person next to them, and was that a man's jacket the young one was wearing? Handy was now in among the crowd of girls from Cathy's class standing over by the cigarette machine. Whatever he was saying to them was causing them to laugh, and though the lounge was loud Francie could make out those disgusting pig noises they were all making now.

– Where is it they have you going Francie?

It took Francie a second to hear what Mickey said. He turned around to his nephew and looked at him before answering.

– The Town, initially.

He took up his drink.

– I've to drop the car in for a service at Meegan's garage round the back of The Wall. Except I've to bring ten grand in a bag. It'll all kick on from there I imagine. Out back of Meegan's they'll transfer me to a van, take me to one of their safe gaffs, in Bay Estate most likely. Alternatively Cox's Demesne. I'll be searched and put into a jumpsuit. Eyes taped over. Another transfer. Most likely into a small woman's car driven by a woman. There may even be a babe in arms. Certainly there would be if I was running things. Needless to say I'll be in the boot. From there we'll head to wherever the fuck, northbound obviously but probably a long spin around the place for the craic. Which is to say boys that I am familiar with their procedures.

– I heard it was Lisburn you're headed to.

– I'll believe it when I see the wide plains of the Down Royal, Nephew, her bright green flats and those fine specimens that constitute the sport of kings. Other than that I'm making no assumptions.

– What do you want us to do?

– Nothing you can do boys. Just to know about it. If they try to pin some shite on me I am asking for nothing on my behalf other than your pure disdain and total utter inner scepticism. *Confessed during the course of questioning to being an informant for The Crown.* You will know the truth boys. That is all I ask. The wherewithal and the whatnot to say bollocks to that.

– To Francie, said Mickey, ach sure you'll be grand so you will. You're stressing over nothing.

– To Francie, said Kaja.

It was around then that Pat Behind The Bar eventually came downstairs from his flat overhead. When The Regulars at the bar saw him they squealed with laughter. Plainly the man had gone to trouble. Shaven, the hair washed and untangled, jet black from the Just For Men and wearing a white shirt that would hurt your eyes it had been so starched and ironed. A chorus met him as he descended the narrow steep steps.

– The man of the hour!

– Where's this exotic bird of yours anyway Pat?

– She hasn't flown off on you now has she?

– Look at him, henpecked already he is, the state of him!

– Tell us Pat is she all pink or have you seen the bit of white yet yourself?

– Sure isn't it the white meat that's the best bits of a bird anyway?

– Hey Pat do you stand on one leg while you're at it?

– Is it the big beak on her that has you riven wild Pat is it?

– What does she think of your own big beak Pat?

– It's not too yellow for her is it Pat?

Pat, his face burning, lifted the side of the bar and came in behind it only for his expression to freeze in its mould, that particular blend of alarm turned to obedience that would have told you without the need to look that Nailer was standing there at our backs, and all now turned to him.

– Well, if it isn't my sylvan chorus.

– Nailer. Nailer. Mr Nailer. Nailer.

– Any news for me boys?

Nobody said anything.

– Ah relax, I'm only codding yiz. Take the night off men. I want youse to enjoy the show which I have to say I am looking forward to immensely.

People shifted aside to make room for him to step up to the bar and extend the flats of his hands on the counter. Pat took a pint meant for someone else and put it down in front of him. Nailer turned to talk to the men.

– Tell me, are youse familiar with the flamenco at all?

There were some murmurs.

– Well you should be. It's the music of our Andalusian cousins boys, Provos in their own rights. The original ones in many respects. And this is their dance, the dance of the outcast, the persecuted classes, the gypsies and the Jews in particular. Our brothers and sisters in other words. Sure if we didn't have two left feet on every man, woman and child, we could have invented the blasted thing ourselves.

Everyone laughed. Nailer took up his pint but placed it back down on the bar without drinking from it.

– My theory about these things relates to the weather. You need the bit of heat for a dance like that. For the arms to open up like wings and the body to flow. Allow that manner of spirit to enter into it. Explains why we ended up with the thing that passes for our native nonsense, that arms down by the side carry-on which I don't know about youse but I never liked at all. Young ones shivering in the cold is how that got started. Some nun screaming at them. Out on The Blaskets or some stony field in Connemara.

Again people laughed. Nailer stood upright again, became a bit ruminative.

– But this flamenco boys is something proper. I was reading about it there before I came out. Seemingly the gypsies came up with it on catching first sight of the flamingo. We're talking Spain in the time of

Colombus here. They would have been as outcast and downtrodden as they come. And this was their response, can you imagine? There's the whiff of revolution about it. Something elemental about it, a molten thing, hard to explain exactly. As if they're making their way across the scorched earth and sand. To get to the sea, they have the vision of it in their eyes, it's like a blindness leading them on. Driving them out of their minds almost. The music's not much use at all to them. It tells you only that you're lost. Reminds you there's only going to be one end to this thing . . . and we all know what that is don't we?

– Constitutional politics? someone said.

Everyone laughed, even Nailer.

– Death, my friends, death! Like our own poor pink friend in the docks, a thing of beauty shivering away in that muddy harbour. Here, I bet you fellas didn't know that in Egyptian mythology the flamingo was believed to be the actual sun god? Can you imagine that mindset, can youse? To be looking out your window and convinced that right there, that fine creature balancing up on one leg was none other than God Almighty himself? You see we've lost touch with that degree of animism in modern times. I blame the Industrial Revolution. Now, don't get me wrong. I'm all for the Enlightenment so I am, as much as any man. Newton, Descartes, I wouldn't argue with any of them. But Jaysus, the world was a mysterious place before they arrived on the scene, and there was a lot to be said for it, that's for sure.

Nailer was thoughtful for a second but became aware of the silence and noticed the blank faces of the men looking back at him. He stood up, laughing.

– Here, I'll give youse a laugh. Another thing I just read before coming out. You'll never guess what this Egyptian sun god was called?

No one said anything and Nailer stood smiling at them.

– Ra.

The men all laughed.

– Up the Ra! someone shouted.

– Up the Ra indeed, can you believe it? You couldn't make this stuff up men, I tell you. And it makes you almost weep to think of its fate. Because obviously a thing of beauty like that won't last long around here, that's for sure.

Everyone looked back at Nailer.

– What will you do with it Nailer? asked Gene Lawless.

It took a second for Nailer to comprehend what was said and he stared at Gene, more sore than angry.

– Jesus Gene. Do you think I'm like that Jeffrey Dahmer lad? Christ, I wonder sometimes what image youse have of me at all.

– Sorry, sorry. I must have picked you up wrong there.

– I'd say you did Gene.

– Sorry Nailer.

– Do youse know your Gibbon boys?

– Bits and pieces, someone said.

– The abridged version, someone else said.

– No harm, no harm, I believe they made a good fist of it, said Nailer. But Gene here clearly has me marked down as some sort of Commodus, who as you know succeeded Marcus Aurelius. Not a patient man, by all accounts our Commodus was a sporty lad. A whore for the crossbow in particular, going around shooting them at children, babies in particular, the smaller the better, morning, noon and night he'd be at it apparently. He used to send out his men to steal them for target practice. Seemingly he'd have them pinned to the wall with the crossbow, barely recognizable from the sheer density of arrows that he'd put into the poor little mites.

Nailer paused, looking absently at the floor.

– Mind-blowing, isn't it? The cruelty of history, the frightening thing being that the vast majority of it we don't even know about. . . . Anyway, one day Our Commodus seemingly cuts the head off an ostrich with arrows he had designed specifically in his workshop. Starts waving it about in the faces of the senators.

– Jesus. Mad cunt.

– Which begs the question boys. Do I strike you as such an entity?

– No, God no.

– Again, I was only joking. I apologise.

– No offence taken Gene, you're grand. Sure I'm only giving you a hard time. Anyway, enjoy the night men. You boys are our watch. They have their Black Watch and we have youse. So keep the eyes lit and the ears not far from the ground. You're doing God's own work boys. The heart of this here thing youse are, no matter what anybody says. Have youse got that?

Pat Behind The Bar placed the rest of Nailer's drinks down in front of him and said he'd drop them over, but he was distracted by the appearance of The Spaniard arriving in through the front door. Nailer noticed the big blushing face on him and laughed along with everyone else as Pat hurried from behind the bar to go and greet her.

– Ah love striking an old leaky vessel, said Nailer. Is there a more ridiculous sight on God's earth?

The whole room was now looking at The Spaniard and it seemed to take a minute for her eyes to adjust to the murk. There she stood then, blinking, like a figure from history, in paraphernalia that was either comic or poignant, take your pick, a bright red headband, a yellow flower the size of a fist over her heart, the colourful dress which splayed out below the waist, and dark hair pulled so tight it was as if someone was grabbing a fistful of it from behind. When she saw Pat approaching, her relief was appreciable, and he brought her over to show her the set-up he had spent all day working on, the large speakers he'd borrowed from the brother-in-law in Monaghan, arranged like small ogham stones in a half-ring to demarcate a stage. She was delighted but straight away set about rearranging things. Pat stood around uselessly before retreating to the bar to deal with the growing and dissatisfied backlog of customers. An expectancy was building and not many would have noticed Francie leaving, head down and with purpose weaving in and out of the crowd blocking his way. When his progress was checked by a tug on his elbow he would have been as surprised as anyone to turn and see the young Murphy girl looking up at him. He had to lean in and down to her to hear what exactly she was trying to say to him, before indicating that she should follow him out the side exit so that he could hear her better. Handy must have noticed them too because he also started to make his way across the lounge, impeded by the dense crowd and the odd person grabbing a hold of him and trying to chat with him. By the time he made it to the door the young Murphy girl was already coming back inside. Handy stood in the doorway, blocking her entry.

– Well, will you look who it is? A Murphy out in the wild. Quick, call David Attenborough, I have a documentary for him!

She stared back at him, trying to go past him but she couldn't manage it. He had moved out a bit and now had her cornered against the wall of the little porch area, still holding the door open with his shoulder. He was angry but, as could happen with Handy, seemed to change abruptly in his demeanour, he was now amused by something which had only just occurred to him for the first time. He smiled as he looked young Cathy up and down.

– You know, you're not bad looking actually. You've a nice wee body on you. Not bad at all I must say. I like the boots as well by the way.

– Do you want to borrow them?

Handy laughed, genuinely it seemed.

– You've got a mouth on you too, that's for sure.

His demeanour changed once more.

– What were you saying to that old fart out there?

– What do you mean?

– Come on now, don't give me that jip. That Francie fuck, what were you saying to him?

– Nothing.

But she was smiling a little herself now, maybe she couldn't resist it, and Handy went from looking her up and down to leaning right in close to her face.

– I warned you little piggy. You'd want to be careful so you would.

He stood back, the inner door opening a bit but still there was no way past him. He was smiling at her again.

– My brother said your father cried like a little girl when they shot him. He was on his knees begging them so he was. He even offered to suck them all off.

Handy turned and let the door close over the girl's frozen face. He went to the bar. There were three pints on the counter meant for someone else and Handy took two of them up in his hands. He headed back over to where he'd been standing with the crowd of girls. It might have taken another few minutes before the young Murphy came inside the lounge again. If anyone noticed they might have described her as looking a bit shocked, reeling perhaps, but also determined to stay, and why shouldn't she?, she wasn't afraid so she wasn't, no she'd show them, in particular those little bitches who were looking over at her, that Handy fucker back in among them now, all of them looking at her, laughing at whatever he was saying to them, the evil bastard, well she wasn't going anywhere, she wasn't going to give them the satisfaction of it, so she stood there over by the cigarette machine, shaking and angry, her narrowed eyes teary, no doubt relieved at the darkening of the spotlights and the change in music signifying that the show was about to start.

When The Spaniard emerged on to the little clearance that made up her stage, Pat flicked a switch and the speakers erupted into the low rumbling hum of the Andalusian cadence. She walked slowly, placing one foot in front of the other as if balancing on a high wire, but when she tried to speak the microphone squealed, making everyone grimace. She took it up again and it squealed again but not for as long this time. Staring out at the bemused audience she said she wanted to dedicate this performance to the beautiful creature who had decided to come among the community for unknown reasons. And she wanted to also dedicate it to the community itself which had welcomed her into its arms these past few months and made her feel so at home. Somebody said something to Pat and there was some laughter from around the bar. The Spaniard waited for silence before speaking again. Did anyone know that the flamingo symbolizes balance and harmony? Well, it's true. So maybe it is a good omen that such a creature has decided to come to this broken part of the world at this time. Perhaps it is an omen and a reason for hope. That balance and harmony and love can be restored. Again someone must have said something because there was more laughter from the area of the bar and Pat stood staring in a mortified glower. The rest of the audience sat still, no reaction out of them, either not following what The Spaniard was saying or bored and impatient for her to just get on with it for Christ and heaven's sake and quit with all this speechifying, that's what politicians were for and lord knows there was plenty of that already for people to be putting up with, Jesus could we not get one bit of a break from it, this was our night off so it was, give it a rest for heaven's sake. Perhaps sensing this, she mumbled some more into the microphone, which squealed again in disagreement, but she continued anyway, saying that it would be an honour for her to demonstrate through her native dance a language that spoke of lost love in the voice of the downtrodden, of their search for a place in the world, for harmony and peace because, my friends, flamenco is for the soul, a balm for all the hate that existed in the world and a plea for love. Again some of the audience seated near the bar laughed at whatever smut was spoken, but the majority just stared back at the woman, causing Pat to hurry over to put on the music, turning up the volume so that it would obliterate all background noise. The Spaniard stood back into a pose, resting like a statue before working up slowly into a rhythm with those castanet yokes clicking about her like narky birds, the sound reverberating inside the back of people's skulls, then appearing to lead her, hypnotized, around in a circle according to their own wilfulness, wild things going at each other in a fury of argument. The place was, in fairness, now captivated by the spell she cast, even the womenfolk who stared initially at her with resentment, but who now had their mouths hanging down like everyone else. A few may or may not have noticed that the only person in the place whose eyes were not fixed upon the stage was Handy Byrne. Some said afterwards that they noticed him continuing to eye the young Murphy girl where she was standing by the door, herself completely mesmerized by the performance, her small body swaying to the strange music. The thing went on for a good thirty minutes, interrupted only by Pat hitting the button for the next track, during which times The Spaniard stood in a rigid pose, arms aloft and eyes closed, her lungs panting like a pair of hounds and her neck region laced with sweat, the sheen of her skin sparkling in the overhead light, her chest rising and falling quickly.

At the intermission young Cathy approached the bar to get a Coke, and as soon as he saw this Handy was out of his seat, appearing at the counter beside her.

– Here, put some vodka into her Coke there Pat, it's on me, and here give me a bit of a refill there while you're at it.

He put a tenner down on the counter.

– I'm fine thank you very much, young Cathy said to Pat.

But who was Pat going to listen to, and in went the vodka into her drink. The girl walked off in protest.

– Here, give it to me, Handy said to Pat. I'll bring it over to her.

Later there were those who claimed they saw or thought they saw or heard someone saying they thought they saw Handy reach into his pocket and put something into the drink, a small white pill perhaps, or maybe powder, accounts differed, but whatever it was he came around the bar with the glass, having squeezed a lemon into it and given it a big stir with his famous trigger finger. He caught up with the young Murphy before she got to the door.

– Here, he said, handing her the drink. Peace offering.

He laughed, full of the charm now that he was also capable of.

– Hey, listen, I'm sorry about what I said about your old man. I made it up. Admittedly I'd have a bit of a tendency to do that. I was just trying to get at you. Hurt your feelings. My brother said nothing about your father so he didn't. Sure he wasn't even there so he wasn't, he was in the Maze at the time, you can ask anyone.

The young Murphy ignored him, but she did accept the drink before he turned away and went back over to the other side of the room. And it was noticed that after a while she started to drink from the glass, awkwardly, several quick sips in succession, getting over the taste of the thing, quite possibly her first-ever vodka, and people watched with interest as she weighed it in her buds, not liking it, tolerating it, liking it, feeling the strength of it, what was later said to have been not mere alcohol, and even at the time you could make out the different swaying of her body as it became more pronounced, the effect of it on her young system, and some people might also have noticed that Handy continued to watch her closely. When the intermission was over the lights went off and the music came back on again Ms Gonzalez reappeared and the spell of her performance was once more cast upon the room and all who were in it. The exception was the young Murphy one who, after moments of increasing unsteadiness, now barely able to stand straight, made a quick and urgent beeline out the back door leading to the car park, nearly tripping as she went, the world suddenly spinning around her. A fair number might have noticed it and would have laughed at the sight of her, a teenager new to drink, the body rejecting it with violence, O it was all too familiar to everyone in the building so it was, sure the young have to learn somehow, though one or two others would have also noticed that, following after her in rapid stealth, as close to her as her own shadow heading out the door, was none other than Handy Byrne of The Byrnes, local republican legend and all-round revolutionary hero, who all that time had been making his way to the rear exit, getting closer and closer to her, like he was stalking her, arriving perfectly at the last moment to the spot where she was and, ready to act as her swaying and unsteadiness kicked in causing her to rush outside, was in position to be out the door straightaway after her and into the cold night of darkness.

11

FRANCIE HAD THE majority of the details correct but not all of them. There was Meegan's garage all right. There was the ten grand in the bag all right. There was the body search and the layover in Cox's Demesne. But there was no jumpsuit and no woman's car nor crying babe in arms and he drove himself to Lisburn in a loaner. He didn't need to be told to take the long way, coming at Lisburn via the back roads through her upper-middle-class section, in past the golf course and the sprawling residential areas, right into the leafy unsuspecting centre of Her Majesty's loyal heartland. He didn't know the area well and, self-respecting pro that he was, spent some time meandering this way and that to make sure there were no eyes on him. It was near noon when he finally pulled up in front of the particular house in the particular cul-de-sac in the particular housing estate, the blinds down, the wheelie bin outside full to the gills with pizza boxes and beer cans. Our Francie was as surprised as anyone when it was none other than the legendary figure of Casio himself who answered the door, in shorts and flip-flops, a sleeveless vest, and wearing a Chicago Cubs baseball cap.

– Ah, the Newry man. We were wondering when you might show up. Here, come in and have a cup of tea.

Francie walked in and as he did Casio stepped out past him on to the porch to have a good look around. From inside the hallway Francie stood watching him, the big hairy back of the infamous inquisitor and tout catcher pushing up through the neck of his vest. He couldn't help noticing in himself a sense of the ominous as Casio turned and, closing the door to the outside world, ushered Francie to walk on ahead of him along the corridor to the kitchen. Two of his crew were in there, sitting at the table having breakfast. They barely looked up as Francie was introduced to them by Casio. Rooney and Drill Bit were their names. One of them was friendlier than the other.

– You came up from The Town Francie? asked Rooney. How was the border?

– Still there anyway.

– Right you are. For how much longer though right?

– Give it a rest, said the other one, Drill Bit. It's too early for politics. Christ. Me head is hanging off me so it is.

– Were you stopped at all Francie?

– No. I went the back way and then the long way.

– Sit Francie, said Casio. Make yourself at home. The boys here will wet the kettle for you. There's waffles and shite.

Francie took a seat at the table. Casio left the room.

– Cup of tea Francie? said Rooney, getting up.

– That'd hit the spot nicely thanks.

Over the sound of the kettle being filled they heard some rapping from upstairs, what sounded to Francie like banging on the radiator, then a loud groan. Rooney turned off the tap and they listened in silence.

– He's up anyway, said Rooney. Good sleep seemingly.

– Here I'll get it, said Drill Bit, getting up. It's my turn anyway.

He put a rasher into his mouth as he stood and downed his tea. He was a big unit, muscle-bound in a sleeveless Orlando Magic basketball top, his skin sunburnt, the back of his neck in particular. Away out the kitchen door with him, heavy boots on the corridor and the thud of them on the stairs. Francie could hear an upstairs door opening and slamming shut, a confusion of human noises, Drill Bit shouting something, another voice of somewhat higher pitch answering back to him in what sounded like a pleading manner in its cadence, some more banging, heavy footfall on the ceiling directly over their heads, muffled cries, a struggle which didn't last long, certainly less than a minute or two. In the meantime Rooney had put off the kettle and made the cup of tea for Francie and a fresh one for himself. There was an interlude of quiet in which he brought the two mugs of tea over to the table and he and Francie sat while Rooney finished off his breakfast. Another minute passed and the heavy steps could be heard descending on the stairs and then the door opened. Drill Bit came through it rubbing his upper arm.

– Y'all right there big man, said Rooney to him.

– Aye, said Drill Bit, holding out his arm. Fuck me, he said, inspecting the underneath of it.

– I thought I might have to ascend the steps myself there, said Rooney. Give you a dig out.

– I think I pulled a muscle. It's sore, the cunt.

– You should put some ice on it.

– Ice or the deep heat do you reckon?

– I find ice to be the best myself, your only man really, especially for those soft-tissue-type injuries, assuming that's what it is. Granted the deep heat is what you want for tears and the deeper bony-type injuries. Ligaments and what have you.

– Well that fucker could do with some then. Cuz tears and bony injuries is what he has now.

– Is it the boy from Cullaville? Francie asked.

Both Rooney and Drill Bit looked at him.

– We never know where they're from Francie, said Rooney.

– Don't care neither.

– It is, as they say on the telly, immaterial.

– Have yiz started with the interrogation yet? asked Francie.

– We gave him a few slaps if that's what you're asking.

– Has he broken down at all, said much? Youse have been here now, what, a few weeks certainly at this stage?

Again, the two boys just looked at him.

– Talk to Casio Francie, said Rooney. For any of these higher-level questions. We just do what we're told.

– Where'd the fat fuck get to anyway? asked Drill Bit.

– In at the box no doubt. He was bitching that he never got to see the end of that other thing.

– That's because he fell asleep. The snoring out of him.

– *Universal Soldier* Francie, have you seen it? The Cas man claims we should have woke him for the part when Jean-Claude Van Damme and Dolph Lundgren finally meet and start going at it. He was rightly sore about it this morning.

– Well we'd want to get moving, said Drill Bit. That fucker up there's wrecking me head so he is, I swear to God.

– Relax the cacks. We'll have this cup of tea and then we'll have the chat with the big man.

Rooney turned to Francie.

– So Francie I hear you got M.O.C'd.

– How do you mean?

Rooney and Drill Bit looked at each other, grinning.

– Och he's a cute hoor that fella. Drill Bit here calls him the hand wringer.

– Aye. Any fucken heat, said Drill Bit, and as he said it he held his head back and mimed the action of someone washing their hands.

– It would have been Pontius Pilate himself who ended up on the cross if M.O.C. had been in on those negotiations.

– O he's a slippery wee cunt so he is.

Francie thought about what they were saying.

– In actual fact the idea of involving me in this matter had been put to him by Nailer.

– Nailer? I heard he was losing it.

– Aye, added Rooney. Senile they say.

– I can assure you the man is all there in terms of his faculties and, though he takes counsel, does what he wants.

– Right. That's what he'd have you believe all right.

– You're referring to the matter of the boy upstairs I presume?

– Also known as he who never existed in the first place.

– Which is why we figured we'd be getting a new groupie from up your way, said Rooney. Always the way so it is. A bit of heat in the political realm and our doorbell rings. This time it's you Francie.

– The thought did cross my mind.

– If it's any consolation you're not the first.

– And you'll not be the last. No offence like.

– I'm tempted to ask about my predecessors.

– Temptation is a terrible thing all right.

– How long do youse reckon we'll be here?

– It is dependent upon the whim and gut of Casio.

– The gut certainly.

– It has a mind of its own that thing.

– Big mind.

– Huge.

– Here, we'll try and pressurize him, said Drill Bit. He'd be happy to stay here another month otherwise.

– You see, Francie, he likes to get away from the wife and sprogs.

– You'd understand it if you saw the wife.

– And the sprogs.

– They're wee jaunts these things to him.

– Perks of the position.

– Wee holidays. Like going to Mosney, minus the rides.

– Allows him to expand his mind even further, said Drill Bit.

– Big mind, said Rooney.

– Huge.

The two boys got up and went into the next room, leaving Francie alone at the table. It was another hour before he went looking for them only to find the three of them in the living room watching a video. Rooney offered him a can of Tennent's and Francie, declining thanks very much, took the spare armchair in the corner. Nothing much happened for the rest of the afternoon other than a Chinese delivery. It was one video after another. Kung fu flicks mainly, they had a whole stack of them in an untidy heap in the corner. Anything with Jean-Claude Van Damme in it, seemingly Casio had got into him recently and was now a major fan. Bruce Lee featured as well of course, as did Chuck Norris and a rake of others. Their eyes would be practically glued to the box and the hours rolled into one another as the fall of evening could be appreciated behind the darkening curtain. They rewatched *Universal Soldier*, seemingly for Francie's benefit, and after that *Bloodsport* and then *Kickboxer*. Drill Bit went to Xtra-vision to rent out *Double Impact* for later on because neither he nor Casio had seen it and Rooney claimed that it was in his opinion the best Van Damme by some considerable distance. At one point Francie went out to the kitchen, where Casio was over at the oven making chips. Francie closed the door behind him and cleared his throat to let Casio know he was standing there. He waited until the big man turned to face him, an oven mitt on, holding the metal tray.

– I was asking the two boys earlier about the plan.

– What plan would that be Francie?

– Regarding the detainee.

– You mean that toerag upstairs?

– Aye.

– Go on.

– Well I was just wondering if we should discuss strategy.

– Strategy?

– I presume that's why I'm here, no? To help with the interrogation. An extra set of eyes and ears. Local knowledge et cetera.

Casio looked at Francie for a moment. He held out the oven tray with the chips.

– Are these done do you reckon?

He nodded at Francie, who took one of the chips and put it in his mouth.

– Aye, more or less.

Casio turned and reached up to the cupboard for a plate then emptied the chips on to it. He took up a bottle of ketchup and smothered the chips with the sauce. He then turned and faced Francie.

– Francie, I don't know why you're here to be perfectly honest with you. I don't know if it's a good thing or a bad thing or if it's neither one nor the other that has you here. The way I look at these things is very simple. We're all doing what we were told and that's about all any of us can do.

Casio took up the plate of chips and held it out to Francie again.

– Do you want a chip?

– No thanks.

– They're not bad actually. McCains is the best I reckon. Of the oven-baked ones certainly.

– Healthier I'm sure.

– So the ads on the telly say.

The two men stood facing each other, Casio leaning back against the counter. Francie waited a moment before asking what was on his mind.

– Why am I getting the impression that sentence has already been passed on this kid?

– Like I say Francie, and maybe you didn't hear me, I only do what I'm told.

– Why am I even here then?

– Again Francie, just in case you didn't hear me the first time, I don't know why you're here.

– What about due process? I must have missed it.

– Aye Francie, you must have missed it.

Casio looked long and hard at Our Francie and in that stare was all the hardness of the man and all the coldness of the man that he had long heard about and it was the first glimpse Francie got of the real version of him. But, in fairness, the moment of tension didn't last long and Casio held out the plate to Francie again.

– Here, given that you're so interested why don't you take these upstairs to him.

Francie took the plate.

– I can try and talk to him. I know his oul doll actually.

– What did I only just say to you? He's a toerag Francie.

– Which is not to my knowledge a capital offence. Like I say, I know his oul doll. That might be the way in. The pressure point. We can find out what he knows. Maybe root out a few more of them. Or at least get info on how The Branch made their approach to him.

– Francie, Francie, Francie. Take these McCain's oven-baked chips and deliver them to the little toerag upstairs. You will find him in the back box room sitting in a puddle of his own piss. It really does not get any simpler than this.

Francie went up the stairs with the plate of chips. When he had reached the landing he stood and watched as Casio disappeared into the living room to join the two others. He waited for a second before rapping on the back bedroom door and entering. It was dark and it took his eyes a second to adjust. The floor was bare linoleum which stuck to the soles of his shoes. Over beside the radiator was a figure wearing a hood over his head who retreated back into himself as Francie walked in. The stench in the room was awful. Human waste. The air warm with it, as if the oxygen had gone off. There was a mattress on the floor which even in the darkness looked filthy, a large stain in the centre of it. Francie went over, his sticky footfall on the lino making the figure by the radiator huddle even further into himself as he got closer. Francie put the plate on the floor within reach of the kid, then stood upright in front of him.

– You can take the hood off when you hear the door close.

No response.

– Did you hear me kid? You can take the hood off when you hear the door close.

– Who's that?

– You wouldn't know.

– You're not one of them.

– I am actually.

Francie stood looking down on the kid, who he could tell was trying to work out where he recognized Francie's voice from.

– I know you. I know that voice. Who is it? Please. I haven't done anything wrong. They told me I could come home. Please mister. They told me. I did nothing so I didn't. I'd nothing to do with that job they keep going on about. Handy Byrne said he might need a driver but then he never got back to me. Next thing I know it's all my fault.

Francie said nothing. God, the air was bad. It took all his focus not to gag on it. The captive figure was moving forward on the ground now, as far as the chain would allow him.

– Please. I'm begging you. Please. Mister. Please. I'll do anything so I will. Tell them I'm sorry.

– What are you sorry for?

– Nothing.

– No, go on. What are you sorry for?

– Wait. Are you that Francie fella from Newry? I promise. I'll do whatever. I'll get you money. Me ma has a whole pile of it stashed away.

– What are you sorry for?

– Everything. The smack. The hash. Whatever. Please, mister. I'll do whatever. I'll leave and stay away this time. Or stay, whatever youse want. I'll go to Thailand. Australia. Wherever the fuck. Whatever youse tell me.

Francie stood looking at the pathetic figure for a minute. It was hard not to feel bad for the kid, but that's life. You make your choices and it plays out. Same for everybody.

– Who did you speak to about Warrenpoint?

– Nobody!

– I'm not talking about cops. Who did you speak to about times, dates and all that?

– I didn't know any times or dates. Whatever Handy told me. That was it.

– Just Handy?

– I swear! Nothing except what Handy told me. He rings me and tells me there's a job on but then nothing. That was it, I swear to God. Please.

Francie let a whole minute or two pass. After a while the Donnelly kid dropped his head and let out a groan that was hard to listen to before banging the back of his head against the radiator. Francie crouched down on his hunkers and waited for the kid to calm down a bit.

– A young girl has vouched for you. Do you have any idea who that might be?

The hooded figure looked up at him but didn't say anything. Even with his face hidden it was obvious he had no idea what Francie was talking about.

– The young Murphy one who lives on your road.

Again the figure remained fixed on Francie, the big black hood over his face. The surprise on the lad was easy to discern even under the hood. He didn't say anything, the black shape of his head utterly still. When he finally spoke his voice was uncertain, rambling, as if someone had knocked the wind out of him.

– But she hates my guts . . .

– That much also seems clear. Which is the main thing giving her words weight.

– But . . . what would she know about it?

– That doesn't matter. But she came to me and vouched for you, said that you were most likely innocent.

They looked hard at each other then, though the kid would at most only have been able to make Francie out as a shadow in front of him. Neither of them spoke and then the figure on the floor bent over. Francie had been hoping for some sort of reaction but even he was surprised by this. At first he didn't recognize the sound coming from the kid on the floor. It was a strange music, something from an animal, and then he recognized it. Weeping, genuine weeping. Like someone learning something far too late about the world. Francie waited for a minute before backing away and opening the door. When he spoke next his voice was a little gentler.

– You can take the hood off when you hear the door close.

He shut the door after him, before going down the stairs. Casio was waiting for him at the bottom. He handed Francie a piece of paper.

– You're to call this number at eight o'clock. Not from here obviously. If no one picks up, call again at half past.

12

NAILER WAS AS surprised as anyone to see Rehab the Murphy lad appearing like a ghost up on the security monitor in the corner of the kitchen. The lad had left hours earlier and now here he was coming back up the laneway, frozen where he stood in the glare of the security lights, staring at the ground. The dogs recognized him and, Nailer noticed, barely barked, crouching down like they wanted to play with him. Putting aside the book he was reading, Nailer stood up and, grumbling, put on his boots in the hallway before stepping out on to the drive. Jarlath and two of the other men were already out there, blocking the way. What was surprising was the Murphy lad wasn't alone but had someone with him and, seeing this, Nailer told Jarlath to lead the two of them into the living room, not the kitchen, but the living room, and to throw the kettle on. A few minutes later Nailer himself came in bearing a pot of tea and a plate of biscuits. Rehab had stayed outside on the drive, so it was just his sister, young Cathy Murphy, who was sat on Nailer's couch. Nailer placed the tray on the low table in front of her.

– I've mineral as well if you want.

– I'm fine thanks.

Nailer poured tea into badly chipped mugs and retreated to the armchair in the corner. He watched as Cathy clumsily put milk in her tea, her hand shaking. He could see she was tempted by the biscuits but didn't want to take them. There was a scratch on her face and the side of her neck was covered in an enormous bruise. Nailer took all this in but didn't say anything about it. Though it was the height of summer he'd lit a fire some time ago and it was a bad one, giving off a thick smoke. He took up the poker and, reaching over, stirred it a bit.

– I won't ask after your mother.

– Don't.

– Your brother is a great worker you know. There'd be a fondness there. And a reliance as well to be truthful.

Cathy, having been nervous, now looked at the old man with anger to the point of tears in her eyes.

– He was the smartest boy in his class you know.

Nailer put both hands up in the air, his eyes closed.

– It was a terrible accident what happened. And Lord knows I've done my best for the lad. And yes on account of your father believe it or not, who I remember fondly. Again, believe it or not.

– And he happens to be cheap labour too.

Nailer laughed.

– Ah, so that's why you're here.

He laughed louder.

– Look it. Tell your mother I'll go an extra tenner. The truth is he's worth it. And I wouldn't want to lose him. The pigs for one thing would be devastated. They're Berkshires and they know they're minded.

Young Cathy looked at him. Money hadn't crossed her mind but the extra bit of it would be welcome, no matter where it came from.

– Fifty.

Nailer smiled. He stood up.

– Twenty, and I wouldn't want to lose him. Now if you'll excuse me, I'm expecting a phone call.

– I have information.

She was staring up at Nailer. He took a moment before sitting down again. Cathy drank from her tea, staring at him over the top of her cup.

– I see you've noticed my cuts and bruises. Do you want to know where I got them from? Or, more to the point, from who?

Nailer glared at her. Cathy smiled.

– No, I didn't think so.

– Look, what information do you have? I've to go now in a minute.

– Darren Donnelly may or may not be an informer. But I know for a fact Handy Byrne is.

She pulled back her hair and bared her neck to show the full extent of the bruising.

– In addition to being other things that is.

Standing abruptly, Nailer picked up the poker and turned to the fire again. It was as if he was alone in the room now, raking at the embers roughly until the flame had caught hold. It still wasn't a great one, but it would do for now. Ridiculous that he felt the need for a fire at all given the recent sun they were having. But a chill in the bone is a chill in the bone and you can't just leave it there. Putting down the poker, he turned and, without saying another word and without looking at the young Murphy one, left the room, going out to the kitchen to put on his coat. Behind him he could hear Jarlath ushering the girl out, telling her that next time she wanted to talk about her brother's wages she was to phone well in advance first.

13

LISBURN TOWN CENTRE was dead. The shops were closed and it was hard to imagine them ever being open or any sort of thriving occurring there. It was your typical British town, characterless, sure you could be anywhere, Scunthorpe, Bristol, Southampton. High street chains, a load of tack essentially, capitalism with a small, miserable c, was this what they had to offer? All shuttered until the next day, the whole scene depressed him to his bones. Francie had made sure he was there well in advance for fear of not being able to find an unvandalized phone. But there was no problem in that regard and when he called the number at the appointed time Nailer picked up straight away.

– Well, have the gentlemen of the jury reached a verdict?

Francie stood for a second. He could hear Nailer's breath on the receiver and guessed he'd been in a rush. Probably it was that phone box halfway up Gullion. If The Brits weren't too afraid to leave their barracks they'd be well advised to stake it out. Francie took a pull of his cigarette and let the smoke hang on the air in front of him.

– He's certainly a toerag Nailer, that much is true. But other than that I don't have a strong intuition going against him. Maybe we might just give them this one.

There was silence on the other end and for what seemed like quite a while both men stood listening to the sounds of the other in the receiver. Francie had time for another pull of his cigarette before speaking again.

– You should also be aware that I have received information from a third party which throws further shade on the matter. Maybe pointing in a different direction, closer to home shall we say.

– I thought I told you to be careful there.

– True, it's only a whisper. Possibly bollocks. But either way my instinct is to pass on this one, just to be safe. Besides, he's only a kid.

Nailer didn't say anything. There was the sound of his breathing coming closer and then he cleared his throat, holding the phone away from him. Francie could imagine the scene. That fine vantage point from Gullion, looking back down over the coast, indented by the silver sea, the lights of The Town sprawled out like some major European capital in the distance. And though the phone went dead then, with not another word spoken, Francie stood with the receiver still up to his ear, smoking his cigarette down to the end while listening to the dial tone. Then he put the phone down and climbed into his car.

The next day the routine in the house was more of the same. A late fried breakfast, the kitchen an absolute mess, cans everywhere, ashtrays full, the stale air. The whole span of afternoon spent in front of the VCR. They watched *Nowhere to Run* and *Hard Target* and *Timecop* and bits of *Street Fighter* for what felt like the tenth time, then in the evening it was *Sudden Death* and *The Quest* followed by *Maximum Risk*. The following day more of the same. They fought over who went to the offie, the video rental, the Chinese. Francie would have been happy to get some air, but Casio wouldn't let him, and mostly it was Rooney who ended up going. Francie found all this lying about a challenge. The sheer and stultifying boredom of Internal Security Squad duty was, he realized, its one unassailable constant. For a restless and hyperactive man like himself it was pure hell sitting around like this for hours on end. If they weren't watching videos they were playing cards, and always there was lager, tray after tray of it, and clouds of cigarette smoke, the windows shut, the curtains pulled. The total opposite in other words to the buzz of an operation, the stalking and planning, the round-the-clock obsessive surveillance that had been Francie's day to day for years now, the thrill of the chase, always on the move, your quarry constantly in your sights and in your thoughts and honestly the only thing in God's universe that mattered, before finally arriving at the climactic act itself, what you hoped would be the perfect culmination of all this planning, its smooth and ruthless execution, the sharp end of what for those months represented the only and true purpose of your entire existence, to be the final word on some poor sod, consigning them to the hereafter, hell, heaven or purgatory, while in the process striking at the heart of The Crown and the British State and Empire, nefarious as it was, withering on the vine of history as it was, colonial, decrepit and doomed. Well, there was none of that now, that's for sure, and for long stretches of time Our Francie sat observing Casio and his two acolytes, increasingly disdainful of their immature enthusiasms and what he could not fail to observe as the utter poverty of their imaginations. True, he tried to fight these thoughts, putting them to the back of his mind as much as he could, but it got harder with each can of Tennent's, each pizza, each kung fu flick, each morning and every stultifying day. In particular, he found the cut of Casio to be a major disappointment. For starters the man lacked gravitas. Nor did he have much to say for himself, and Francie was continually surprised to see him overruled in the matter of choosing the next video. Where, Francie wondered, was the terrifying figure of myth he'd been hearing about all these years? The sheriff of the republican movement in front of whom the weak and traitorous were said to tremble and cower, the fierce warrior of justice who all told must have shot more men than General Dyer? The potent mind, who saw everything, covered all the angles, kept all connotations in his brain all the better to catch you out in your snivelly pathetic little lies while, like the archangel Gabriel, being able to stare deep and with an unblinking gaze into the revelatory substance of your soul? Where was the steely soldier whose purpose, once settled, no pleading or haranguing could reverse, inflamed as it was by righteous indignation, commanding the respect of those living and those who, so cowering, could only concede that their end was close and that they had met their match? Francie could not quite believe that the person in question was this big lazy lump on the couch in front of him, content to sit on his hole all day long accompanied by his two galoots watching karate movies until they had the words practically rhymed off verbatim, the face on him lit up like that of a small boy.

Francie slept on the couch, but badly, hardly closing his eyes. At some point in the middle of the fourth night the door opened and there standing fully dressed in front of him was the imposing figure of Drill Bit.

– Up you get Newry man, we're heading out.

Francie got up quickly and threw on his shoes before following Drill Bit into the kitchen to find the table had been set and plates of food left out.

– Breakfast Francie? said Rooney, who was at the stove with the frying pan on the go.

They had barely been eating a minute when Casio walked into the kitchen, where Francie was sitting with the two boys.

– Will we get a move on men?

– I'll grab the car, said Rooney.

And suddenly they were all action. Drill Bit stood up and stretched, leaving the kitchen. Casio was standing at the door, looking at the still-sitting Francie.

– Is it a written invitation you're waiting for Newry man?

Francie hopped up without eating a thing and went after them down the hallway before following Drill Bit up the stairs. He got up to the landing as Drill Bit opened the door. On the floor of the bedroom, over by the radiator, Francie got another glimpse of the pale kid who he now appreciated without the hood to be all of seventeen, eighteen years old, though he did not look particularly familiar to him. His face looking up at Drill Bit was lit pure with pallid fear. Drill Bit went into the room and put a hood over him, but not without a struggle, the young fella shouting, pleading with them, please please, and again, please, before his voice became muffled under the thick hood.

– Get up you wee shite, we're moving, Drill Bit shouted at him, and gave him a box around the ears.

The young fella cowered against the wall and offered resistance through his body weight and a tight grip on the radiator. Drill Bit started to lose his temper, flailing out with his fists and kicking the youngster furiously, screaming even louder at him. Casio rushed up the stairs. He came from behind Francie and went into the room, slapping Drill Bit quickly on the back of the head, shouting at him to stop, stop, then pushing him away with surprising strength. The kid was by now curled up cowering like a scrawny dog at the radiator, and Casio crouched on his hunkers in front of him.

– Kid. Now listen up, this is important so it is. You've not met me before, I'm only after just arriving down from Belfast tonight to take charge of this situation. The Leadership sent me. Now first of all let me apologize for the over-physical glad-handing of my junior associate here. I did not know about it and will give them all a stern talking-to. Later they will be disciplined over it, I can assure you of that. Now, listen to me, I'm not supposed to tell you this but we're letting you go kid. Your ma's been on the television and the radio and fair fucks to her it has had the desired effect. The Americans are involved now son. So in other words today is your lucky day. Do you hear me lad? You're going home to see your ma. So this is how it's got to happen. We're going to go for a wee spin.

It has to be a bit roundabout for our own safety kid OK? I'm not going to lie to you, it's going to be rough on you because we're going to have to drop you in the sticks. The arse-end of nowhere son to be perfectly honest about it. Again, it's for our own safety. I mean we can't exactly leave you by the main road, now can we? There's cameras and police everywhere. But you're a strapping lad and this time tomorrow you'll be in your ma's having a fry-up and a cup of cha and the fire lit. Now all you have to do is do what we say and we'll have you home in a matter of hours. We'll even lend you a jacket for the long hike you have in front of you. All right son? Good lad.

The hooded head stared back at him and may have given the slightest of nods. Francie had the urge to go to the Donnelly kid and grab hold of him, share the relief that seemed to fill the room, but instead he stood quietly. Casio was in control here and Francie was happy to hold back. He had already done his part and things were going to pan out as they should. Now they met no resistance from the kid in getting him up and walking him down the stairs before stopping at the front door. Rooney had reversed the van right back up against it. Francie and Drill Bit had the kid by his arms, his hands tied behind him, Casio ahead of them looking out. They did the transfer quickly and slammed the door shut. The kid was put lying flat on the floor, Francie and the two lads sitting up front, and off they went out of the estate and then out of Lisburn altogether. The kid on the floor didn't move. Sure enough they went on a winding, seemingly random journey through the night and around the outer regions of Down and into north Armagh. But Francie didn't mind in the slightest. It was a clear night and the sky was dense with stars. He had to fight the sleep away, the sheer exhaustion he was feeling perhaps merely a separate form of relief that the entire episode was at last coming to a close. Short of the town they took a turn off down a regional road towards a forested area. There was a dirt track, and the car went along it for a good bit before stopping. They got out and opened the back of the van.

– Out you get lad, Casio said.

Drill Bit and Rooney reached in and dragged the lad out. He could barely stand upright by himself out of fear and deconditioning. Casio took his bally off and the kid, tape across his mouth, looked back at him, but he was also afraid to look at him, and closed his eyes again.

– Now, said Casio. I need you to walk in that direction over towards the forest there. If you keep going on that track you'll eventually arrive at a wee village. It'll be light mind by the time you make it. It might take you a couple of hours son. But eventually you'll come to a phone box and you'll be able to get through to the emergency services and they'll put you through to your ma, the police, whoever the fuck, that part is entirely up to you. I am also authorized to inform you that this is your final warning. Upon your return you must abide by the rules. No more nonsense, OK? Next time you might not be so lucky. And stay away from them Coolock boys. OK? They're bad news. Now off you go with yourself. Good luck kid.

And they stood and watched as the young lad went with a very unsteady gait down the laneway, gathering speed as he went. Francie looked up at the sky full of stars and, breathing deep but perhaps not understanding why, found the relief flooding through him like warm rain, his mind and thoughts easing like a fist had been unclenched inside his skull, he felt like shouting out in praise, the realization that he had been straying entirely wrong in some of his recent thoughts, the whole thing made him practically chuckle to himself, what he recognized now as the dark temptations of pure paranoia, and with not a little circumspection for having short-changed the benevolence of the universe, the righteous path, and above all the decent wisdom of the republican movement to which he had dedicated his life and energies. Beside him he saw Rooney lean into the boot and take out a couple of shovels. Though Francie did not instantly appreciate the significance of the act, he accepted the one that Rooney handed to him without questioning. And then he watched as Drill Bit hurried along the dirt track in silence, his steps sticking to the grassy verge of the path, soundless as an animal, gun in hand, trailing expertly after the kid who was staggering from one side of the pathway to the other. Casio also took a few steps down the track and stopped, before shouting out after the kid.

> – Good luck to you son. Hi just think, this time tomorrow you'll be with your ma. Getting your big fry into you and a big steaming cup of cha. You'll sit next to a raging fire, a blanket over you. You'll be elected son. Don't worry about a thing. Your ma will be smiling back at you, tears will be running down her face so they will, she'll be so happy to be having her eyes set on you after all these weeks, her wee fella returned safely to her, still her babe in arms. You'll be elected son. Don't stress nor worry about a thing.

You're going to be elected son. You're going to be elected.

And as he said it, and as the three of them moved forward themselves, bearing the shovels, on the dirt track, they watched the dark shape of Drill Bit further on ahead of them as he now arrived in silence at the space directly behind the young staggering lad and they watched as he raised his gun to the back of the youngfella's head and he fired and he fell.

14

IT WAS M.O.C. who finally confirmed the rumours about the ceasefire. Not that it should have come as a surprise to anyone. Speculation had been rife for months, and there was a restlessness about the place, murmur and counter-murmur, rumblings that something was clearly afoot behind the scenes, of a process started seemingly by the priests. The fact that nobody from around here knew anything only made matters worse, introducing a degree of uncertainty into the fabric of people's conviction, a restless tension that got into our bloodstreams, inflaming everyone's imaginations and generally upping the paranoia levels all over the shop. No hard details could be confirmed, it seemed that nobody knew anything, but there was no want of suspicion, that's for sure. Whatever anyone thought they did know they voiced aloud in vehemence like children reciting their catechism, old certainties tinged with blood, full-throated though, as everyone knew right well, hollow at the same time. A lot of nonsense was talked in other words. People wrapped themselves in the tricolour and wept, arguments broke out, and even fights. Lines were drawn in the sand only to be erased again, what would and would not be acceptable to the rank and file, certain terminologies that were treasonous even to think of uttering them, though it was plain they now existed on the tips of people's tongues and at the forefront of their minds. Passionate disagreements broke out followed by sullen brooding silences, friendships were bruised or even ruined altogether, new hatreds kindled out of the thin air, while underneath it lay an all-too-familiar fear. That the nationalist community was, and not for the first time, being fed sly succour by the political class. A two-faced commitment to the nationalist agenda only for the purpose of winding the whole thing down. That some silver-tongued treachery was afoot, leading the way to some manner of compromise, a cooperative-type federalism with the emphasis on community activism, socialism and civil rights, while all the time subtly, slowly, steadily moving further and further from the traditional tenets of the separatist nationalist agenda, militarism and physical force republicanism. That the process of dissolution would be as silent and sly as decimating and irreversible. That we were in fact being led like cattle to the captive bolt, to decommissioning and permanent ceasefire (like the disastrous one of '72), constitutionalism and parliamentarianism, the Unionist veto and – God in heaven forbid – a return to Stormont.

Word was due to be leaked out to the media at midnight, so M.O.C. arrived that evening at The Arms with a job of work on his hands. The place was packed to the gills, The Regulars all standing with their backs to the bar, the crowd twenty deep in front of them, every Cross man with a big head on him in attendance and the active service units from the surrounding locale represented by at least one man, if not the whole pile of them. Camlough/North Louth, Castleblayney/Keady, Armagh, Monaghan, Downpatrick, Castlewellan/Newcastle and Kilcoo. The boys from the Cooley Peninsula were in attendance as well, as were the East Tyrone lads, and everyone remembered now what a loud and cantankerous crew those boys were in particular. M.O.C. stood in front of the crowd, his canary yellow jacket yellowing the face of him further under the sickly lighting, surrounded by a new small detail of bodyguard, a coterie of Belfast thuggery. Someone noted later how jaded the man looked, how tired and perturbed and stressed out generally he appeared, and didn't he have plenty of reason to be? The glares of dissatisfaction beaming back at him, the distrust and frank rancour that would have been slap-bang in his eyeline, and no he wasn't imagining it. It was real rancour, you can be sure of that, and he was getting it from all angles. For a while he said nothing but just stood there looking out at us, possibly cowed, certainly cautious, before finally coming out with it. That all activities were to cease. *All* activities? someone asked. Yes. All activities, he said. Or most of them anyway. Seemingly this was a joke because he laughed, though nobody else in the place did, on the contrary, the wall of faces looking back at him could not have been more serious. M.O.C., smiling, came forward now, in all placation, as if stepping out from behind an imaginary pulpit.

– Look it. It's pure tactics, that's all it is. I mean, it's not like we're going away or anything. We're just testing them. We want to see what we can get out of them, how they react. If they're serious about negotiating an end to this, well, this is us saying to them right, off youse go then, we've done our bit, it's your move now.

He stopped there, waiting for someone to say something, his eyes darting to all corners of the crowd. Nobody said anything.

– Look it. I'm aware that there's plenty of fellas talking and plenty of rumours flying around and that's why I wanted to come here and talk to youse in person. And I'm here to tell you that a lot of what you're hearing is spurious nonsense so it is. And I'm sorry to say it but you'll be likely hearing plenty more spurious nonsense over the coming weeks and months. Well, shite and rumour is what it is. Shite and rumour. That's them trying to divide us so it is.

M.O.C. had been walking in a little circle but now he came forward pointing his finger to the ground.

– So I want youse to hear it straight from me right here and right now. There's no one talking about stalemate other than The Brits. That's the arrogance of the colonialist mentality right there so it is. And none of this, I repeat, none of it, is us in any way shape or form giving in or, God in heaven forbid, surrendering. Not one iota. Do youse hear me?

He paused for a second, looking out at us with wild eyes.

– And I'll say something else. Before any one of youse even has to ask the question.

He took a step forward, making a big show of looking straight in the eye as many as he could.

– There's no one talking about ending the armed struggle, that's for sure. Instead of people sitting on the sidelines and in pubs such as this talking about ending the armed struggle they should be talking about continuing the armed struggle for the rights of the Irish people to be a free and united nation once again.

Large murmurs of agreement greeted what he said though probably not with as much vigour as he might have expected. There was a hubbub as people muttered to the person next to them and took up their pints. M.O.C. seemed to shrink back into the shadows a bit, not too dissatisfied perhaps, and the meeting would probably have dissipated had someone not shouted out from the crowd in a very clear voice that instantly quietened the room.

– In that case why are we even talking about a ceasefire Mairtín?

It was Bernard Brady, one of the East Tyrone boys, and all heads turned to him. M.O.C. stood still for a moment then took a couple of steps forward, eyes locked on Bernard the whole time. Everyone in the building knew Bernard and respected him. A small enough fella, he was only the second in command over there, but there was no doubt who was the real soldier in that outfit. A renowned, possibly even famous, volunteer at this stage, he was still on the run from the Maze breakout in '84 with at least nine dead Brits to his name in the interim. It is said that Bernard spent more nights sleeping under the stars than under a roof, that he knew every square inch of the borderland, both sides of it, and every farmhouse knew not to turn him away if he came knocking.

– Well, it's good to talk Bernard, do you not think?

– Not when it seems the whole thing has been decided already.

– Nothing's been decided Bernard. Nothing.

M.O.C. was very grave now, as if he was personally aggrieved and immensely saddened.

– As I said there a minute ago Bernard, and maybe you weren't listening, this is all tactics so it is. Pure tactics. To get them to lay their cards on the table. See where we're at. We can always go again.

Bernard stood up. A lithe, wiry man, the back of his head and neck red from the recent sun we were having, his anger could be plainly appreciated in the way he stood rod still, every muscle clenched. He had a known temper and was prone to deploy it.

– Tactics?!

M.O.C. looked at him for a second before responding. There was a hint of a smile on his face, like he was back teaching school and indulging an inquisitive student.

– Yes Bernard. Tactics. Pure and simple.

– What sort of tactics is it when you just stop off your own bat?

– I'm only the messenger here Bernard.

– I don't give a shite what you are Mairtín, it sounds like surrender to me. We should be taking it to them, and that's what we should have been doing all along. I'm sick of saying it so I am. Ramping it up is what we should be doing. Not stopping and taking a wee break like we're tired. Well I'm not tired, you might be tired

M.O.C., The Brits might be tired. But *I'm* not tired so I'm not.

For the first time that night there were genuine cheers around The Arms. M.O.C. exchanged glances with his thugs and even gave them a wry smile. He took his time walking over to the Tyrone corner and standing in front of it, waiting for all the cheering to die down. Bernard Brady sat down, but he wasn't finished and stood up again.

– It's a big Tet type of job we should be doing Mairtín. That's what is needed around here. If the Vietnamese can do it against the biggest and most technologically advanced army in history then why can't we? Tell me that.

More cheers. Bernard sat down again, receiving claps on the back, though clearly a bit embarrassed by the attention at the same time. M.O.C. waited for the noise to quieten. He was standing directly in front of Bernard now. Strangely, he seemed to have grown in confidence and even appeared to be enjoying himself. Those in the crowd who knew M.O.C. well would have known that he probably had the argument won already. This is the way he goes on, and as always, the contempt was well hidden, but if you knew what to look for it was there, appreciable in the face especially, the way he smiled at you, perfectly at ease, not an absolute bother on him, gathering his thoughts, arranging them, deciding how exactly he wanted to slice you up, did he want to do it this way or that way, or maybe this other way, the eyes in particular had it in their coldness, their narrowed focus on the man he was preparing to address.

– You know why Bernard. You know why and stop pretending you don't. Certainly don't be giving me any of your guff about Tet Offensives. You've been at the same meetings I've been at and if you want to lie to these men here then go ahead. The truth is that if we had the requisite level of weaponry for a Tet-type situation it would be a whole different proposition altogether so it would. We'd be Tet all the way. Tet Tet Tet. Every day of the week it would be Tet. There'd be a Monday Tet and a Tuesday Tet and a Wednesday Tet, however many Tets you'd want to squeeze in Bernard until The Brits were pushed into the Irish Sea. But I'll do you the respect of being honest with you Bernard, and also your comrades here. Out of respect for what youse have done in the past and continue to do. Are you ready Bernard? And are the rest of youse ready for a bit of grown-up adult-type reality?

M.O.C. leant over slightly to address Bernard directly, his hands in his pockets. The politician was now the angry one, his patience exhausted, like he was only wasting his time and honestly was now done with the whole thing.

– Speaking of Tet Offensives is pure fantasy Bernard, and you know this. It's like a child dreaming of unicorns so it is. You know as well as I do what happened with the Libyan shipments. I'm sure the rest of youse all know by now as well. And you probably also know that Gaddafi is none too happy about it, so there'll be no more Libyan shipments so there won't. Meaning that it is simply a fact that we cannot go down the route of overwhelming force. So youse can talk and youse can dream of Tets all youse want. I'm telling you now that it ain't going to happen so let's say we come to an agreement right here right now, that you stop giving me your guff and I'll stop feeling that I have to talk to youse like youse are children.

M.O.C. stood looking at Bernard, who was not happy about it, his body language fidgety, he looked down and about himself, frustrated to be sure, he shook his head dismissively, for he still had his anger, but it was a useless anger now and he didn't know what to do with it, and anyway it was all he had. He mumbled something to one of the men beside him who also shook his head and all of this M.O.C. took for acquiescence. He continued looking at Bernard for a while to emphasize his victory over him, and to make sure there was no more life left in his resistance, or no overt life at any rate, before drifting back to the centre of the room. He was in a relaxed mode again, almost affable.

– Look it lads, the only question is whether we can win with the path we're on and *only* that path or if we need to supplement it with something different for a while. It's worth talking about, that's all the leadership is saying. Even our volunteers in prison are saying it. Not all of them granted, but a fair share of them, perhaps even the majority now at this point in time. Remember The Brits have already given up big concessions so they have. Admitting like they did not so long ago that they have no selfish or strategic interest here. That was big so it was. That was progress right there so it was.

M.O.C. stopped again and stood looking around at the faces directed at him.

– Prisoner release is on the cards as well so it is.

Again he paused, waiting to see if anyone else had something to say.

– In the meantime, all we're saying is that the boat is not to be rocked.

There was possibly a bit of menace in the air now. You could feel the chill. Nobody had to nudge each other to point it out and everyone in the room knew not to say anything. M.O.C. stood looking out at us before breaking off to exchange another glance with his thugs. He turned around to the room again, back in his more relaxed mode now which he could turn on and off like a tap.

– Look it. There's a lot going on behind the scenes so there is. The Yanks are involved. I can't say much more than that and who knows where it'll take us. Maybe nowhere, and we'll be right back at it and we'll be back telling youse to go out there now and do your worst. In which case we've lost nothing. But we'll at least be able to tell the world that we tried and it'll be on them then so it will, The Brits and The Unionists. The main point is we have to put on a united front. There can be no messing. It'll make us look bad in front of the Yanks. Which will only jeopardize our negotiating position going forward. So we're only saying to take a bit of a break. Relax. Have a few pints. Go fishing. Whatever it is youse do apart from hanging around this place. But the boat is not to be rocked, OK?

And with that, he bade the room a good evening and in a somewhat abrupt fashion went upon his way. After he'd gone there was at first a heavy quiet in the air. Turning around to the bar, each person swam in their own thoughts. It took a while for the tension to dissipate and the different groups to mingle. People weren't happy, that's for sure. The Tyrone lads in particular. People gathered around Bernard Brady, telling him they agreed with him one hundred and ten per cent, fair play Bernard, fair play, we were right behind you there so we were, you had him there Bern, O you had him on the spot so you did, you had him against the ropes, teetering he was, the snake, sure you wouldn't trust him as far as you could throw him, that fella, fair play Bernard. But bit by bit the hubbub rose and the topic of conversation changed to other things, mundane things admittedly, relating to farming matters for the most part, the awful bother created by some of these new EEC regulations, the lack of rain, the foot and mouth outbreak in Wales. Pat switched on the sound system and soon you had to shout to get your point across. It ended up being a good night actually. A bit of trouble broke out between the Tyrone and the Cooley boys but other than that it was all relatively good natured.

15

FRANCIE WAS THERE as well that night, in his capacity as OC for South Down. For the most part he didn't say much, sitting off to the side in splendid isolation, although his general demeanour was noted. As M.O.C. spoke, Francie kept shaking his head, making perfectly obvious his dissatisfaction at what he was hearing through little grunts and tut-tuts, guttural dissents that might cause you to look over at him periodically but not otherwise take much notice. In actual fact though, no one was too surprised. Lately there had been more of him about the place, in The Arms in particular, and nobody knew exactly what the story had been with the man ever since that whole business with the Donnelly lad. Certainly there was no word of him out scouting any ops lately, he seemed to have given all that up voluntarily, even before the ceasefire was announced. The other thing he had given up was the non-alcoholic Beck's, and was instead most nights on the whiskey. Mickey, his nephew, was also in The Arms to hear what M.O.C. had to say for himself and had chosen, it was noted by many, not to sit with Francie but rather alongside Kaja and the rest of Handy's posse. Not that these young pups were paying much attention to what was being said up the front, sure they weren't even listening half the time, spending the whole evening messing around with each other, making each other laugh, flicking each other's ears, pinching and nipping at one another, wrestling round the side of the bar, putting each other in headlocks, ignoring the constant shushing and bitter ire directed their way from some of their older, more sombre comrades. Mickey was the best behaved of the lot of them, dolled up like The Fonz, the biker jacket on, the hair slicked back, they were headed out to the nightclub in the Carrickmore afterwards. A popular lad, Mickey, he was up chatting at the bar with a few of The Regulars for a while after M.O.C. had gone. Idle enough chit-chat, until it was pointed out to him the sorry state his uncle was in. Mickey shook his head and said sure didn't he know? And wasn't it very sad altogether? A pure tragedy was what it was, Francie being back on the bottle after all this time. Duly, he went over to check on him, but he practically had to shake Francie to wake him, slumped over as he was in the seat, his head resting on his arm.

– Well Uncle, what way do you reckon?

Francie squinted up at him, wondering at first who it was.

– Ah, will you look who it is. The nephew. Is it a Cross man now you are son?

Mickey laughed, but Francie just stared up at him.

– Sit.

Mickey looked around but remained standing. Francie straightened himself up, running both hands along the side of his head, opening out both his eyes as wide as possible, Mickey watching him closely.

– What time is it?

– Nearly time for home Uncle.

– Ah leave me alone will you? You're getting more and more like that sister of mine.

– That M.O.C.'s some boy isn't he Uncle? As one of the boys said there, he'd flog you a used Durex so he would.

Francie didn't reply for a while. He was even drunker than Mickey had thought. He used his fingers to stretch open an eye that was still half-closed, a bit sticky from a bout of conjunctivitis.

– Thanks for the mental image Nephew. It'll take me a while to get rid of that.

– What way do you reckon it'll pan out?

– Bollocks and bollocks and more bollocks. That's what I reckon son.

– O yeah?

– Sit. What's the matter, are you ashamed of me, Nephew?

Francie took up the remainder of his drink and squinted at it. Mickey looked around and then took a seat across from Francie.

– Seems promising enough, I would have thought. The whole business with the Yanks. They'll be for us definitely. Top of the morning and all that shite.

– Nonsense, son. They're looking to end it. Wind the whole thing down.

– That's what some people are saying as well right enough. You'd never know though. The Brits could be surrendering as we speak.

– The Brits are going nowhere child! NOWHERE.

Mickey looked around, embarrassed by Francie's sudden eruption. There were plenty listening in now. Mind you, it wasn't difficult, Francie was coming a bit more to life. This time when he took up his whiskey he finished it, not taking his eyes off Mickey. Plainly he didn't care who was listening to him, his voice elevated more than necessary. He was smiling now.

– The politicos have won out Nephew. And for what?

He laughed.

– Jobs for the boys in suits, that's what. In Stormont no doubt. After that, the UN possibly. It could have been a whole different carry-on so it could. But that ship set sail long ago. Like a fool I am only just realizing it myself these past few months.

Francie took up his glass again. Even though it was empty he held it up to his mouth trying to drain it, before slamming it down on the table in frustration.

– The more I think about it the bigger fucking eejit I am becoming in my own estimation.

– You don't mean that Uncle.

– O do I not?

Francie was just staring at Mickey now. He raised his voice even more.

– In truth this thing was over years ago Nephew. Whenever we started shooting women and children for no reason.

– Jesus Francie. Quiet!

– I will not.

– You on about Donners again?

– Him and a rake of others Mickey. You could line them up from here to the Divis flats, the poor fucks.

– But sure they were touts, traitors to The Cause Francie!

– Touts my hole. What cause were they betraying exactly, can I ask you that?

– I'm not following Francie. *The* Cause. Brits Out and all that craic.

– Brits Out my arse. If we wanted that it would have been done by now. We didn't have the stomach for it. That's the truth of it so it is. Settled instead for the chance of being the Big Man. So as the likes of Nailer can be the local don. Who does he think he is anyway, Marlon fucking Brando?!

– Jesus I'd be careful there Francie.

Mickey leaned over and put an arm on his uncle's shoulder, whispering so that nobody could hear, no doubt reminding Francie what he had been constantly telling Mickey for years, that not alone did the walls have ears but they had good imaginations too, which they would gladly use to fill in any gaps, so come on Uncle, time for home, he'd put him in a cab so he would. But Francie in his body language didn't pay him much heed. He shook his arm away.

– Cathal Goulding was right all along so he was, and we should have stuck with him. We veered away from our principles Mickey. That's what happened. Pure and simple. I ask you this. What does your average man in this establishment know of Marx or leftist theory in general? The answer is nothing, not even the basics. This crowd are too busy fumbling away in the greasy till so they are.

– Uncle!

– This was the mistake we made early on Mickey. Instead what do we have? Tell me that Mickey.

– Come on Uncle, you've had enough now, you're talking shite.

– A rump of thugs is the answer.

– Francie. Come on.

– We could have been the mujahideen Mickey! Principled. Ruthless. United around a common goal. Instead what are we? Look around you. Sure you heard them there talking yourself as soon as M.O.C. was out the door. What concerns them the most? Here, let me answer my own question for you.

Francie stood, somewhat unsteady, and placed his hand over his chest, and now he had the attention of half the bar.

– We, the republican movement, hereby declare that it is our sacred and noble duty to . . . smuggle shit.

Francie bent over laughing at his own joke.

– Sit down Uncle!

Francie sat but, laughing, he stood up again. Practically everyone at the bar was paying attention to him now.

– We, the republican movement, hereby contend that it is our sacred God-given duty and right to . . . smuggle pigs over and back across the border. And sheep. And grain. Don't forget about the grain. Or the diesel!

Francie fell down in his seat again, cracking himself up with the laughing, and went to take another drink of his whiskey, forgetting again that his glass was empty. He put it down in anger and leaned over into Mickey's face.

– That is what we do Nephew. Scooting over and back across the border. Grain and cigarettes and any fucken thing. And we kidnap young fellas and we nut them for what exactly?

Francie tapped his index finger hard on the table.

– This is the republican movement Nephew. This is who we are. This is why we shot that pissing man in Dungannon who was no doubt a decent skin with a decent family. We're smugglers Mickey. Smugglers and thugs. And petty fucking criminals.

He stared over at Handy, who had climbed up on top of Kaja's shoulders and taken out his gun, waving it around.

– And psychopaths.

– Jesus Uncle, come on now!

– I'll not. I've done more in one week in the service of republicanism than most of the men in this room.

Mickey stood up. He leaned in to Francie again, telling him again to calm down, to chill, and that he'd be back in a few minutes to give him a ride home. Francie waved his hand at him dismissively. Mickey walked away shaking his head. He came back over to the bar where all The Regulars were sitting, watching and listening.

– Is your uncle all right? Gene Lavery asked him.

– What? said Mickey. Ah he's grand. He's just knackered so he is. The last few weeks have been wild. Sure, he's barely kipped. To say nothing of the fact that he's not a whiskey man in general. He was on the wagon there for years so he was. He can't handle it.

– He doesn't seem too happy about things, said PJ Moley.

Mickey laughed excessively, like a hyena.

– O he's a character isn't he? The shite he comes out with. Don't worry, I'll get him home now. No disrespect was intended. He's a big admirer of the way you boys carry on around these parts. *You can trust the boys from Cross to get the job done*. He's always saying it. Just ignore him sure. You know Francie. He's harmless so he is. Pure harmless.

16

THE ONE THING that M.O.C. couldn't forestall nor rightly ignore was The Widow Donnelly who, statue to misery though she had been these past number of months, now had a bit of life about her. And not only that but a bit of company as well. No longer was the woman going at it full bore and solo in the hysterical rendering of her delusionist and demented grief, but now whenever she appeared in front of the cameras she was for the most part accompanied by a more sympathetic figure, a much younger one, a girl no less. It was in fact none other than young Cathy Murphy who people started seeing now on a regular basis up there on their television screens standing beside The Widow Donnelly as she faced down the phalanx of microphones and the soft and sympathetic if not downright leading questions emanating from the biased, gullible and blatantly left-leaning liberal reporters who had streamed into Cross from all directions to cover the ceasefire and assess the local mood in what they predictably, perennially, lazily described as this hotbed of republicanism and rabid nationalism, so-called bandit country. Initially it was more of a mere curiosity to see the young one up there, but as the days passed and the television interviews totted up it could be better appreciated the constructive conciliatory type of role she was playing in this their little double act, a silent figure initially but whose presence seemed to have a becalming effect on the older woman, softening her voice and easing her spirit, stilling the harsh and untelegenic manner into which she had slipped in recent times, twisting and contorting her once-fine face and bodily features as she railed at people, jabbing a sharp index into their sternums and accusing them of representing incarnate evil itself, the blackened soul of Satan. Though all of that carry-on was plainly still detectable not far below the surface, she had now about her somewhat the semblance of dignity, or at least something approaching it, the sort that being wronged confers, or certainly imagining that that is so, a style of stateliness if you will, and a sense of control, even discipline, as if the young Murphy one was continuously whispering into her ear, like you'd do to a beast of burden near the end of its days, begging and bargaining with it, pleading with it, beseeching it to please stay the course for just one more mile, a half mile damn it, give me whatever you can give me because I need you woman because by God I cannot do this on my own. The young Murphy one didn't speak herself for many days, but when she did, when her moment finally came, when she was called upon by The Widow Donnelly to tell her story and prodded on by the wily newsman, she did so, slowly at first in the halting tremulous tones of a child, O very convincing, very convincing altogether, before she changed the gears of her articulation, appearing suddenly to hit her straps and tell the whole world what it was she had to say. It only took a little while then for her story to become the bigger story. Because when she spoke she spoke of one night in particular, a night everyone in Cross could well remember, the night of the flamenco in honour of the flamingo, and the crowded Arms with the whole parish in attendance, by implication all implicated, and how after the evening ended everyone had filed out the back of the place and, despite seeing with their own eyes the sad and obvious state of what had happened to her, proceeded to go on their way looking in the other direction. In clear and particulate detail the Murphy girl recounted for the world the specifics of that night, the last one of her girlhood as it turned out. She spoke of the initial excitement and the promise and the joy of the flamenco, and the wonder and pride of seeing her very own Spanish teacher up there on the stage, transformed for the night into the exotic and the magical, but how this was obliterated by something unnatural that was put into her bloodstream by malicious scheming hands, a potion, a cocktail, some concoction, powder perhaps, she wasn't sure exactly, but whatever it was, it caused a nausea that came on her rapidly and she spoke of the spinning darkness which accompanied it and she spoke of the desperate need that got into her for fresh air and the rush and the fierce urgency that was placed upon her, the absolute imperative of acquiring it pronto and she spoke of the momentary relief then of being outdoors, away from the noise and under the swaying stars and the black night and the cold indifferent span of the universe looking down on her in its expansile motion getting further and further away from us and how peaceful it was and how still and how miraculous it all seemed, until a sudden hand out of nowhere pushed her and grabbed a fist of her hair at the back of her head so that her eyes watered and her scalp burned and at the same time she spoke of how her arm got clenched into a tight knot right up behind her back so that her shoulder nearly popped out of its socket and how an unseen foot caused her to trip over it and down on to the ground she went and she spoke of the unrelenting pressure that was bearing hard on her lower back pushing her on to her knees at first and then her belly on the cold mud and her mouth filling up with dirt as her face was ground down into it and she spoke of how cold it was, the dirt and the grass on her bare skin, the cold earth and the muck getting pushed up up up into her face and her eyes and her nostrils and on to her tongue stifling her cries and she spoke of the loosening of her underthings and of being completely numb as her horrified eyes could only stare into the dark earth, arms that weighed a drugged and useless ton by her side, and she spoke of the weight of him now climbing on top of her, the weight of pure hard-core local republican legend, and she spoke of the clumsy uncoordinated effort of him and she spoke of the pain of his introduction into her body, the raw and searing force and pressure of it, and she spoke of his stale breath from pints and curry chips moving over her and biting into her neck and her cheek and her ear as his chest leaned on her skull smothering her and she spoke of his short pathetic panting which she thought would never end and she spoke of his sweat dripping down on to her forehead off his fore-head and she spoke of the salty taste of it on her lips and she spoke of her bleeding mouth and the other bleeding afterwards after the abrupt finish of him as he lay there like a dead weight of dog on her rapidly panting away before moving off her and she spoke of the shame she felt at not being able to move not even an inch after he'd gone off back inside and she spoke of the line of people of this town who walked right past her looking the other way as she lay there huddled and completely exposed on the grassy verge of the car park as they left for home with the clear ac-knowledgement and the knowledge in their eyes of what had happened but how quick they were at the same time to look away again to hide their understanding of it as they stepped around her and over her pretending to see noth-ing, not a thing, no thing, absolutely nothing so they didn't, sure what was there to see?, a typical enough sight in many ways, a bad feed of pints, a sick child not being used to alcohol, sure that's all it was, it has happened to us all at some stage, sort of funny actually, no hilarious is what it was, and then, to the baited breath of all, and even over the voice of the reporter trying not to defame anyone on live television, she went ahead and spoke the name of her attacker and she repeated it loud and clear practically shouting it into the microphone, screaming it as loud as she could to get it out out out out into the world and make it travel as far as possible, it was the name of Handy Byrne of the Byrnes. He was the one who attacked her, the animal who had mauled her, the beast that had bespoiled her, and for what reason, why did he do this she asked into the camera, why did he single her out? Perhaps because she knew something. Perhaps because she had seen something. Perhaps because she had seen him do something he didn't want people to know about, such as meeting with a policeman for example, a Branch man by the looks of things, who scarpered quick, and why, she wondered, why would he have done that? And when she said this last part in particular there was only a stony grey soil of silence in The Arms, an initial small silence that immediately rhymed with a louder inner recognition of the truth that was quick to spread outwards into the vacant parts of belief and fill it up to the brim, a recognition that was uniform across the faces of every one of the people present for ten, fifteen, maybe even twenty seconds. But that small bit of time collapsed quickly in the gathering murmur with people rushing quickly to be the first to cover it over instead with their strident disbelief to obliterate with anger its whole memory and existence with competitive clamorous outshouts of outrage directed at the television screen and the image of the pair of them two hussies up there, look at them, the state of them, two slags and sluts is what they were, spreading their filthy lies about one of our bona fide genuine modern-day nationalist heroes, a soldier and a marksman of the highest order, from a respectable, no legendary family, whose blood has been spilt in buckets in the service of Irish republicanism, and then spilt again and then again and then again, and go on, just compare him now with the likes of them two hussies, go on, compare them, a hero and patriot with the likes of them, the spawn of a bad-tempered informer, a half-Prod to boot, and a crazy wench of zero morals whatsoever, sure you only have to look at them, the pair of them, the state of them up there besmirching not just the Byrne family but in fact every single man woman and child who would deign to call themselves a republican or an Irish nationalist, with all the sacrifices and hardships that this entailed, with all that went before them, untold heroism and martyrdom and all manner of things, well they were a disgrace so they were, a pure disgrace, up there casting a pall across all of it, what people held and hold most dear, The Struggle and The Cause and, in front of the entire world as well, bringing shame, shame, shame they were on the people of this town and the proud people of Ireland, and in particular on her nationalist communities, past, present and future.

And now look, they were suddenly everywhere seemingly, these women, you couldn't get away from them, the odd couple, the rape victim and the grief-demented mother, but no, let's call a spade a spade, two bitches is what they were, two hussies and slags, the younger one becoming more and more the leader of the pair, whispering into the older woman's ear, emboldening The Widow, giving her heart and hope and purpose, but also urging her, baiting her, admonishing her to get her act together for God's sake, to get a grip woman and clean yourself up, to pay attention to your bearing and general deportment, your demeanour, your manner and your image, getting her to present a far more presentable version of herself, telling her to dress better, to get some exercise, to lay off the vino rosso, the brandy and the schnapps, to go and get the hair done, and her nails, do a bit of Pilates or go a for a brisk morning constitutional and give up this ridiculous fasting carry-on, and instead make sure she had her breakfast, her lunch and her dinner, to lay off the fags and the downers, to get a good night's sleep and to dream and Christ of almighty to live again, don't let them bastards win, that's what they want so they do, to have you down as a hag and a slag, a demented witch, a nutbag, to put you down and keep you down, well fuck that she said, you have to exist now so you do, you have to exist on an even keel, be measured in your passion to reveal all the more the searing pain of grief, to become in other words and in the process an all-round and better emblem of our Cause. Their story catching fire by the day, she accompanied The Widow everywhere, they travelled down south to appear on *The Late Late Show* and across to England to go on any TV or radio production that would have them. *The Terry Wogan Show*, *Newsnight*, *Panorama*, *Question Time*, *News Extra*, *Prime Time*, *TV-am*, they gave impromptu press conferences as they went, on footpaths getting into taxis, outside airports and train stations, they would talk to absolutely anyone so they would, their words in print being carried everywhere ahead of them, giving extensive in-depth detailed and supposedly heart-rending interviews to the *Belfast Telegraph*, the *Irish Times*, *The Sunday Times*, the *Independent*, the *Guardian*, the *Observer*, and across the pond to journalists from the *New York Times*, the *Washington Post*, the *LA Times* and the *Wall Street Journal*, their stories being translated into French and German, Italian and Spanish, the Scandinavian languages, the tongues of Eastern Europe, being heard or read about as far away as the Antipodes, the Malay Archipelago, the continental land masses of Africa and the Americas, from Cape Town to Santiago. And yes indeed, why not go over to the White House to warn the man living there of the type he was doling out visas to and getting himself involved with? Why not take him up on his recent invitation? And while you're at it why not meet with the Speaker of the House of Representatives and that nice chap who called saying he was from something called the Ways and Means Committee and that other man they had also never heard of who said he was the leader of the Congressional Black Caucus and warn them too about these so-called freedom fighters and so-called revolutionaries and so-called civil rights reformers, yeah right, Che Guevara my hole, Nelson Mandela my hole, Václav Havel my hole and Mahatma Gandhi my hole, because in reality they were nothing but a gaggle of petty criminals is what they were, smugglers, thugs and psychopaths. And rapists too, let us not forget. Well, worldwide shame they were bringing on Cross in other words, you couldn't get away from the pair of them, stalking the community from every television screen, reminding them constantly of things people naturally only wanted to forget, admittedly low deeds done for a higher purpose, things that have a tendency to happen, even unfortunate regrettable things that probably shouldn't have happened but which, let's be honest here, were, alas, inevitable really, and which unfortunately are always going to occur in zones of conflict, things which you are always going to get, no matter how careful you are, with any of your physical-force revolutionary-type movements where yes admittedly there is the occasional shortfall in absolute moral perfection that does indeed happen from time to time but is really just unfortunate and yes unintended, sure we all make mistakes, regrettable yes, but completely understandable and in many respects the really quite reasonable price to be paid when put up against the utopian salvo of ultimate delivery. No wonder everyone wanted them to disappear, even the political class, especially the political class, more than anyone the political class, throwing as they were now an almighty spanner into the works of the ongoing behind-the-scenes negotiations, they were only giving sustenance to the Paisleyites and the Apprentice Boys and the plentiful right-wing contingent and downright racist sectarianist naysayers in among the so-called moderate Ulster Unionist Party, shaking their abstinent heads while saying No, Ulster says No so she does, Ulster says there can be no deal with child murderers and child rapists, Ulster says No, not in a million fucking years, Ulster says that the fiery waters of hell shalt freeze over first before there's any accommodation sought or achieved with that brand of typical papist paederasty so no, away off with you, Ulster says No so she does, No to Dublin, No to Downing Street, No to the whores of Rome and Babylon, and No to Satan himself. There was genuine alarm at the prospect of the trip to Washington. We can't be letting that woman get within groping distance of that philanderer was the political consensus. Who knows what that randy man would make of her? The sight of this otherwise good-looker who was just his type with the big hair and the generally fine and shapely body that was just about still appreciable beneath her Oxfam clothes and becoming again more and more so by the day. What was needed was a procedural, some certain strategy, a plan of action, but in the meantime what had to suffice was only the relatively mild community-level approbation and continual low-pitched type of harassment that was all we good and ordinary people from around these parts had at our disposal, approaching The Widow from behind on the quiet days in her busy calendar when you would still find her sat alone on the street, perched on The Square by the Monument to the Martyrs when young Cathy was for whatever reason not around to guard her back. Think of crows picking at each other, a cawing herd of them, taking small nips of flesh each and every time, going for the eyes especially. Be quiet woman, whispered the passing voices, you're making a holy show of yourself so you are, and us as well, so be still now woman, be still and quiet you old crone, do you hear us now do you?, shush now, whisht, that's enough so it is, you've had your say so be quiet now, don't you know that you're doing The Brits' own work for them so you are, you're playing into the hands of Paisley and Robinson, and we'll tell you this much, if you're not careful, you'll meet a similar fate so you will, yes indeed you'll go the same way as that little bastard of yours, that little toerag and waste of space, that's right, that little piece of scum you called a son, you'll follow him into the cold earth so you will, an early grave and no mercy to be shown, so be quiet now, do you hear us now, do you hear us woman? And as she remained resolute and silent in the spot where she sat the only response The Widow could produce was a grimace, but one which was followed on this occasion by a barely appreciable trickling of tears falling at the eyes to hear confirmed for the first time within the substance of these taunts and whispers the first unofficial semi-official confirmation of the worst version of the truth regarding her son's present state, his existence or rather non-existence, that he was indeed buried in the bog, in a cold unmarked grave which may or may not be identifiable and ever found in the future by whatever pointless tokenistic commission might be set up, well good luck with that, because there'd be no chance there, zero, zip, of finding the little fucker's bones in that featureless marshy terrain where he was put without mark or memorial, out there in the back of beyond, in the bog, well under the bog by now he was, dead and surely gone, halfway to hell at this stage, and good riddance, well it was as good as official to her now so it was, his fate and what had happened to him and it was noticed by many looking on and passing by that her face did indeed appear to register this information, the tears trickling lightly and then a bit more noticeably, as if there weren't too many of them left, but still the woman held her head up high and believe it or not even smiled as she started to weep still more openly now but soundlessly and freely into herself, and seeing this, noticing it, there would admittedly have been among some but certainly not all of those who bore witness to it a small, unwilling though not insignificant hint of admiration for the majesty of this woman's pure maternal fury.

17

NAILER, A MUG of tea in front of him, sat behind his little table up against the back wall. Irritable, he hadn't even bothered to remove his field wellies, and now, looking down at them caked in muck and seeing the trail of it they'd left after them was another source of serious annoyance. He was one of only two seated men in the crowded kitchen and nobody was saying anything, the atmosphere just like the man himself, tense and moody, sore and bruised, the other standing men not even making eye contact with him, O they all knew what he was like and no need to pretend otherwise. On the other side of the window was a rhythmic scraping as the Murphy lad worked seemingly in a blind fury shovelling gravel into a wheelbarrow. For the longest time there was only the tight rhythm of his shovelling action, the heaving lift of effort followed by a quick grunt. Something becalming about it. Scrape heave thud. Scrape heave thud. Nailer decided to focus on it rather than on those in front of him. He didn't like to be surprised like this, getting set upon practically, out of the blue without a drop of warning, for starters it wasn't good for his blood pressure, a perennial concern for him, a silent killer seemingly, or so he'd been reading recently, responsible for all manner of ills it was, strokes, heart attacks – and they all knew it so they did, if he'd told them once he'd told them a thousand times, they knew right well he didn't like to be surprised like this, and every single one of them was now avoiding his gaze the cowards.

Christ, was a phone call too much to ask in this day and age? Apart from everything else it was the height of discourtesy. And then there was this bunch of old-timers who had accompanied Gerry Byrne up here completely on spec. Hardened, sorry-looking cunts, Nailer hadn't seen them in years and God knows what rock Gerry had found them under, their nerves shot to bits, their systems malnourished, surviving down these years on cigarettes and nightmares. Gerry Byrne himself was the only other seated man, at the table directly across from Nailer, scratching the place where his missing fingers should have been. His younger brother Handy was standing beside Kaja, leaning against the far wall like a child in trouble, as innocent as an altar boy.

– We have to do something about these women Nailer. The hippy and the little bitch.

Nailer, who was dunking his tea bag up and down, didn't look up. He tensed as Gerry spoke, putting his free hand over his face.

– They were on the news again last night Nailer. Every time they put a microphone in front of that little slut she starts coming out with more of this nonsense about our'fella. A tout now seemingly as well?! I couldn't believe what I was hearing! About one of the Byrnes of Cross?!

Nailer sat motionless, continuing to dunk his tea bag.

– Which reminds me, said Gerry. Can we close that window? That's her flesh and blood you have lurking there, probably listening to every word.

Still Nailer said and did nothing other than continue to stare down at the cup in front of him. Gerry looked back at his accomplices and put his arms out. Had the world gone completely mad or what? He turned back to the older man.

– Look it. If it makes you feel any better, I'm sorry for barging in unannounced like this.

Nailer took his time but eventually his eyes drifted up to look at Gerry.

– Can we have the room please?

It took a while for the place to clear, the group of men smirking at each other as they stepped out on to the backyard. Their murmurs and laughter of relief were soon to be heard outside in the night. The only other sound was the scrape heave thud from the Murphy lad's shovel.

– It's common courtesy Gerry. Common courtesy. It was only a question of picking up the phone. Not too much to ask I don't think. I'm a creature of routine these days. I don't like to be surprised. Christ it could be anyone at the door, the Gardai, The Brits, the bucken UVF. Everyone knows this Gerry.

He waited another moment, eyes on Gerry the whole time, before finally getting to his feet and leaning over the sink to shout out the top open part of the window.

– Thomas! Thomas!

The scrape heave thud stopped.

– That's enough of that Thomas. Will you go down the bottom of the field there and do a sweep of the hedges. Give them a good whack, will you? Good lad. Then you can hit the road. Come back at eight in the morning and we'll sort out that other thing. The job with the fence. Tell your mother you'll be gone all day.

Nailer closed the kitchen window and took his seat again. He went back to playing with his mug of tea. The silence left by the absence of the shovelling was arguably more obtrusive. Gerry had forgotten how touchy Nailer was. He himself hadn't been out this way in years. A legendary operator, the older Byrne brother had been retired from Provo business ever since the fertilizer bomb responsible for his capture took away half his left hand. You wouldn't see him much about the place any more. He lived in one of the council houses on the outskirts of Cross, his was the corner house at the back of the estate that every thief in the six counties knew to steer clear of, its front lawn strewn with scrap metal, dismembered and lobotomized trucks that looked like they'd been brought in for interrogation and then ripped apart with an unnecessary rage.

– You're tempting trouble there, Nailer. His father before him, the Prod mother, now his squealing pig of a sister. How much evidence do you need? I don't have to tell you what my old man would have done with the likes of that. We wouldn't even be having this conversation.

He stared at Nailer but the older man seemed to find this amusing, he was in fine form altogether now.

– Ah he's a good lad so he is. One of God's creatures

Gerry. Harmless. And I do admit to being a bit superstitious regarding that type of thing. Always good to be insightful about what we don't fully comprehend. Believing as I do that we are here for a purpose. Like it or not.

– Like it or not? That's a good one.

– If we trust the Lord, Gerry. I do believe He has a goal set out for us that we need to accomplish.

– I won't begrudge you your religion.

Nailer laughed.

– Bloom where you are planted, Gerry! Bloom where you are planted! That's the sum total of my religion so it is. And such is The Word as even my miserable cunt of a brother teaches it. Be love unto others and all that shite, certainly the meek. Which is to say that this unnatural creature is the burden I have chosen to take on for myself. I remember his father well so I do. A rangy midfielder when I myself was in goal. He was some player I tell you. Going up for the ball he'd practically soar through the air, the arms on him like an albatross, I've never seen anything like it, before or since. He could have played for the county if he wasn't so belligerent with the selectors. Don't get me wrong, there was never any love lost between us, but there would have been some affection there for the old bastard. Respect certainly.

Gerry didn't react. It was always hard to know how earnest Nailer was being in such matters, to what extent he was mocking you. Either that or the rumours were true and the senile old fuck was halfway to the funny farm. Nailer drank from his tea, smiling to himself. But then he became thoughtful.

– Granted the young one is a problem though.

– A problem? She's dragging our family's name into the mud so she is.

– She does appear to have talent in that regard. Getting her grievance out into the world.

– And again Nailer, a tout of all fucking things!

– She's just lashing out Gerry. They both are.

– Well it can't go on Nailer. I'm here this evening to tell you that I'm not happy about it. None of us are happy about it. I want something done. The Byrne name can't be made a show of like this. We've given too much to be rewarded with this sort of shite coming back at us. Our lad being bandied about in the news, making all sorts of spurious allegations about him. But especially *that* of all things.

Nailer sipped from his tea.

– They're making trouble all right.

– You're saying it like it's the weather, with nothing to be done about it.

– Christ Jesus what would you have me do Gerry?!

Sure there's television men hiding behind every crack and corner in Cross now with all this ceasefire nonsense. And that Donegal fuckwit has me sworn not to lift a finger any which way. Believe me I'm not one bit happy about it. These Belfast cunts. Do you think I trust any of them? I'm as whipped as the next fella Gerry.

– You said it yourself there. M.O.C.'s not from around these parts Nailer. Those boys don't give a fuck at the end of the day. M.O.C.'ll move on to the next thing so he will. But we are from around here. And youse all know the price our family has paid. I don't need to go through the list. You've seen half our blood on the floor. There's a debt there.

– You don't need to be telling me this Gerry.

– Is that so? Because I am getting the distinct impression that I do. Every time I turn on the television as a matter of fact.

– But again Gerry, the question right back at you. What would you have me do?

– Well I guess that's why they pay you the big bucks isn't it? But here, let me make it easy for you. Don't we have a man in with Casio's crew these days? M.O.C. doesn't need to be told in advance.

– Jesus Gerry we can't touch children. That's a no-no right off the bat.

– I'm more thinking about the hippy bitch.

– Sure she's wired to the moon that one. A space cadet. She'll burn herself out soon enough.

– That Newry prick, what's his name? You know, the sickly looking cunt. Is that not the way? Back in the day it would have been certainly.

– The Squad? Sure they're a law unto themselves.

– Exactly. They don't need the say-so from Belfast. Ceasefire or no ceasefire. There's a job of work there Nailer and when it's done it's done and everything carries on and nobody ever asks them lads any questions. Sure, knowing Casio, he'd do it just to get out of the house for a few days. Certainly if you throw a couple of grand into the mix.

– I don't know.

Gerry stared hard at Nailer, his anger turned on like a tap. Anyone looking in the window could feel it. He stood up and leaned towards the older man.

– Well you fucking do now.

Nailer didn't move an inch, his face fixed rigidly in front of him, reddening with emotion. He could feel the other man's breath on his cheeks, perhaps the speckles of moisture from his words. The table tilted as Gerry removed his fists from it before turning and walking slowly down the kitchen. Nailer stayed where he was. It used to be said that nobody would dare speak to him like that. Well, that's what used to be said anyway.

18

THE FIGURE WAS indistinct initially, like a structure of some sort, planted there at the gate of the fence demarcating the backyard of the complex. The chatter stopped in ripples spreading backward from the group of men as they noticed it, just as they were about to set off walking in that direction. It put an end to their merriment, whatever they were muttering and gossiping about when Gerry came out the back door and joined them in trying, without speaking, to identify what it was, the creature or shape in darkness over there just beyond the reach of the floodlight. It was an odd thing whatever it was, some manner of troll or local legend come to life, all superstitions now available to their imaginations. It was only when they adjusted their eyes and took another few steps forward that they identified Rehab the Murphy lad, standing immobile, entirely blocking the yard gate, a pickaxe gripped in both fists, his shadow splayed monstrous across the ground in front of them. The men understood that they would be torn limb from limb, Handy in particular cowering behind the other men. Just a second ago he, Kaja and The Young Goss had been laughing at something. The night held its breath and every live thing in the field sensed it, the violence that the Murphy lad was capable of. God knows what would have happened if Nailer hadn't appeared around the side of the house behind them.

– Thomas! Thomas! What are you doing lad?!

His words had no effect at first. The Murphy creature seemed to have been transported beyond reach, in thrall to his rage, breathing heavily through the nose, snorting snot like a bull readying itself to vent its fury at the world. And if that's what he chose to do no man on earth could have done anything about it. He would have to be shot and by now there were at least three shotguns aimed at him. This would be him now, finally, Rehab Murphy and his sorry history, how it all ended. Nailer, stepping on to the gravel, walked quickly around the static group and approached the gate.

– Thomas! Go home now. Do I have to dock your wages, do I? Thomas! Thomas! Do you hear me do you?!

It took a bit of time but the lad seemed to snap out of it, his gaze coming back to Nailer, finally acknowledging him as master. A barely appreciable change came over his body language, a slight slump of the shoulders, but it was enough to make the air bleed with relief. Gerry shouted at Nailer.

– Christ Nailer. You'd want to control your livestock a bit better there.

A few laughed but Nailer said nothing. The incident had frightened him too and he looked every bit the elderly farmer, a face of concern. He walked over to Thomas and took the pickaxe from him. Go home now, he told him, and said he'd see him in the morning. Then, noticing the tears that were running down the creature's face, he added not unkindly, only if he felt like it. The men were free to walk through the gate now. Their cars were parked around the side of the house. Gerry called out once he had safely passed through the narrow gap allowed by Rehab's static frame.

– If they're rabid there's only one cure for them Nailer.

As he said it he had two fingers pointing at side of his own head.

– I'd be happy to oblige if you want.

Handy laughed at that, his nerve and good spirits recovered. He was jittery, energized, mouthy again where all evening he'd been quiet. He muttered under his breath but for everyone's benefit, *Rehab you batshit rabid fuck.* No one apart from Kaja and The Young Goss laughed, the rest of the men were more sombre and as a group moved past where the Murphy lad was still stood rooted to the spot, each man daring to glance at his face at the closest point, a fork of floodlight glare on it, the swollen lips, the misshapen nose breathing heavy through it, the snot mixed in with other secretions, tears streaming from the eyes, big fat mucousy ones, from a grief that was soundless and depthless, the whole sorry history of his existence, and his family's existence, visible in his trembling shoulders. It told some tale and under other circumstances a few of the men might well have pitied the lad, but mostly they were disgusted by him as they hurried past. When it was Handy's turn he took a step closer to him. Rehab barely registered him. With one hand Handy reached behind himself, presumably for a concealed weapon, either gun or knife, and with the other he held out two fingers and waved them under the downward gaze of the Murphy creature's face.

– Hey Rehab . . . do you want to smell your sister, do you?

The Murphy lad's entire bearing stiffened, he stood with his eyes still fixed downward, but perhaps widening, the disbelief larger than the fury. Almost all the men shouted at Handy.

– Jesus Handy, are you stupid?!

Gerry was quick to pull back his younger brother, who was laughing now, finding the whole thing hilarious. The Murphy lad didn't budge though. Kaja was beside Handy now, he had taken out his army knife and was standing ready. But there was no movement from the giant and they walked on laughing. Nailer in particular was enraged, he screamed at Handy to get a grip, are you stupid altogether, Christ Almighty?! Gerry pushed Handy and even punched him slightly in the shoulder, the younger lad laughing at that too, as Gerry made sure to keep him ahead of him as they went in the direction of the cars. Before disappearing round the corner of the house Gerry turned back to Nailer a final time, again his two fingers pointing to his head.

– Sort it out Nailer. Sort it fucking out, or I will.

19

FRANCIE CAME THROUGH his front door and stopped dead in the hallway. The radio in the kitchen was on, as was the light. It was, he supposed, a possibility that he had left both on, but highly unlikely. Plus there was the fact that the music playing appeared to be some romantic pop tosh and he only ever had the dial tuned to the news. There was now another noise getting louder, and he was slow to recognize the reassuring sound of a kettle coming to the boil. He walked up the hallway and pushed open the door, surprised to see the politician Mairtín O'Cuilleanáin with his back to him at the sink, in the act apparently of making tea. Francie cleared his throat and M.O.C. turned around.

– Ah Francie. Sorry to frighten you but there was a nip in the air and I hope you don't mind but I let myself in.

M.O.C. then laughed.

– I can't very well afford to be seen loitering around outside the house of a known republican militant now, can I? Especially at these historic times.

There was broken glass on the floor which Francie could see had come from one of the window panes of his back door. Looking out, he saw a couple of large figures standing in his yard smoking.

– And I've taken the liberty of making myself a cup of tea as well. You'll have to wait if you want one yourself as I could only find one mug!

Francie said nothing but continued to stand there. Having heard the voices from inside the house the two figures in the backyard had turned and were now looking in through the window from outside. M.O.C. seemed to be in great form, laughing to himself as he dunked the tea bag up and down. He turned to Francie and was smiling as he looked around the kitchen.

– One cup. One knife. One fork. One plate. One bowl. Jesus Francie, you've got the whole thing worked out haven't you?

– I don't like waste.

– And rightly so, rightly so! No, I have to say I envy the simplicity, I do. Sit.

Francie accepted the invitation to sit at his own table but kept his coat on despite the heat from the Superser that M.O.C. had also put on. The politician had his own jacket off and draped over the back of his chair, his shirt sleeves rolled up. The handle of the mug was broken so he had to use both hands to sip the tea he'd just made for himself. There was a container of Francie's various pills beside him which M.O.C. now picked up.

– They're keeping you busy, aren't they Francie? My God. Cholesterol. Diabetes. Blood pressure. All you're missing is cancer for the royal flush.

Francie gave a wry laugh.

– Who knows with these medical people. Sometimes I take them and sometimes I don't.

– And then throw in the stress on top of it all. You should be taking it easy at your age so you should.

– Aye. Chance would be a fine thing there.

– Ah Francie, you're not depressed now are you?

M.O.C. laughed as he picked up one of the pill packets and read the side of it.

– My mother used to have to take these ones I think. I hope you're consuming plenty of fibre with them. That was her bugbear.

– You got my message I take it.

M.O.C. put the pills back on the table. He was looking at Francie with that angry look that he could turn on and off seemingly at will.

– The girls in the office said something about you having called. Hence I came, though I'm not sure how I can be of service.

– Well you seem to be the only one with influence out at the complex these days.

M.O.C. laughed, genuinely it seemed.

– It sure doesn't feel that way so it doesn't! Jesus, that's a good one so it is, because it seems to be that when I make a simple request it is the exact pure opposite of it that happens.

– You're referring to the matter in Lisburn last month.

M.O.C. stared at him. It really was remarkable the way he could do that, the laughter cut, the severity coming on like a switch. He would have made a great stage actor.

– I wouldn't know what you're talking about there Francie.

Now it was Francie's turn to laugh. Do these boys ever get sick of their little games? Him and Nailer. Christ they're like children half the time. He took a deep breath, deciding to come right out with it.

– I'm inclined to believe the young Murphy one is right in what she says.

– Well, there's no argument there Francie. Violence against women is a terrible thing. I am very much against it so I am.

– I meant the other part. That he's a tout. I could be wrong. But still. I find her highly credible at the same time.

M.O.C. continued to look at him in that severe manner, then he broke into laughter. So much laughter that it brought on a fit of coughing. Just when it died down it started up again. Francie sat watching him. If this laughter wasn't for real this man was some operator. Finally M.O.C. gained control, as if he'd ever lost it in the first place.

– They're all touts Francie! Every single one of them! Jesus Christ, don't tell me you didn't realize that? I have to say I'm disappointed so I am, I had thought more of you. *Francie knows* and all that.

M.O.C. shook his head, his laughter now just a wry smile.

– Every single one of them, Francie. Trust me. You don't go to war on a piece of land this small without compromising every single bone in your body. If you don't believe me wait fifty years and you can read all about it in the declassified papers.

– I have a strong suspicion they'll go for the Donnelly woman now. Possibly the Murphy girl as well after that. Certainly the brother is in danger. Which is why Handy's status is relevant. His brother Gerry is on the war path over it.

– Well what do you want me to do about it? I'm a politician Francie, in case you didn't know that. My hands are clean so they are.

– Like I say, you seem to be the only one with influence. Nailer doesn't want to know.

M.O.C. stood up. He spoke as he rolled down his shirt sleeves and buttoned them.

– Francie, Francie, Francie. There was one way of making this whole thing go away from the very beginning and youse didn't listen to me. You. Nailer, the rest of youse. You had your chance to nip it in the bud. All you had to do was let that little shit go and that slapper of a mother of his would be back to staring at the bottom of a gin bottle. But youse wouldn't listen to me. Here was me trying to give youse all a bit of real-world guidance and honestly I feel like I'm wasting my breath half the time. Youse have your wee western going on that youse seem to think you're all starring in. Well, youse are on your own so youse are. And so is everyone connected to that sorry tale of which, for the record, in case anyone's listening, I know not a thing. All I know is that I tried so I did.

M.O.C. stood looking at Francie, the way you would at a child.

– And the other thing I know is that around here a problem either goes away of its own accord or it gets buried in the bog. My advice to you Francie would be to simply do what you're told. Heroism doesn't suit you so it doesn't. No offence but you just don't look the part.

Annoyed now, his patience shot to bits, M.O.C. put on his jacket and went to the back door and opened it, before turning one last time.

– And one more thing Francie. Don't contact me again OK? That was the only reason I came here today. To tell you just that in person. Don't contact me again. Under any circumstances. Have you got that Francie? Good lad.

20

DOWN THE DOCKS it was a blue night still, not yet a black one, the sky limpid, weightless, every shape blocked dense and exact right up against it, the dusk at least covering up some of the desolation. If you looked you could have found three figures stumbling over the strange planetary terrain. Whatever moon this was it was remote in the system, no one came this way any more, if they ever did in the first place, certainly not even the tide which glinted far off, needled by bits of light from somewhere, but otherwise just a flickering memory of the day. Out in front of them the acres of mud thirsted for the long-disappeared sun, damp but slaked, black as oil, soggy under foot. The stench of raw sewage filled their nostrils, the stumbling figures were spread out, one of them lagging well behind the other two and howling every time he put his foot in the mud. It was his own fault. For starters he had on completely the wrong footwear. On up ahead Kaja and Handy, both booted up, were far more nimble. You'd swear Kaja in particular had inbuilt knowledge of the place, Handy had entrusted him with their tackle of choice and he held it out in front of him, an angling pole with a hoop at the end of it.

– Here, chucky, chucky. Here, chucky, chucky.

– It's not a chicken Kaj.

– Chucky Our law, hi.

They had found purchase on the mudscape across from the Navvy Bank, climbing down on to the flats to the right of the quay which was empty obviously. Just the one rusty bucket moored, God knows how it got there, how long ago it was, well it was stuck now, that's for sure, Cyrillic writing on the hull locating its place in ancient history. Here at least some of the grassy marsh jutted in, sprouting rushes like dunes, pure oily mud underneath though, some sort of attempt at knitting the earth back together. The only source of noise was the stumbling figures themselves, pinted up, tripping, cursing, laughing. Every wrong foot landed them in a plop of muck. Mickey roared again from some distance behind his companions, his voice carrying grief in it now.

– This is pure cat so it is!

Ahead of him Handy laughed and shouted Bingo! Mickey sat down cursing on a mound of reeds, his foot stuck. In his opinion this was one seriously bad idea from the get-go. Say what you like about Francie but he never had him doing things like this. With difficulty he extracted his soaking foot out of the sucking mud with a plop.

– I thought it was a rock so I did. Shoes is completely wrecked now so they are.

Kaja was the closest to him.

– Serves you right for wearing them anyway.

– I thought we were going to Tivoli's so I did. Not this shite.

Kaja had already gone on. Mickey got to his feet, squinting to discern the disappearing figures of his two associates in the late-dusk mist. He had no heart for following them but out of a poverty of imagination he continued to do just that. It was a conjurer's terrain, too much give in it, not enough, the puddles duplicitous, shallow, depthless. Every footfall needed to be gauged. The mud was ancient, alive, it would be a slow drown all right, the pull of the black earth sucking you down into it, nothing to grab on to other than your bad memories. Your last view of the world would not be pretty, the grinning face of Handy for example waving you off as you slid into purgatory. On the far side of the peninsula lamps of light studded its tail practically all the way out to Greenore. But behind them, at some distance, the houses had their backs to them, not wanting anything to do with whatever they were up to, an occasional odd pane of glass telling some lonely story. Further on the three boys went out into the strange marsh. Little choice now anyway. Mickey put another foot wrong and went up to his ankle in mud. He was at the end of his tether now.

– THIS IS PURE CAT SO IT IS.

At least Kaja and Handy waited for him. By the time he got up to where they were, Handy was sitting on an abandoned shopping trolley eating a slice of bread from the loaf they'd lifted from the corner shop not long before.

– It likes Mother's Pride in particular seemingly.

Mickey went over to where he was sitting. Then leant over on his hunkers, panting.

– Speaking of Mother's Pride, I hope Wheelie Bin is knocking around The Square when we get back.

Handy stood up and started to walk. Kaja went after him, but stopped to wait for Mickey. While he waited he practised casting out the angling hoop.

– Here, chucky, chucky, here chucky chucky.

– Again Kaj, it is not, in point of fact, a chicken.

– Nice spicy wings out of the wings you'd get though. Yum yum.

Up ahead Handy spat out the bread he was eating in disgust. Mouldy. Kaja shouted out to him.

– Hey we should bring her to Mullins after.

– Who? said Mickey, behind him. Wheelie Bin?

– The bird you spa. See what they can do with it.

– Nice fillet burger all right. Heavy on the mayonnaise there Kathleen.

– A Mullins right now would hit the spot.

– So would Kathleen.

– Would you though? In all seriousness? She's as old as my granny so she is. Who's dead by the way.

– Plus more mileage than Wheelie.

– Debatable.

Mickey howled. He had gone into the mud again. He stopped and, in a rage, took off both of his shoes. With a roar he flung each of them as far as he could. Kaja stood admiring both his throws.

– Will you look at Fatima Whitbread there.

Mickey laughed at that, genuinely. He didn't care now. Up ahead Handy had stopped to urinate and they could hear the hiss of it against the damp earth.

– Would you by the way?

– Who, Fatima? Absofuckinlutely. Great arse on her.

– I was always more of a Tessa Sanderson man myself. The skimpy shorts. I'd say she's a demon in the sack.

– Come on the fuck. I'm starving so I am.

They caught up to where Handy was standing, doing up the buttons on his jeans. Kaja called out to him.

– Hi what do you say we grill this thing out at Nailer's by the way? He has the big pit. Pluck it to fuck and carve it up. Nab one of his sows while we're at it. Streaky bacon hi. Lovely jubbly.

Handy looked back at him, all serious, almost angry.

– It would ruin the joke so it would.

Mickey was now standing beside Kaja and Handy was staring at both of them. For some reason he was particularly sore on this point.

– The old man is to find out about it like everyone else.

Kaja laughed.

– To say nothing about the fact that he'd skin you alive so he would. Forget about this freak of a bird, the man has an unseemly affection for those pigs.

Handy stood upright, the shoulders back and a frown on his face. His companions started to laugh already, knowing an imitation of Nailer was coming.

– *Have you ever seen the Salar de Uyuni Mickey? Have you hi? As Marcus Aurelius used to say to Julius Caesar, shove it up your hole Julius.*

Even Mickey laughed, despite standing there in his socks, sopping wet with muck. Say what you like about Handy but he was a funny bastard. Some mimic too. The three of them walked on then, quick to revert to silence, each of them in the world of their own thoughts, before Mickey stopped, his foot gone into another sinkhole, though not as bad as the previous one. He was well beyond caring now. When he caught up with them again the two boys were standing looking around, disorientated, their bearings completely lost now. They had reached a point where the long reeds formed clumps like dunes, made of oily mud rather than sand, the negative of a beach. Hellscape didn't even begin to cut it. Another shopping trolley was in their path, gleaming, the bones on it picked clean like a carcass on the veldt.

– Remind me again Handy, where in the absolute fuck are we?

– The bog.

– Didn't appreciate that The Town even had a bog until now.

– Let me correct that. Under the bog.

– Keep your eye out for Shergar hi.

– O that's one you'll not find. Nailer's pigs had a good feed off of him so they did. Why do you think they're so fast?

– Big long faces on them too.

Mickey laughed.

– Horsey faces and big shites.

But then, with another bad step, he landed his leg in liquid mud up to his knee. This time he did roar in frustration, a guttural thing that came from the stomach. Kaja was standing next to him and at least this time helped him by holding out the angling pole for him to grab with his hands to pull himself out. Mickey stood panting then, bent over on his hunkers.

– What exactly, may I ask, do you intend doing if we ever get close to it? I mean, assuming your hoop contraption does in fact do the actual trick.

Kaja, grinning, pulled back his jacket to reveal a big hunting knife in its holster. Brand new, it gleamed in the light.

– Got it in Jocks, he said. Russian army. No spoons or tin openers or any of that other shite on it. Just the blade. Could saw through a tree with it.

Mickey shook his head, laughing, before walking on, ahead of Kaja this time.

– Youse are mad cunts so youse are. Mad absolute cunts altogether.

21

ON THE THURSDAY after the Monday a group gathered out the back of The Arms, sheltered in a huddle by the oil tank. It was a wild near gale of a night but no rain surprisingly and the air itself was as warm as fumes. Not nightfall yet but a purple furious sky attendant. The group of men stood watching out for the lights on the Lower Pass, finally spotting them and following them as they snaked along the back mountain way towards them. When the van pulled into the car park everyone got into it without saying much.

Sheila McGoldrick had been only too happy to confirm that The Widow Donnelly was on her own that night. No visitors, no relations staying, certainly there were no friends calling in to her, that's for sure, or, Christ in heaven forbid it, journalists. Who would have been calling in on her anyway? As Sheila pointed out, sure the woman was on her own every night, you'd no doubt find her off her face from midday onwards. The sherry or the gin, take your pick, whatever was handy, still in its brown paper bag from Culligan's offie. The slut had gone to seed completely so she had, as long as there were no cameras around that is, and even then when they were pointed at her she was only just about able to put on a face for them, but which unravelled soon enough I'll tell you, said Sheila, she was a disgrace so she was, a pure lush was what she was, and the state of the place that had become a cluttered mess all around her, gone to hell completely, the whole house and the beautiful garden that poor old Jim used to be so proud of back in the day, it was his pride and joy so it was, he would have been up and out in it, from morning to night practically, tending to it, practically hoovering it, snipping the grass with nail scissors practically, the man was a pure obsessive perfectionist when it came to that garden, but now look at the state it was in, gone to shit completely and overgrown with weeds, the only bit of it presentable the few acres The Widow had sublet to the Lynch lad. And there were rumours there as well so there were. O yes, there were indeed. That she was always trying to entice him up into the house, lure him, bait his base instincts, the understandable urges of a youngfella, but he mustn't have been as stupid as he looked in fairness to him that fella, he must have known what was good for him and what was not. So yes of course Sheila was only too happy to oblige Jarlath when he met her by chance in town and asked her for the bit of help, and Jarlath was only too happy to take it. She was reliable was Sheila. An educated woman, a secondary school teacher in The Louis no less, as well as a bridge player and a golfer. And no fan of Marie Donnelly that's for sure, the cunt, despite them being nextdoor neighbours this twenty years. Didn't she laugh in Sheila's face over that highly regrettable Killen Cup incident. When Sheila put in a score, not a great score, could have should have been a great score, but she'd been unlucky with a few putts that lipped out because of a bit of malrepair of spike marks and then that gobshite she was playing with from Greenore putting her off her swing on the thirteenth, coughing when Sheila was at the top of her backswing causing her to put it straight into the water which she never ever did on that hole. She was practically guaranteed a par there, sure you could have practically marked it down on the card in advance. So in her opinion it was not the worst thing in the world to correct these details herself on the scorecard afterwards when the Greenore gobshite gave her her card back and Sheila volunteered to drop them both into the box. She only wanted not to get point one back on her handicap, she didn't think she'd actually win the bloody thing. And of course the gobshite from Greenore heard about it afterwards and rang up to point out that there must have been a mistake, because there was no way Sheila could have won and in fact she remembered her having a different score. Well, the shame and mortification were one thing, the reputation of her of being in any way like that, some sort of God forbid thief or cheat, and her an educated woman, a teacher in The Louis et cetera, but it was quite another thing altogether when that bitch of a Donnelly woman hears about it and starts in on her, lording it over her with a sudden new-found superiority, the slut, and then what does she start calling her from that day on? Seve. As in *Morning Seve, how's it going Seve, well any craic Seve?* And the look on the bitch's face laughing her hole off the whole time, nothing but pure malice behind it. The cunt, the fucking whore. And never mind but her with that little scumbag shithead of a son that everyone was always giving out about all over town selling drugs and joyriding and robbing, out till all hours of the night causing trouble and mayhem and giving jip all over the place. Seve my fuck, you absolute malevolent pain in the fucking hole you, I'll get you so I will. So when Jarlath bumped into her down the town a week or so ago now and asked for a very small very minor favour altogether it was no big deal for Sheila to say no bother Jarlath, no bother at all, sure all he wanted for her to do was to keep an eye on things for him that week, that's all he was asking, it was no big deal at all, almost nothing really, just for her to keep an eye on things and make sure there were no cars on the driveway other than The Widow's own banger of a Ford Escort, ha! suitably named that's for sure, and then at Jarlath's urging when he rang Sheila again on the evening of the night in question for her to go further than this and to make one hundred and ten per cent certain of things by going around the back of the house and peering in the window to absolutely one hundred and fifty per cent confirm with her own eyes that yes indeed the hussy was on her own as usual, swilling away as usual, knocking it back and tipsy as fuck as usual, away with the birds as usual, completely distracted, jerking and twitching like there were flies buzzing around her head, whatever was going on inside the mad bitch's head.

So the Hiace went on a loop of the town and then out the back way to the forest road, where the lights of Cross grew distant behind it. As it traversed the lower reaches of Gullion and passed the higher-up houses on it, everyone in the van ignored the brief glimpses and bits of inner domesticity that were on view, the mood way too sombre for any interest in that sort of thing, the van entirely lacking in curiosity about any of it, everyone just sitting listening to the howl of the near gale wind that had mostly quietened now for some reason and the rattling on the roof of the van which told the humdrum story of an unremarkable, intermittent and somewhat half-hearted rain. Eventually we came to the long laneway by the stone cross and the turn-off to the old Donnelly farmhouse, switching off the lights of the van and pulling into the long drive to go up it slowly. When we got to the courtyard the van emptied and the light in the hallway came on immediately and, somewhat surprisingly, The Widow Donnelly herself appeared at the opened door. Plainly the woman had made an effort with her appearance, she was in eveningwear, her coat on over it and, holding a glass of red wine, she stood looking out and down at the group of men she was now seeing surrounding the bottom step of the porch, seemingly finding the whole scene amusing. By now everyone had put their ballies on, and The Widow was smirking away, almost grinning at us in fact.

– The Halloween costumes is unnecessary boys. I know each and every one of youse.

She laughed.

– Christ, I can smell the booze from up here.

She drank some of her wine, evidently half-cut herself.

– I've been waiting for youse. I was wondering when youse would come knocking. I figured it might be whenever we started going on about child rape.

She took another drink from her wine, swaying slightly.

– I was all ready for youse last night as well but youse didn't show. The same thing the previous night, and the one before that. I've been waiting weeks for youse and here youse are at last. I find the nights a long hell you see. I wouldn't wish it on anyone, even that snobby bitch next door, who by the way you can tell her she can stop sneaking around my back garden now. But youse will be doing me a favour actually.

She drank more wine and then paused, looking at us over the rim of the glass.

– He is a tout by the way. That young Byrne lad. Youse do know that right? A proper one this time. Not like my Darren or any of the other ones. He's been meeting with a man from the Branch. Young Cathy seen them with her own eyes. It's true, whether you want to believe it or not.

The Widow leaned forward but didn't move and nobody wanted to be the first to approach her. For what seemed like an age nobody said anything and it was easy to see that it could have stayed like that. There was no law to state otherwise and it was almost pleasant standing there, everyone in position like stage actors, the swirling warm breeze, the rain having stopped completely. Nothing had been committed to yet. The future was open still. But then something gave, and as a group everyone moved as one towards her. The widow raised her hands.

– Stay back, she said, her voice raised.

We stopped.

– I'll go with youse. But on condition youse don't put a hand on me. I'll go with youse. I'm ready. I've given away the dogs and the house is sorted so it is. I'll go with youse. How do I look by the way? I wore this outfit on my wedding night, for the afters of it. We danced till daylight. My Jim sang Cole Porter into my ear. *You'd be so nice to come home to.* It was a great night and he was a good man. A fine man my Jim. A gentle man. And he loved my Darren as if he was his own. Well, tonight I'll join him in the earth. I'm looking forward to it actually, the peace and quiet of oblivion. I've suffered enough. I'll go with youse so I will. But

> don't dare put a damn finger on me or I swear to God I will absolutely lose it. You don't get to do that so youse don't. You don't get to lay a finger on me. That's the bargain I'll strike with yiz. But I'll go with youse, so I will.

She knocked back the wine, draining every drop from the glass, then turned back to put it inside on the hall table. She reached inside again to switch off the main light in the hall and pulled the door closed, stooping to put the keys back in through the letter box. Turning, she straightened herself and stepped forward like a model on a runway, slow and graceful, picking her footsteps carefully as she descended into our custody. Everyone kept their distance until she was among us and then we surrounded her from all sides. She kept her eyes open but didn't make a sound as a hood was put down over her and her hands tied up behind her back or even when she was thrown on to the floor of the van. We headed south, everyone in the back of the van silent looking down on The Widow as she rolled this way and that on the bare floor. Not once did she complain, but there was no more laughter out of her. No one took off their ballies and everyone sat surrounding her like hangmen, heads bowed. The van drove beyond the nearest farm lights of Mullaghbawn on the old road to Forkhill and then cut through Jonesborough before chancing the N1 for a short stretch. At Blackgate it turned off and headed to the Long Woman's Grave, where a parked car came into view, a Datsun by the looks of things. The van went up the road slowly and stopped near it. The car's side door opened and the familiar form of Francie emerged, sober and serious. There was no sign of Casio or any of the others from that crew, but presumably they weren't far away and certainly no one was of a mind to sit and wait for them, that's for sure. Francie took a final pull of his cigarette before stamping it out. Then he reached in and popped the boot and came around to open it completely. The van emptied, with two of the boys helping The Widow Donnelly step down out of the back doors. But she insisted on walking unaided, and unsteadily she went on her feet. Not a word was said and Francie remained where he was, looking not at The Widow but at the ground in front of him, his face empty of expression, everyone noticed it and commented on it afterwards, the man seemingly bled of all concern or purpose, a man who was simply going through the motions now at this stage, doing as he was told, the boot open beside him, lined black by bin bags taped to the lips, like a throat waiting to be fed, and he stood there not helping but allowing it to happen, patiently and not moving an inch as The Widow Donnelly, only partially being led, mostly made her own way in silence towards him.

22

ADMITTEDLY THERE WOULD have been some people who thought the whole thing hilarious. A gothic show or something from way further back in history. An offering of some description, a sacrifice, an immolation. Some humour to it too admittedly, whether you wanted to acknowledge it or not. Plenty shrugged. Boys will be boys, there's nothing surer. And anyway what do you expect the Devil to do with all these idle hands lying about the place? Form steeples out of their fingers? Join their hands in prayer? It was raised on adventure and mayhem the likes of these young pups were, and all that now turned off suddenly like a tap. Sure there had to be some sort of outlet for it. So it was only natural so it was. And anyway what of it? The tree huggers might not like to hear it but the creature was bound to die soon enough, that was the reality, plain and simple, there was nothing more definite, certainly not in this climate which was completely unnatural to an exotic being such as that, it was only a matter of time before it took ill with pneumonia, died rigid from hypothermia. And be honest, a part of you had to appreciate their showmanship, the ghoulish pomp and the sheer devilish humour of it, the mischief and yes, why not, the pure imagination. Close your eyes and you could practically hear their manic laughter as they set the whole thing up. Like some barmy gory sculpture. Yes indeed, boys will be boys. Admittedly though the majority were appalled. Of course they were, and that was understandable too. It was disgusting so it was, disgraceful in fact. Nailer in particular was apoplectic, an offence against the gods or Mother Nature, take your pick, and he had the whole spectacle removed and incinerated pronto before any journalists caught wind of it. According to Scrawny Magee – who had heard it direct from Jarlath – the old man was inconsolable in his rage, but also shocked and quite shook too, as if, no stranger though he was to unpleasant acts, he had never seen the likes of it in terms of pure barbarity. Perhaps the funniest thing about the whole incident was that for the longest time, no one even noticed. Anybody crossing The Square early that Sunday morning could have been forgiven for thinking it was The Widow herself still perched there on her upturned mineral crate, perhaps a tad earlier than usual it was true, but in fairness to the woman, there as ever, got up in her usual spot by the Monument to the Martyrs. An untidy mess, a dirty clump of a thing, sleeping perhaps, get up you lazy hag, was she dead?, certainly not moving, wrapped in a stained blanket, held up by a pole, rags and ragged, and a stench that made you choke on the very air you breathed. Many would have passed before anyone dared or even bothered to take a closer look. And this was what people spoke about afterwards, even those who hadn't seen it with their own eyes. A gruesome find indeed, it was at first not clear what manner of species it was, dismembered from what whole sum, its bits promising some weird jigsaw, or what accumulation of injuries or damage it had accrued, but once the various parts had been assembled in the mind's eye, it was hard to shift the image, again even for those who'd only heard about it, the pole keeping the entire contraption upright, making it seem quite a bit bigger than it was in actuality, what at its very heart was nothing but a shrivelled pathetic clump, bloodied, the neck not only broken but more or less severed, practically hanging by a thread to the small body, and underneath – what made it recognizable – the dirty pink, the poor damp thing, a clotted horror, feathered, and that curved distinctive beak pointing downwards at the ground.

23

THINK AGAIN OF crows. They seemed to be everywhere. A plague of them, or maybe they had always been this common. The unnatural heat we'd been having was driving them wild and they went at it riven, with their harsh violence towards one another, whatever was at stake for them, no doubt not a whole pile but worth marvelling at all the same, their language of hate, you could recognize their particular grievance in it, adhering to its own set of rules. What had passed was local history now, intertwined with it, and everyone knew some version of the facts, the word had spread the way these things do, a form of currency that tightened in everyone's throats, developing its own form, the familiar weight of silence, a pressure felt physically in the neck and the back, the memory of it, like the act itself, seeping into the black earth. An endgame was in the works, everyone knew it and everything seemed portentous, ominous, decided ahead of time. It was the summer of the heatwave, record temperatures that had spread out across the span of the continent, and this time we were not to be spared. The grass bleached to straw and children played with the cold relief of water on the street until the hosepipe ban was brought in. Animals started to drop where they stood in the fields, dehydrated, languorous, stupefied, flocks of flies covering them. And then one day Gullion erupted like Vesuvius and the mountain was aflame, so quick that arson was questioned in the furious raging of her lit gorse flickering bright orange and the thick body of cloud emanating from her, dominating the landscape for miles around and sitting heavy in a bad mood over all the adjoining counties. There was no getting away from the taste of it in your throat, the sting of it in your eyes, your lungs heavy and blackened from it, you could hear the crackle of the fire all the way from town, like gunshot or the snap of bone. It was not true that we were going to hell, it was coming to us. The authorities came with their trucks and hoses and worked at it gamely enough but with an obvious futility. They asked for volunteers and some acquiesced and were given a whispered pass to join the official lines to cut the lower gorse back to stop the spread. But there was no slowing it and after a while the decision was made to leave the mountain to burn, to focus on cutting back the growth along the roadways, banking on the flames not vaulting the gaps. It turned out to be the right decision but for a period of time nobody knew for sure and the mountain squealed at our willingness to abandon her to her fate, the raw flame not as appreciable now but still present at a continual low level, the smoke constant, the great Gullion's vengeance stewing on itself, O she would not forget this, that was for sure, our treachery reflected in her flayed and scalded back. With the full rage quieted finally and the last elements of flame extinguished she sat in judgement, sore, deeply ashamed, her skin charred and covered by a thickened straggle of the black gorse, skeletal infant scaly trees skinned alive, bark-stripped, sticking up and out of the black earth like cartilage, bodies shorn of flesh by some long-buried incendiary material that had been kept and minded and nobody wanted to know about. She seemed disposed to return them now to the world, figures from the past, figures that knew no fondness in the collective recall, figures that the world wanted only to forget, the pathetic and the damned, the maimed and the perpetually silent.

Handy and his crew had never been around The Arms as much. They were practically living there, Handy drinking more and more, developing the bit of flab about the face and midriff, losing by the day that baby-faced assassin look, leaving only the viciousness, the suspectful eyes, the ready sneer. Up to no good in Pat's new beer garden out the back, they ruined it on him, after all the money and effort he had put into it, vandalizing the new bamboo furniture, setting off firecrackers, squibs, they pulled up the shrubs and the root veg patch he had planted for his nature-mad youngfella, burned his fake tropical ferns and yuccas. When they got bored with that they toyed with the animals, any of the stray cats and dogs that hung about the place, luring them in with scraps then scourging them for the want of anything else to scourge, no creature was safe from their messing with blades and coat hangers and plastic bags and cigarette lighters. Pat's youngfella's jar of tadpoles matured and the frogs came spewing out of it, lit up and hopping around the back. The screams of the wee lad almost rupturing the place then when he came in off the street to find a bored Kaja had crucified the young frogs on the barbed-wire border of the yard's perimeter wall. Handy in hysterics laughing at the trouble Kaja had gone to, an impressive brand of artistry under other circumstances, he had hung them in a row like medieval siege victims, stretched out across the level gap from barb to barb in a grotesque elastication of their arms and legs, impaling them with finesse upon the spikes, their guts torn, semi-ruptured, innards pulled bursting at the seams, Pat's youngfella speechless standing in front of Kaja's gory composition, Handy wetting himself laughing.

Jesus Handy Jesus Kaj Pat said when he heard the roars of his young lad, but the two boys weren't listening, Kaja too busy bent over in concentration for the final touch, with his cigarette lighter out, trying to set the paraffin-soaked creatures on fire. He went to each one in turn with the lighter and after some frustration had going a stunning conflagration. It was admittedly some sight. Devil's hands all right. Devil's hands.

24

IT WAS THEREFORE no doubt a good thing that the Dungannon job was back on. Word leaked out from Nailer's crew and, laugh all you like, but it caused a change in things around here, giving a sense of purpose and meaning back to people, something for them to get up for in the morning and go about their day with a bit of a skip in their step. Dungannon was the op Francie had ruined on Nailer months back with his urinating man, a bank job seemingly bigger than the Brinks Mat. No surprise then that Nailer wanted another crack at it. Word was M.O.C. had even OK'd it, though he'd been given little choice. It is said that Nailer had him rightly on the spot, convincing him of the pure need for something like this in terms of the local morale which, as M.O.C. knew only too well, had taken a serious dip in recent times. Nailer even talked up the possibility of a schism, what the politician wanted perhaps least of all in the world. Not to mention the value of the loot itself, because a haul like that would set you right for a decade, talk about a war chest, said Nailer. M.O.C. took his time about it but came back with the green light. Say what you like about him, he's no fool. Some speculated that of course he would also have had his own line of reasoning. Especially when it was heard he wanted Nailer to spread the spoils about a bit, specifically in the direction of East Tyrone, that he wanted Bernard Brady to lead it.

The following Friday the whole crew gathered out at Nailer's, what you might call his inner circle, most of them standing about the back kitchen, leaning against the sink, the sideboard, the bare wall. Pat Mitchell was there, as were all the usuals, 'Lee Trevino' Murphy, Jarlath Heneghan, Joe The Bus, Scrawny Magee and a rake of others. Maurice McCabe (aka Taxi) had gone off with Handy to pick up Bernard Brady and everyone waited for them. There was a tension, but a good one, about the place, people were giddy and eager to be getting on with things. There had been too much lying around of late, too much inertia, giving in and giving over to the so-called best way forward, excessive sway lent to the ways of others, the politician, the statesman and the diplomat. Nailer himself could be found sitting in his usual spot at the back wall like a lord, a mug of tea on the small table in front of him, in great form. The night was an impenetrable pane across the window but if you came closer you would see that it was in fact the burnt loins of Gullion, as black as tar. Craning your neck you would find that day was not in actual fact done, the last bit of light getting slowly smothered, and at some remove the lights of Forkhill and the Cooley Peninsula starting to come on. After an age of waiting there was the noise of cars pulling up and voices out in the yard. The back door opened and in came Handy and Taxi, accompanied by Bernard Brady, who had come on his own. After the formalities Handy went in next door to the snooker room where Kaja and The Young Goss were playing, while Bernard went over and sat at the one empty seat directly across from Nailer. The Tyrone man looked around himself, nodding approvingly, both men pleased to see each other.

– I like what you've done with the place Nailer. The off-white. It's a while since I've been here.

– Too long Bernard, too long. And thank you, I do appreciate that. None of these savages ever notice things like that and, I don't mind telling you, some thought would have gone into it, you know, the colour scheme et cetera.

– No, no I can see that so I can. You don't get that type of harmony by chance.

– Seashell grey they call it.

– Fuck me, are you serious? That throws me right back to hell so it does.

Nailer looked at him, confused.

– Elocution lessons, said Bernard. She sells seashells on the seashore.

Nailer laughed, as did some of the others standing around. It was true that Bernard had a bit of a stutter but it wasn't that pronounced, and anyway, it had been many years since anyone had slagged him about it. Nailer poured from a teapot into an empty mug in front of Bernard. He pushed a tin of biscuits closer to him as well. Nailer's fondness for the younger man was clear. Practically everyone liked and respected Bernard. A slight, wiry figure, tough as pig leather, though you wouldn't guess it to look at him. He was clean and washed and gentle appearing, wearing a nice lumberjack shirt tucked into his jeans and new Desert

Storm boots with not a speck of dirt on them. A whiff of cologne even emanated from him.

– You're looking well Bernard.

– Thanks be to God.

– Did Handy fill you in?

Bernard took his time answering. He drank from the tea, then put more milk and sugar into it.

– He did.

– What did he tell you?

– The essentials.

– Such as?

– That there was a job of work to be done. Handy cash going. For when the taxman comes calling. Says you could do a fair bit of damage with the proceeds. Maybe a mini-Tet type of thing could be on the cards after all.

– Not that mini Bernard.

– Good to rein in the expectations though at the same time.

– The part about handy cash is certainly correct.

Handy called out from the snooker room.

– Did someone say Handy Cash? That's my porno name so it is.

He was standing in the doorway, holding a snooker cue. People laughed. Kaja, behind Handy, was bending down to take a shot, and from the sounds of it missed. As he waited for the laughter to die down, Bernard was staring at Nailer.

– Dare I ask?

– Ask away Bernard. You're among friends here so you are.

– Is it sanctioned?

– Official as they come Bernard. I would give it to you in writing if I could.

Bernard laughed at that. Nailer leaned over to pour more tea from the pot then sat back before speaking.

– Being serious though, he was in earnest about wanting you to lead it. Our political friend. In fact he requested you specifically. You and young Handy.

– Is that so?

– He must be trying to get into your good books. Handy's too.

Bernard leaned forward to put more sugar into his tea, shaking his head in disbelief.

– Does that fucker not realize what this will do to this little process of his? Christ, it will blow it to smithereens so it will. That's the main reason I'm up for it to be honest. Anything above and beyond that is a bonus. Especially if it gets us a few of them new bazookas the Russians have come out with. I seen them in a magazine there.

Nailer laughed.

– You'll have RPGs out the ears so you will Bernard.

Bernard laughed then looked seriously at the older man.

– But even if it doesn't. I mean, be straight with me Nailer, am I missing something here? It's too good to be true so it is.

– He reckons he can handle the political fallout.

Bernard took up his tea again.

– Maybe he can, said Bernard.

– Maybe he can, said Nailer.

Both men sat quietly, looking at the floor, thinking. Bernard sat up straight and smacked himself on both thighs. Well, fuck it, he said. He raised his hand to his mouth and spat on it, then extended it to Nailer.

– I guess we're going to find out aren't we?

Nailer put down his tea and spat on his own hand. He reached over and shook Bernard's.

– I guess we are Bernard. I guess we are.

25

WHEN M.O.C. POPPED in unannounced to The Arms later in the week he bought, to everyone's shock and surprise – and for possibly the one and only time in his life – a round of drinks. He stood a little back from the bar then, watching everyone closely in the mirror behind the hanging bottles, observing, studying us even. But that cuts both ways and people were able to study him as well. It had been a good few weeks since anyone had seen him but in fairness the man was looking well, and was actually in fine fettle altogether despite all the stress and strain, the thick-haired head on him mat and firm, well-oiled, he looked rested, tanned after his recent holiday in the Arans where he said he got plenty of you know that unbroken type of sea sun, that dry salty island sun that you can get lucky with the odd time coming in off the Atlantic and God isn't the Arans the most perfect spot in the entirety of the universe then? People nodded and hummed back to him in agreement, docile but also a tad wary as M.O.C., all smiles and charm and benevolence, said he just happened to be passing by and thought that he might just pop in for a few minutes to chew the cud and perhaps take stock of the local temperature, vis-à-vis various community matters in particular, matters of varying degrees of importance but which, nonetheless, were all fully deserving of his utmost attention. But also, in addition to that, and now that he was back from his holidays, he thought it would be a good time to get people's views on things in general, the bigger picture so to speak. That it was always good to take a fresh look at things, especially when you are back from a break like he was, with the mind and the body well rested. Does a man good so it does. And he also wanted, he said, to keep people up to date on his council work, to make sure they understood that despite his recent short and long-overdue break away from the grindstone he was still beavering away on our behalf, on a variety of issues, nothing was too small, whether it be the erratic (to say the least) wheelie-bin collections or the knock-on effects on community services of this godawful heat we were having recently (particularly the impact it was having on the elderly), and not to even get him started on the state of poor blackened Gullion, it was a disgrace so it was, an absolute disgrace what happened there, sure there was still even now smoke coming out of her burnt rump and carcass, bringing into sharp focus needless to say the matter of the completely derogatory speed and insipid manner of the emergency response, or rather the complete lack of speed and the complete lack of emergency response, he said, laughing, because it was patently inadequate so it was, and without a doubt left a whole lot to be desired. It went without saying, so it did, that he would be raising hell about it at the next assembly meeting. Certainly it wouldn't have been like that if it was one of the Protestant areas up in flames, that's for sure, no leave it with him, he'd put a rocket under them so he would. Metaphorically speaking of course, he added, laughing. Walking around in a little semicircle, M.O.C. changed tack then, verging on to more delicate matters, though in truth you would have barely noticed the gear switch, the man barely missed a step, seasoned pro that he was, his tone being still quite casual saying that while he was here he might as well take the temperature in regard to the larger-scale-type events too, vis-à-vis the situation in general so to speak, the lie of the land across the board, the, yes, big picture so to speak, regarding this whole ceasefire malarkey. He wanted, he said, to get the general view of things from the community perspective, the state of play et cetera as regards the local orientation, the average viewpoint and demeanour, what people around the place were saying, the body politic as it were or, to put it plainly, the amount of jip they were giving, either for or against, their general disposition so to speak. Had Nailer been around much for example? Had there been many meetings up at the complex at all? If so, who would have been up there? Had the Tyrone boys been seen around much at all? He'd heard all right that Bernard Brady was hanging around a good bit. Which was completely fine by him of course, it was in fact more or less his idea so it was, and he was very fond of Bernard, very fond of him altogether, no he was just curious that was all. And, while he was at it, what did we ourselves think about the situation, the prospects for some type of political settlement being on the cards? Were we open to considering it at all? Would we welcome it? And again, what about Nailer himself, was he trying to sway people one way or the other? It would be completely fine if he had been by the way, it would be perfectly understandable, completely natural in fact, sure wasn't he one of the leaders of the community? No, M.O.C. was only just being curious, that was all, but, more than that, and here his tone became a bit more serious, he particularly didn't want to get ahead of himself, he didn't want to be too far out in front of where the locals were at, and where they were comfortable. This was the way politics should work, he said, he himself personally would actually encourage any debate or doubts being expressed openly about the running of things, the direction they were all headed in, or the strategy that was being deployed, he would want to hear about any dissent or disagreement, because in his opinion it should all be aired out in the open anyway, better out than in, isn't that right? Isn't that the sign of a healthy movement? We're not the politburo you know, and, after all, he himself was only trying to represent the community according to the best of his albeit limited ability, he could no more tell the man on the street what to think than he could dictate marching orders to the drummers of the Apprentice Boys band. And if there were any naysayers muttering away in corners, well, he wanted to know exactly who they were and what it was they were saying, he wanted to give them their due, to hear them out, for they no doubt had understandable concerns and very reasonable points to make. And that was all totally fine by him. In fact, it would be a bit odd if that weren't the case. It would be a pretty piss-poor reflection on the self-confidence of the movement if that were not the case, such as, and again, not to pick on them, but to use the Soviets as an example. Because, if he had his way, the movement would be a thriving hotbed of argument and counterargument, debate and dissent. So he'd like to hear out these renegades, these naysayers and alternative, if not to say original, thinkers. Again, who were they? What were they saying? It was important that people listen to them. They might have things that neither he nor the leadership had ever even considered, valid points that needed to be taken on board, accounted for, drilled down on a bit, discussed in depth, then either be taken on as part of the orthodoxy or dismissed with total self-confidence, reason and good debating manners all round. And he was the very man for this, he welcomed it a hundred and ten per cent, he looked forward to it, relished it, enjoyed it. So again, what did we think ourselves? Genuinely. Youse are the crucial voice in this whole thing, did we not know that? Arguably the arbiters of it. And here he stopped and looked intently into the mirror and at the wary faces looking back at him but trying to avoid his gaze at the same time. In many ways the future is in your hands, he said. Youse are the opinion leaders, the makers and breakers of the consensus, the small, no offence meant, but absolutely critical links in the chain. What did *we* think of the whole thing? Maybe he himself was wrong in his own thinking. Honestly, he understood the difficulties we all might be having. The internal doubts and the arguments that people must be having with themselves and with each other, perhaps keeping them to themselves or muttering them under their breath in dark corners. He didn't mind sharing that there were some mornings he thought this and then other mornings he woke up thinking something else, the pure and complete opposite of it. He laughed. So he knew, so he did, O God he did, he knew right well what people around here were going through, that internal bit of confusion that they were feeling, that awful sense of worry that they were giving up in some ways, that they were God in heaven forbid surrendering and letting the side down, the republican tradition, all the mothers and fathers who went before them and whose ghosts were rearing up in front of them now, to say nothing of all the martyrs, our prisoners and the great and decent silent majority that constituted the hard-working mainstream republican nationalist community. People weren't to feel that way of course, because we weren't surrendering one iota. No, we weren't. One hundred per cent we weren't. But these feelings were only natural and debate was good and healthy so long as it was all kept in house. That was the crucial thing. That's how you get to the next stage. United. As one. You see, that's the essential thing. There can't be any schisms. It can't be like it was with The

Stickies back in the day. Everyone has to move forward as one. Or not at all. If everyone did that it would be win-win so it would. Win-win-win every day of the week and twice on Sundays. Sure we'd be sick and tired of winning. And even if it was decided to give the ballot box a proper go and it didn't work out well he himself would be the first to make the case that the movement could and should go right back to militarism. He'd be clamouring for that in fact, virulently in favour of it, as strident as anyone calling for it, the return to war. He'd take it upon himself to make the address at Bodenstown if he had to. He'd stand over Wolfe Tone's grave and wholeheartedly apologize to his memory and the memory of all the republican martyrs, and in that hallowed and saintly presence he would forswear the path of non-violence as the bad idea it was from the get-go and do all he could to make amends and reignite the military effort, to personally, if he had to, push The Brits physically into the Irish Sea. He laughed again and left a bit of silence that wasn't filled. Looking around the mirror of reflected faces, M.O.C. took his time before bringing his little lecture to an end. Taking a few steps towards the door he paused before turning again to us. Sure as Nailer himself has said on many occasions, he said, they haven't gone away you know. The faces in the mirror murmured in agreement and, to a man, everyone present raised their glasses in the air.

Throughout this little speech of his, M.O.C.'s eyes flitted frequently to the corner where an irritating and somewhat incoherent grumbling dissent in a sort of snorts met many of his words. Nonsensical interruptions that he did his level best to ignore. It was of course Our Francie, who was scuttered drunk. This by itself was not in the least bit surprising to anybody, as Francie did lately tend to stray into The Arms on an almost daily basis to sit on his own or occasionally in the company of his nephew Mickey. The word was he wasn't in with Casio's squad any more, nor of course were there any ops for him to be scooting around after, all of that sort of thing having been put on ice. The man was at something of a loose end and, it was observed, wore that vacant look upon his face that was all too common around these parts during those uncertain days, bled as it was of any belief or sense of purpose. People generally left him be, he was harmless enough at the end of the day, the cut of him as he got more cut, the dark glowering face on him as he descended further into the malted depths, tending to become more bolshy as the night wore on, irritable and irritating in equal measure, but generally incomprehensible in his ravings for the most part, a pain in the hole essentially, as he took to spouting off and shouting out to anybody and everybody and nobody in particular, answering imaginary interlocutors, assailing those who were not there at all other than in his own mind, shouting at them, railing at them, his speech slurred, saying things that people couldn't specifically make out half the time though certainly you might have got the gist. But that was generally later in the evening. Before that he would be a rather mute pathetic presence about the place, taciturn, locked-in, his disposition a complete downer, and it was plain to see the devil of depression had entered into the man's soul. It was hard for anybody now to recall what he once was, an up-and-comer and a go-getter, an all-knowing hungry type of individual with a certain self-confident vim and vigour about him, what up until recently had been his trademark drive and purpose. He was completely dispirited now so he was, and it was sad to see in many ways, dejected as he was, dissolute and self-damning, certainly not a happy camper and it didn't take much detective work to get to the root of it, the manner of his mania, the explanation for his dissolution, the utter other side of reality into which he had slipped, especially as he had no qualms about telling everyone. He was, he claimed, only now realizing what a fool he was all along, to have been, as he bitterly put it, the only true believer in the crowded church. That he hadn't known the charade was a charade at all, because nobody had bothered to tell him. That all along he had been too sincere in its pursuit, too eager in reciting his lines while not appreciating that he was only in a play. Or perhaps it was the wrong play, a different one to the one everyone else was taking part in. His was the socialist nationalist version in bright green Technicolor, with trumpets blaring and confident drums being beat to fuck, an epic earnest four hour director's-cut job, a bit of a bore to be truthful, while everybody else, he saw now, had all along been participating in some independent gangland flick, a blood-sport movie revolving around petty crime and the stuff of the day-to-day, exhilarating though that may have been. And now that the whole thing was done and dusted all the man could hear when he put his head down at night and closed his eyes was the deafening roar of silence descending upon him and the sad look of each of his victims staring straight back at him out of the void, their gaze as haunting as birdsong over Flanders. He claimed to see them during the daytime too, them mouthing their questions back at him, taunting him and mocking him, laughing at him, delighting at the pure fool he had been and wondering aloud with great amusement whether their disappearance into the cold earth and his own inevitable trip to hell as a result will have been worth it at the end of the day. His urinating man. The old retired gent and his wife. Even the wee Donnelly pup. And besides them a whole pile of others queuing up behind to get their digs in. The man had no rest from it, morning, noon or night. Sometimes he'd be just sitting there balloted, the fat tears streaming down his face, you'd pass him on the way to the jacks, blubbering like a hungry mutt, pleading to the visions appearing in front of him in the murk telling them he was sorry, I'm sorry so I am, forgive me, please. Mickey told us his uncle hadn't been sleeping right, not a wink in weeks, his nerves shot to bits, his victims' voices a banshee's lure that kept him up at all hours, torturing him, needling him, baiting him, they wouldn't relent or leave him alone, give him a moment's peace or let the matter rest, and he couldn't take it any more, and he couldn't keep it to himself any longer, he was done with all that so he was and he wasn't afraid to let everyone know about it. People tried to ignore him but it was getting harder. His behaviour put a strain on Mickey in particular who more and more had to come in and carry his uncle out of the place, apologizing profusely for his carry-on, the things Francie was wont to declaim aloud as the night wore on, all manner and shade of heresy, the shouting and the roaring out of him, his general comport and the obstreperous way he had of acting about him, over there in the corner of the red lounge mumbling away in this indiscriminate fashion as the drink took a fierce and sorry hold on him, its grip whitening into a firm bony claw from which there was little chance of escape. Occasionally, Francie even got physical, but laughably so, he'd knock into you on purpose, the slight frame of him, it was hilarious really, the way he'd lean in and out of his way to get you with his hip or elbow and then fall against the wall in the narrow passage, sure he'd do more damage to himself, staggering backwards then, dazed and meandering about on his way to the jacks or the bar. Pat stopped serving him and even banned him outright but it didn't matter, he'd sneak in when no one was looking, hanging out in the shadows, it would be more hassle to kick him out then so he'd be left alone, to drink the dregs of left pints, or sip away at his own naggin, then fall fast asleep in the corner. People warned him or told his nephew Mickey to warn him, but alas to no avail. And now here he was with his carry-on in front of M.O.C. who through the entirety of his little speech was in fairness doing his level best to ignore Francie until the moment when he made it to the end and the part about going to Bodenstown if he had to, clamouring for the return to arms if he had to, virulently in favour of it he would be, strident for it altogether, and him standing over Wolfe Tone's grave with his fist in the air and the other one across his chest as he wholeheartedly and without reservation apologized to the martyr's memory and the memory of all the other ones who died and suffered for The Struggle and The Cause and in this saintly presence forswear once and for all the path of non-violence and democratic constitutionalism as the bad ideas they were from the get-go. When he'd finished Francie was on his feet giving a round of applause.

– Wolfe Tone my hole! he said.

This got everyone's attention, but Francie wasn't finished.

– You can fuck Wolfe Tone so you can. And you can fuck Patrick Pearse and you can fuck James Connolly. And you can fuck Kevin Barry and Michael Collins. And you can go and fuck Bobby Sands as well while you're at it. They perhaps were the biggest eejits of them all. They died for nothing so they did. Nothing. Jobs for the boys in suits and that's about it. That's what they died for. Jobs for the boys and the likes of you M.O.C.

Even M.O.C., professional politico that he was, accustomed to being heckled as he was, found his patience snap at this point. Fuck Bobby Sands? Christ, what next? Apart from anything else it was simply bad manners. M.O.C. looked over at Francie sitting crooked on his seat, steaming, the world swimming in front of his eyes. At a glance from M.O.C. one of the Shinner thugs went over to where Francie was.

– Y'all right there Francie?

– I'm fine thanks, and how about you my fat friend? Are they feeding you right?

The two of them stared off for a few seconds before Francie spoke.

– Here, I've a question for your boss over there. Ask him does he remember the exact moment he became a sell-out, or was it just more of a slow gradual type thing? No seriously, I'm genuinely curious so I am. Go on, ask him. I'm thinking of writing a book.

Francie started chuckling to himself. With effort then he stood up and shouted over at the bar.

– Because that's what you are M.O.C. A sell-out. You and the likes of you.

Francie sat back down again, almost collapsing into his chair. M.O.C.'s thug, who was halfway back to the door, turned around once more, but M.O.C. told him it was all right Wally and, laughing to himself, he took his time and, hands in his pockets, as chill as they come, walked slowly over to Francie, coming to a stop in front of him, where he looked down at the sickly drunken man.

– Say that again Francie. You say that again.

– Sell-out.

M.O.C. smiled at first and then laughed loudly, and the whole room laughed too.

– Francie knows. Isn't that what they used to say boys? *Francie knows.* What a joke that turned out to be?

With his hands in his trouser pockets he leaned over to speak into Francie's face.

– The state of you Francie. Sure you can barely even stand upright. Tell me this, does Francie know the time of day, does he? Does he even know the day of the week or the month? What about when to keep his mouth shut, does Francie know that? It is said he used to know these things though personally I always had my doubts. You see I've had my fill of the likes of you down the years Francie. I've seen yiz come and I've seen yiz go. Goulding and his ilk. Farrell. Devlin. McCann. All you lefties and Connolly-ites. Fantasists and pub talkers the lot of youse. Eventually all ending up in the same place, places exactly like this, sitting in puddles of your own piss.

M.O.C. turned around, his hands in his pockets, as he smiled back at the room, before coming closer to Francie again.

– You watch yourself now Francie. That would be my wee bit of friendly advice to you. And it might be my last bit of friendly advice to you. On account of your, eh, shall we say, service to The Cause. Because, let's not forget Francie that I know. That's right, I know all about you Francie. I know what you did and I know who you did it to. In fact, we all know. So you watch yourself now, do you hear me Francie? And you can take that any way you want to by the way. You can take it as banter or you can take it as a warning. It might even be a final warning Francie.

M.O.C. stood back and addressed the room again.

– Which begs the question, doesn't it lads? Does Our Francie know anything? Did Our Francie ever know anything, any damn thing at all?

He laughed as he headed out the door then.

– Aye, Francie knows all right. Francie knows.

26

FRANCIE WASN'T SEEN for the rest of that week, or indeed the one after that. No one knew where he was. But on the following Saturday he was spotted sitting alone out on the low wall by the bus stop, on the Main Street side of The Square, not far from The Monument to the Martyrs. Nobody passed any remark initially other than to notice that he was still there a couple of hours later. No big deal you might say, it was a fine late-summer's day and why wouldn't you want to be lounging around in it, soaking up this unnaturally fine weather we were still having, allowing all that vitamin D to seep down into your bones, especially if you were a chalky scrawny specimen like Our Francie? But as the hours and then the whole afternoon passed people began to wonder what the man was up to. Someone suggested that it had the whiff of protest about it, Our Francie ruminating away like the Buddha not far from where The Widow Donnelly herself had perched, and with that same vacant hollow look about him, hunched over, miserable and wretched, chain-smoking away. Was this him trying to communicate some sort of message to the community, was he out to make a point? Because surely, it was mooted, his choice of location was no accident, not only near The Widow's perch but also directly across from M.O.C.'s constituency office. Was this him expressing his regret at that whole sorry episode, owning up to his own role in the messy business, while at the same time trying to expunge his guilt and wipe the slate clean? Well you don't get off that easily so you don't. You can't just click your fingers and poof, slide the bad memories off you like a snake's spare suit of skin. Life meant life with this business, nightmares all-inclusive, caveat emptor, no returns allowed, if you have a problem with that speak to the management and good luck with that. By this stage everyone in Cross had noticed him, sure you couldn't fail to notice him, and people were understandably getting irritated, even angry. This was him having a go at the community at large so it was. More or less sticking up his two fingers at us, sticking them up and holding them there in front of our faces and the faces of all the good and decent people of Cross, jabbing us in the sternums, blaming us essentially, while at the same time trying to disassociate himself from us as he chilled and lounged about up there on the high moral ground. The hypocrisy was simply galling so it was, nauseating, and also tiresome, this was yet more of the man's posturing, what had become lately very tedious altogether. Well, what a goddamn and utter fool he was if that was the case, to be sitting out there like a sulking child, insulting people in this manner and levelling all sorts of wordless accusations against the community who had put up with enough down the years, to be dealing now with the likes of this being thrown back in our faces.

But no, it turned out that it was none of that because, as soon became apparent, Our Francie was merely waiting for somebody. It took a while for people to cotton on to this but yes, in hindsight, it had been perhaps obvious from the way he kept checking his watch, or looking down the street, standing up and then sitting down, impatient and jittery, then forlorn as anyone would be to be kept waiting like that for hours on end, his attention focused always in one particular direction, in eager anticipation, people now understood, of the arrival of a bus. Whenever one appeared on the horizon Francie stood bolt upright in expectation, his eyes fixed on its approach, only to sit down again in disappointment when the vehicle either didn't stop at all or failed to produce whoever it was he was waiting for. Speculation was rife then so it was. Who in God's name could he be waiting for? Did the boul Francie have a woman, a paramour, a bit of fluff on the side? Chance had some serious sense of humour if he did, that's for sure, Our Francie with a floozy, what in God's heaven was next? Perhaps it was one of those mail-order jobs from Cambodia or Laos or Vietnam, the Philippines perhaps? Or a lonely-hearts dalliance with a landed widow from down the country. Well, whoever it was, she was clearly having the jitters because the hours went by and still there was no sign of her. Poor oul Francie eventually stubbed out a last cigarette and off he went. It was the same then the next week. Nada. Zilch. During this time the man didn't once darken the door of The Arms and in fact hadn't done so since his tête-à-tête with M.O.C. Mickey confirmed that he was back on the wagon and, no, for the hundred and fifty-sixth time he did not know anything about a woman. In fact he told us that his uncle had returned to his mostly monkish ways. Up at dawn and on the road. Driving around the back lanes, spinning here and there, whatever it was the man was up to. The following Saturday it was the same story, Our Francie out on the wall for hours in the sun, albeit another fine day for it, the face on him puce red, increasingly forlorn and the same constant watch-checking and fidgetiness as the previous two weeks, standing up and sitting down at the prospect of each approaching bus, only to lose heart and spirit and all manner of faith. This third occasion though was different because a bus did eventually pull in and judging from Our Francie's reaction whoever he was waiting for was indeed on it this time, it was obvious from the way he acted, solicitous, even nervy, as he waited at the door. Practically everyone in Cross was watching now at this stage, and he would of course have been well aware of this, the main street being nothing but a lengthy many-beady-eyed organism peaking through gaps in blind slats or around the edges of curtains. And who was it that Our Francie had been eagerly waiting for? None other than young Cathy Murphy, who greeted him coldly at first, declining his outstretched hand, the girl was plainly reluctant, if not outright livid and full of anger and even hatred for the man. At Francie's instigation the pair of them sat for a while in silence on the yellow bus bench, the young Murphy remaining very distant with him in her manner, staring at the ground the entire time, Francie using his hands to emphasize whatever pleading he was doing, whatever promises he was making, whatever blame he was accepting, whatever ideology he was renouncing. After a while they rose and he led her up and down Main Street on an easy stroll. It was only then that people could get a good look at the young Murphy one who, come to think of it, nobody had seen for many weeks. In the interim, it was noted, the girl had filled out quite a bit, she had lost some of that childish pudge but had otherwise fattened around the midriff in particular, as well as the lower limbs which were, as was now appreciated, swollen at the ankles. God, was she sick, the young one? If so, what manner of illness or disease was it? Was she dying even? But then it dawned on everyone, slowly and then all at once, the women seeing it before the men, the girl was not sick or dying, but pregnant. Up the duff! someone shouted. It was undeniable, as clear as day, the child was with child. You could sense it in the air as that realization hit home behind every window and every set of blinds and curtain edge in Cross, and here now it was far from hiding it they were but rather advertising it front and centre to the whole town as they continued on this little jaunt of theirs. That's what they were up to, people finally realized with increasing anger, as Francie led the young Murphy one up and down Main Street, parading her in front of all the watching eyes, his small defiance matched by her small defiance, seemingly united now and all contained within the simple action of a weekend stroll, this most mundane of acts, both accusation and evidence rolled up in one. That of a crime on display. A crime being taken out for a walk on a nice sunny day. An attack, an assault, not alone of rape, but of child rape, the evidence right there before everyone's eyes. There was nothing for it but silence, and in the face of such silence the pair of them simply continued on their way about them, the whole town looking on. After a few laps they returned to the bus stop, where they waited for the bus to Silverbridge, and when the time came Francie helped her on to it and he stood at the bottom of the steps until the doors closed over before, waving out the window at him, she took off and went upon her way.

27

DUNGANNON WAS A disaster. A pure trap from the first moment though at first the boys did not realize it. Lured in well, they were initially delighted with themselves, the whole thing appearing to have gone swimmingly altogether only for all hell to break loose on their egress, quickly finding themselves stuck at the bottom of that small cul-de-sac adjacent to the bank, wedged in at the back by a Land Rover that came out of nowhere, sure they had no chance, there was no escape and no let-up in the deluge and the barrage. Obviously they were expected, their arrival evidently and eagerly anticipated down to the exact minute they came running out of the bank, whooping and hollering, loot in arms, *party on hi*, only to find the police waiting for them, dug in and impatient, probably bored out of their minds waiting for them, well hidden as they were, barricaded and camouflaged, numerous and murderous. All of the lads were lifted, half of them shot and wounded first. Dunne. Delaney. Doherty. Kaja. McComiskey. Murphy. But as for Bernard Brady. Well, call in John Stalker because that was shoot to kill all the way so it was. No attempt made to arrest him, a pure cull is what it was. Foot-and-mouth-infected cattle get dispatched with less efficiency. The paras in particular had an added glee where poor Bernard was concerned, surrounding him like the much-anticipated guest of honour that he was, the prize padrone, with the other boys on their knees watching on. They shot him first around the midriff and then, to their great hilarity, in the area of the ball sack, after which they seemingly let him crawl around on the ground in agony and in a bloody circle as they laughed at and taunted him, spitting and taking turns pissing on him, before finishing him off up close with the money shot to the back of the head. The initial news reports were all over the map. One minute every one of the boys was captured or killed then the next minute some of them got away. Then they were all caught again. Christ will youse make up your minds people roared at the radio. Finally the situation was clarified when the news on both sides of the border led with the same item, of a sole escapee who had made it clean away and was now on the run. Do not approach this man, the commissioner said at his makeshift press conference, he is likely armed and extremely dangerous. Boy did The Arms erupt in cheers when the mugshot appeared up on the screen. It was none other than Handy Byrne of The Byrnes, last seen, according to the commissioner, an hour after the shooting out near Kilkeel. Seemingly he had hijacked a car which he used to go off and hijack another one. Word was he was now in the vicinity of the Mournes. That would be the truth all right. The Mournes would be his refuge.

Nailer was apoplectic. The Young Goss was out at the farm all afternoon scanning the police radios, linking in with a group of other lads out and about doing the self-same thing. The television had been taken from the cupboard and placed on the snooker table, all the boys standing around it watching the news. Nailer too, but The Young Goss maintained the man simply could not sit still, he was absolutely beside himself, no one had ever seen him so bad. Stunned and confounded, especially when Bernard's death was announced, Nailer could barely stomach to watch or listen to it. When M.O.C. appeared on the screen, Nailer's fury went up a notch, he started yelling at the screen, calling him a double-crosser, a turncoat and an unreliable snake in the grass before getting to his feet to leave the room, only to stay standing, half in half out, listening at the doorway or pacing up and down his kitchen. Obviously the politician was going to deny all knowledge of anything, categorically so regarding the question of any potential official republican involvement in this alleged attempted robbery, if that's indeed what was going on, he said. The whole sorry affair was, he maintained, now looking directly into the camera, entirely unsanctioned. If there were any known republicans in on it, well, all he could say is that they were doing so off their own bat so they were. Let me repeat that, M.O.C. said, these actions were not and I repeat not sanctioned by anyone within the upper echelons of the republican leadership nor were they in any way aided and abetted by anyone with any credibility whatsoever within the leadership or any representative thereof. You see, he said, relaxing a little in his tone, what you have to realize is that the republican movement is a family like any other. We have our black sheep too, and these boys were clearly on an earner so they were, while possibly being out to ruin the peace process while they were at it. Well, they will not stand in the way of history, that's for sure. As it happened, M.O.C. continued, he actually knew the dead man well. Bernard Brady came from a decent hardworking family, a farming family with strong republican roots going right back to the War of Independence. A patriot is what poor Bernard was, a patriot and an Irish nationalist and a kind and decent man. Honour out the wazoo he had. Yes, it was true that he and Bernard might have had their political differences, and poor Bernard had in recent times been led into dissidency, but it didn't change one iota the fact that Bernard Brady was a brave and courageous soldier and a bona fide republican hero. He was, he said, seriously troubled, no, extremely troubled so he was, by the manner of what appears to have been the blatant execution-style killing of Bernard. Whatever him and his friends were up to there was no reason to assassinate him like a dog in the street the way they do in Latin America, like Pinochet or Batista or one of them boys. There was no excuse for that, he said, and mark my words, the human-rights people will be all over this like a rash, because it was as clear as day that what transpired on the streets of Dungannon today was yet more evidence of the absolute suspension of human rights that was de rigueur round here so it was, and completely and utterly of a piece with the type of discriminatory policing the nationalist community have been putting up with for years, namely the pure and utter disregard that exists around here for the likes of the Geneva Convention, the Universal Declaration of Human Rights, the Magna Carta or any other goddamn civilizing creed which seemed magically to not apply to *this* jurisdiction for some reason and certainly not to one subsection of the community in particular. If this peace process was to win out, said M.O.C., the whole thing would have to be taken out from the roots up if episodes like this sorry and tragic business were not to be repeated and the memory of Bernard and the likes of Bernard respected so that their deaths would not have been in vain.

– Put that shite off before I throw a brick at it.

Nailer, standing out in the kitchen, his back to everyone, couldn't take it any more. The Young Goss jumped up and went to the television. Nailer turned around and leaned back against the sink. The silence was total, no one was inclined to break it. Nailer took a deep and loudly sighing breath.

> – An admirable sight though at the same time.
> When a man of some skill hits his straps and decides to deploy it. Hard to listen to though. Bloody hard
> to listen to.

He marched out through his kitchen and out the back door into the night air. At the bottom of the field he could see the Murphy lad about to feed the pigs, wading into the noisy centre of them carrying two buckets, lit by the tractor lights he'd driven down there and left running behind him, surrounded by a thick ring of sows up to his knees. Even from here the expectancy in the animals' squeals could be appreciated and the Murphy lad was laughing at them like a child, finding it hilarious the way the pigs were rubbing up against his legs attempting to get closer to him, nuzzling into the backs of his knees looking for his attention, the lad was in his element at such moments, calling the pigs by their names as they climbed over each other, tickling him with their snouts, jostling for position close to him. It was an odd melody, unnatural and sweet, the lad's laughter and the pigs' enthusiasm, the animals assuredly loved him, and for a minute it was easy for Nailer to get lost in the scene, its perfection and its blessedness. But that sure as hell didn't last long because beyond the hedge on the far side of the adjacent field a line of cars could be seen on the Carrick Road, and Nailer knew right well from their speed and the screeching as they turned off in convoy that they were coming this way. Sure enough the cars braked hard on the dirt verge at the charred oak before turning and entering the driveway and revving loudly up the hill, getting louder as he lost sight of them passing around to the front of the house and up the drive. There was soon the sound of doors slamming and his name being screamed out but he stayed where he was, getting increasingly agitated. After all he had done for this crowd. Christ. The last of the summer evening, pastoral bliss, and the neck on some people to be coming at him like this with what he already knew would be their twenty-twenty hindsight. To say nothing of sheer manners. Not even a simple phone call in advance. So when Handy's brother Gerry came out the back kitchen door and on to the gravel yard Nailer had no problem turning to face him with his own version of anger. Before Gerry could even utter a sound Nailer had his finger up to his lips motioning for him to be quiet for Christ sake and not to say a damn word and Jesus not to pick this moment of all moments to be an idiot. Having made his point without speaking he turned and went back into the kitchen in a huff, going straight to fill the kettle, making as much noise as possible, before settling himself in his usual spot up against the far wall and, eventually, grudgingly, looking Gerry in the face.

– A quick phone call would have been appreciated Gerry. You know my feelings on these things. It's only courtesy.

Gerry couldn't believe what he was hearing. Surely he was supposed to be the angry one. It was his flesh and blood that was out on the Mournes this very minute being hunted down by dogs. Swivelling around he looked for acknowledgement from the other men standing about, before turning back to Nailer. His rage didn't allow him to sit but then he did pull the chair across from Nailer over and sat on it. He was about to speak but Nailer, eyes lightly closed, again pre-empted him.

– And you know right well The Brits can hear us out in the field Gerry.

Gerry shook his head and turned again to look behind him, he even laughed at The Young Goss who was just standing there uselessly, his mouth open with the tension, the whole thing was surreal so it was. In the next room the television was back on and M.O.C. was still talking on it. Another politician was being interviewed beside him and M.O.C. kept interrupting him, talking over him, disagreeing with him, contradicting him, even laughing at what he was hearing, making a total nuisance of himself in other words, it was some performance. Gerry looked around to see where the sound was coming from.

– Here, can we put that shite off? I've had enough of that cunt.

Nailer nodded at The Young Goss and then there was silence.

– You can't blame the rodent for its nature.

– I never said I was blaming *him*. I just don't like the cunt.

– Come on now. None of this being wise after the fact. It was a sound job, you know what can happen with these things.

– No, in fact I do not know as it happens.

Nailer said nothing. With his thick fingers he started rubbing furiously at his eyes.

– Bucken allergies. They have me at my wits' end so they do.

– God knows what shape he's in Nailer. He's out there possibly bleeding half to death I'll not ask for what.

– Well we needed it. In case they wind the whole thing down.

– *You* needed it Nailer. *You* needed it.

– In any case your boy was taking the lead in the planning.

– Don't blame the headless for their stupidity. We both know well our'fella's limitations.

– He put in his due diligence in fairness. And it wasn't my idea to put him in Gerry, for the record. M.O.C. wanted it, both him and Bernard. He insisted on it, though I admit that I had my doubts.

Nailer paused, looked at Gerry.

– The only one to get away too.

– What the fuck are you implying there Nailer?

– Only that he was again fortunate. That it could have been worse.

– We should send out a crew.

– And then what? Get them all nabbed Gerry? Have another shitshow on our hands? One shitshow on top of the other.

– If that's what it takes.

– Easy for you to say, you've just the one to worry you. I've the responsibility for the whole shower.

– Yeah but he's an important one and don't you forget what my family has done. Especially with all the shite and rumour he's had to put up with recently. You wouldn't be sitting where you are only for us.

– Again, have I ever disputed this Gerry, have I?

– It's not a matter that's even up for dispute. It's established fact so it is. If he dies or is nabbed it's on you Nailer. On my mother's grave I swear to fuck.

– Look it, we can send a crew. I'm not saying that we won't. We just have to be clever about it.

– I'll go with them. To make sure there's no more fuck-ups.

– You can do what you like, I'll not stop you.

At this point there was the sound of buckets being put down outside the window, then a squeaky wheelbarrow being taken up with a grunt and moving off slowly. Those in the kitchen listened, the wheel in need of a good oiling like a small animal pleading for mercy. Gerry knew without asking that it was the Murphy lad.

> – I told you having that toutspawn hanging about the place would bring trouble. Lurking, listening at windows. You've gotten weak is your problem Nailer. I'd have had a bullet in his skull already.

Nailer didn't go in for his customary defence of the Murphy lad. Maybe he did out of earshot and people didn't hear it. Maybe he was simply tired, tired and sick to his back teeth of everything. Or maybe he was just trying to keep Gerry's head from exploding further on its shoulders. Either way he said nothing, and allowed the idea to hang there, the sentiment Gerry had expressed and the tone of voice he had used to express it, and this fact alone, what Nailer didn't say, was noticed and later commented upon.

28

GERRY GOT A crew together made up mostly of his own kind, fellas who'd been retired from Provo business for years, who knew each other from way back, had worked with each other, done time, inflicted hurt and been hurt themselves, and all this was obvious from their manner and bearing, their scarred skin and limbs, their worn, sad faces, stooped men who hadn't a lot to say for themselves, watchful, vacant-looking men, silent, moody fellas going about the place. They drove in batches in vans in forays out the coast and up and around and through the off-roads out the back of Warrenpoint to achieve the vicinity of the Mournes. After each trip they returned empty-handed, sullen and resigned, like men accustomed to the small tragedy of things going wrong. There was the odd skirmish with the searching RUC doing the self-same manhunt for the self-same man and only those with clean records could get through the checkpoints dotted along all the back roads of entry on to the mountainous zone. Turns out one of theirs had been badly injured in Dungannon and word now came on the news that he was dead of his wounds, so the RUC were out for payback, the entire area had the ring of the fortress to it with the mentality of both siege and hunt, it was clear what they would do if they got to Handy first. All day and all hours of the night Gerry's men took turns in shifts to roam in competition with the hounds and the yellow-vested police. When they could they got out and walked the heathered hills, illuminating every gorse bush with a torch looking for signs of their wounded brother in arms, calling out his name in harsh whispers across the quiet night as loudly as they dared, competing with the sounds of RUC laughter in the distance and their whistling to their dogs which moved around them covering a fair range. Coming off the mountain damp and cold the men were inevitably intercepted at the checkpoints, their van searched multiple times, and those inside put splayed flat and spread out on the wet tarmac while the underside and every nook of the vehicle's interior were searched. After an hour lingering cold by the roadside they would be let reluctantly go to continue empty-handed on their way.

The Arms was the base to which they returned after each foray to sit exhausted in the corner. A sullen bunch, there was not much drinking done, certainly no banter or chat out of them, these were individuals who had no use for those types of things. They kept themselves to themselves at the back end of the place, strewn across the L-shaped corner couch with their feet up, taking turns at sleeping, pint glasses filled with tap water on the table, remnants of breakfast, the odds and ends of rasher butties, ketchup-smeared plates, dinners from the chippy, the rubbish piling up around them no matter how much Pat cleared the area. Gerry seemed not to sleep at all and went out on several of the searches himself each day, known Provo entity though he was. He even spent a full night or two on the slopes. When back in The Arms he sat rigid and commanded a church-like atmosphere by virtue of his mere presence. Every entrant into The Arms was looked at hard by him, the intensity of his gaze making it clear that each and all were being held to account and every one of us was just as much to blame for the whole sorry business.

He stared hard into your lying soul. The only slight movement in his face that tic of a wink of his that he had on one side, and each man, woman and child seemed to bring it out when they were in his presence, like a detector switch being flicked on, the eyes full of accusation. Was it you, was it, were you the one who fucked us over, weaseled us, screwed us, is it because of you that my brother is running like a dog across the Mournes, The Crown hot on his scent? Was it your treachery that has him out there wounded and bleeding somewhere, starving half to death? And will it be you we eventually discover hiding at the bottom of this when all is said and done, coiled like a snake in the barrel? Did you do it for a quick payoff did you, a few scummy grand, or was it to save your own skin from some other thing, a gambling debt, a spot of blackmail or a loan arrears? And will you be the one we finally get the truth out of, but only after taking you to a barn, one of those deserted ones out by Cullyhanna or Belleek, will it be you we have to work on for days as you beg for an early end to your sorry miserable existence, and will it be you who they find at the side of the road, a black bin liner over your head, a rent in your gaping skull, the brain fluid oozing out of it, your body booby-trapped so that some use is at long last made out of you, what couldn't be accomplished in your useless miserable wretch of a life? He suspected us all, discounted nobody, and seemed to be asking his questions just by looking at you. He wanted to know every minute detail, who knew what where and when, but this didn't narrow anything down because everyone knew everything of course. When Francie appeared in The Arms on the Wednesday afternoon the full crew happened to be there resting. A crowd had just returned from the search and another was due to head out. They sat on the back couch in silence, exhausted, glum, pessimistic.

Francie though was chipper, in flying form altogether, laughing at something his nephew Mickey had just said to him as they came across the threshold bringing a flash of afternoon light in with them. Nobody had seen Francie since the day he'd brought the young Murphy one for their little stroll together along the main street and here he was now, not a bother on the man, greeting the room like a bishop, all smiles, back to ordering the non-alcoholic Beck's before taking a pew in the far opposite corner, generally looking altogether much better than before if not exactly spruced, but on the way back to the way he had been perhaps. Him and Mickey were the only ones talking and it didn't take long for the two of them to notice this and the eery silence that was like a thicket of fingers pointing over at them from the corner, the unwashed sullen crew of moody searchers staring at them, Gerry in particular sitting rigid, fixated, convinced. Mickey whispered something into Francie's ear, no doubt suggesting quick egress, but Francie stayed and seemed to be savouring the tension like oxygen, he smiled, almost enjoying himself. Gerry closed his eyes but spoke out loud to his companions, and loud enough for everyone in the lounge to hear.

> – Funny how things have all gone to shit recently, isn't it boys? All this trouble that has been cropping up. All these different ops getting ruined. People being arrested. Stashes found. Dumps discovered. Volunteers getting lifted or shot on the job. Funny how it all seems to have kicked off at the same time, isn't it? When certain cunts started moving up in the world, suddenly with their noses everywhere. Funny isn't it boys? Hilarious really. I mean, when you think about it.

Gerry opened his eyes and stared at Francie. For his part, Our Francie said nothing but was not, it was noted, afraid to return Gerry's gaze with interest. On the contrary they sat perhaps thirty feet apart glaring at each other. But when Francie and Mickey finished their drinks it was undoubtedly a good and wise thing that they didn't get up to order any more, but rather took their leave relatively quickly. Not in any obvious haste it must be said, but neither did they draw it out unnecessarily, to linger or chat or chew the cud. They might have nodded at one or two of us where we sat hogging the bar or chatting at the low seats by the side-door nook, but nobody bid them off and they went of their own accord in silence.

29

BETTY MCGUIRKE SAW him first. She was coming out of Boyle's shop with her arms full and the car running, double-parked, a line of traffic beeping at her. It was, she said later, as if he had materialized out of nowhere, like a spotless apparition, and here he was now walking right down the centre of Main Street, his arm in a sling and an oddity about his appearance in general, perhaps it was the immaculately clean athletic clothing, what was later determined to be the Linfield away strip, as white as England, with a large dried blood patch like a poppy over the loin area, hardened into a natural plaster of Paris stuck to his skin. Limping slightly and weighed down by a rucksack hanging heavy off the other shoulder, he kept to the middle of the road, in amongst the traffic, nodding and winking at everyone like the Pope returned on spec to Ireland but minus the mobile this time and the entourage of cardinals. All Betty did was stand rooted staring at him with her mouth open as the line of cars bollicked her out of it until they themselves saw the apparition and quietened too. Maurice McGrath's reaction was similar. He was coming out of Leahy's butchers twirling a bag of chops when he caught sight of him. Maurice said that the first detail he noticed was all the other heads turning, and suddenly the whole busy Saturday street was frozen on the spot with people dead-eyed, stunned, the hush seeming to spread among the cars themselves like a virus, their engines deadening to a hard stop entirely. Nobody uttered a syllable and the air was paralyzed like in the after-instants of an explosion, heavy with an atmosphere of the unknown, the anticipation that everything would be altered now. But Richie Lennon burst it. He shouted out some crudity and, with others following, the air turned to yelps of cheering, the car horns beeping like the day the Rangers won the Merrigan Cup. Richie ran on ahead, across the bridge and up Gullion's lower slope, bursting breathless into The Arms to report what he had seen, the sudden morning light nearly blinding the crowd of regulars who were in early for the build-up to the Charity Shield. People were still deciphering what Richie was trying to tell them when the apparition itself appeared at his back. The crowd of congregants following him were now believers all right, convinced and many deep, and when the harsh light eased somewhat there was the astonishing sight of him for everyone in the dark pub to behold, Handy, grinning back at us in something like splendour.

– Pint please Pat, he said, his voice familiar as a horror story, vivid, somewhat hoarse, surprisingly bright.

Naturally the place erupted and people went in waves to greet him, intent on carrying him aloft, Our Hero, over to the lounge area. But he shouted at us to hold back the fuck and mind the slung arm for Christ sake and the injured side for Christ sake and this people did while noting at the same time the hospital smell off him as we got close and the guttees caked with thick muck. He was given a cordon of space and escorted over to the back settee. When someone tried to relieve him of the rucksack he hissed them away with sudden anger. O that was our Handy back all right. A pint of Fürstenberg was put in front of him and he looked at it for a melancholy beat before near knocking it back in one, the rucksack snug in between his feet. Another pint was produced and he drank half of that too. Jesus that's good, he said, licking the froth from his upper lip. He took another drink. Jesus that's good, he said again and then again. Nobody had ever seen him in such a state of childlike benevolence, the spirits high and giddy, everyone in the room beaming back at him sitting in rings around him expectant for his tale, but even Handy had his limits and he remained stuck in that high jittery state, looking at the faces crowding in around him, practically pinching himself to verify that it was all real, still reeling as he was from whatever run of things he had lately endured, shivering with the sheer relief of things, but in a fair and appreciable degree of physical discomfort at the same time.

It wasn't long before word was got to Gerry and his crew and they burst in to see this welcome sight for themselves. The older brother was immediately less concerned with the arm and the torn side and the general physical well-being of his younger brother than with wanting to know who did this Our'Fella, who was the tout son, don't worry we'll get him for you son, don't you worry about that Our'Fella, we'll get him so we will, which soon switched to questions and more questions being rapidly put to him about the story with the sling and what's with this Linfield gear you're wearing kiddo and a general attempt to delineate the passage of events within the time span of these past number of days. Regarding the failed op, Handy was only partially aware of any detail. All had been going swimmingly until it wasn't, he said, and then it was a shit-show. It was confirmed for him what he had suspected but did not know for certain until now, that no one else had got away, though Handy didn't seem too bothered by the thought of Bernard Brady dead, Kaja and the others caught and looking at a long spell inside. If anything, it prompted a joke.

– Fucking Bernard stuttered at the counter asking for the money. I swear to God. He couldn't get the words out, can you believe that crack? Well, I guess The Brits cured him of that so they did. He'll not be stuttering no more that's for sure!

Handy laughed, and drank, but then became ruminative.

– But seriously. We might have stood a chance otherwise. It delayed everything, probably gave someone a chance to call it in. . . . Bloody Bernard, it was all his fault so it was.

Gerry stared at him, not quite understanding. He had so many questions buzzing in his brain he found it hard to speak. Handy, in front of him, couldn't sit still, fidgeting, taking up his pint and putting it down again, he opened his cigarette lighter and flicked it on and off, laughed for no reason. It was a pure miracle he had got away. By rights he should still be back there in a pool of blood. It was all Bernard's fault. Everything was going great and then he fucked it all up. Standing at the counter with them all looking at him. They would have had plenty of time to call it in. Plenty of time. It was all Bernard's fault. He was lucky as fuck to get away. Being last out of the bank he'd tripped and fallen on the ground. The luckiest trip in history. He heard the hail of fire descend up ahead and managed to hold back, rolling under the wheels of a parked van then slipping away when the firing finished and the police came around the front immediately focusing on Bernard. It seemed like they were only interested in him. With the coast clear he managed to crawl away on his belly, then melted off, walking as fast as he could before running at full tilt. Two blocks away he nabbed a car.

– Someone must have tipped them off when we were inside. It was obvious so it was. They were there waiting for us when we came out. Bored out of their minds they must have been with the waiting.

The room murmured its agreement, and Gerry sat back considering things, weighing them, not saying a whole pile except to interject now and then looking for the odd clarification. Over the next while Handy let out his complete story in dribs and drabs like it was a lame foal scared of the light, stumbling around in front of the rapt crowd, clumsy and uncertain on its pegs. Gerry poking and prodding it, encouraging it, needling it. Handy confirmed what had been reported on the news, the pair of carjackings followed by the ditching of the second one at Bloody Bridge before his attempt at disappearing into the heart of the Mournes. It was harder than he would have thought, he said, especially humping this big bag of his and mostly having to confine his movements to the hours of darkness, bat blind, in the direction of Donard, the bare hills all the while swarming with yellow vests, torchlight and those German Shepherd cunts of dogs who more than once seemed to pick up on his scent, only to lose it in the wind or be ignored completely by their thankfully thick-as-fuck police minders who you could see spread out over the mountain, chatting and smoking and not bothering their holes searching for him half the time, their voices carrying across the range as they had the craic with each other and the air ringing out with the barks and whistles and the pure and elemental trappings of a bona fide man-hunt. Eventually he came across The Wall and finding nooks of loose stonework in it managed to hide by day in the substance of it. Surprisingly warm enough he found it, actually, he'd recommend it so he would. The Brits never knew how close they got to him on a few occasions, just a matter of feet away from him, smoking and chatting the stupid cunts. At night he followed along the length of The Wall by touch and moonlight till he met one of the Upper Bann streams and traced it downward to the vicinity of Hilltown. From there he ventured cautiously within sight of the main road. He slept in a hedgerow in a back garden and then one night in a house he broke into but, before anyone asked, no, there was no phone, the house had been in a state of disuse this number of years and had no working electricity either and for a day or maybe even two time seemed to lose track of itself. He thought he might bleed out from his wound which was now completely infected, he could barely move his limp and oozing arm, the sheer agony that had set in on it ebbing only as the arm slowly seemed to wither and die, and he was almost reconciled to the loss of it entirely but for a late and frantic burst of desperate energy that had him up and out, venturing the chance of obtaining proper medical assistance. It was then that he abandoned all caution and simply walked brazen across the heartland till he reached Daisy Hill. Within sight of its neon signage he had the spark of guile to swipe the Linfield get-up from a clothes line before heading in some state through the casualty door.

– What did you tell them? Gerry asked.

– The truth.

The two brothers stared at each other. Handy started grinning.

– That youse are nothing but a pack of savage cunts.

Even Gerry had to laugh at that.

– That youse would set upon some poor young fool of a lad whose only crime in life was to be a Linfield supporter and him a Catholic, all because he happened to have the grá for that Prod team on account of a dead uncle of his who may have played for them at one time in the far-off distant past. That such a thing was a crime in certain places around these parts. That it was enough to make a lad excluded like he bore the mark of Cain, making him the subject of many threats and various forms of bullying and savage physical beatings down the years. That one night a gang of youse republican bastards took this young lad out the back of the estate for the craic with the intention of shooting him in the kneecaps. But that the gun went off premature and youse dropped him like a hot stone and ran off away with youse like the cowards and cunts youse are.

– Credible, murmured the room.

– Was there no police questioning?

– With luck I had apparently just missed the one detective there for another matter and they put in a call for him to return the next morning, as in today, to take my statement. So I scarpered from the recovery area when they weren't looking. I've been on the road since.

Went across the fields till I hit the other side of Gullion and here I am.

Gerry was silent, weighing it all up, what may or may not have been gospel. The shoulders relaxed then and leaning forward he said well you're home now Our'Fella that's the main thing, you're home now so you are, and the cheers behind him from the rest of the room confirmed loudly what everyone knew in their bones to be true, that it was going to be a good night.

Nailer came in not long after, leaving the Land Rover double-parked out front. He was wearing his new white Reeboks, as bright as headlamps, advised by the foot doctor. People knew to get out of his way, noting the look of thunder on his face, and when Handy saw him he stopped laughing, following Nailer's approach with plain anxiety as the old man went to that corner of the red lounge only to stop well short of Handy, standing instead on the far side of the couch, his presence silencing the corner if not the entire pub. He didn't say anything for what seemed like an age but simply stood there staring at Handy, who struggled to his feet. Reaching down for the rucksack at his feet he came around the small table and leant over the couch, presenting the bag to Nailer.

– It might not have gone to plan exactly boss man but I was able to salvage this much.

Nailer kept staring at Handy for a moment more before accepting the rucksack from him and resting it on the back of the couch to open it. Anyone in the vicinity could see straight away that it was full of money, gorgeous clean bills, tightly packed and rubber-banded. Nailer stared down at the money for a minute, his face practically lit up by the glare off it, before closing the zip and giving the bag to Jarlath, who was standing beside him. He came around the couch then to confront Handy and everyone watched with their hearts in their mouths. He stared at Handy for a long moment before grabbing hold of him and squeezing him into his chest, swaying slightly like he was dancing him. You are, Nailer said to Handy, nothing short of miraculous, and he even kissed him on both cheeks to much laughter and cheering. Pat Behind The Bar brought over a pot of tea but Nailer told him to take it right back where he came from and bring over a bottle of Redbreast instead. We're celebrating, Patrick, he said, and mourning as well, celebrating and mourning, so we need the good stuff. They took over the corner sofa then, Nailer reaching over and grabbing Handy once more, getting him into a headlock, running his knuckles over his scalp. Pat brought the whiskey and Nailer poured himself a generous measure. He held up his glass and waited for silence.

– To Bernard.

Everyone in the pub held up what they were drinking. To Bernard!

It took a minute for the hubbub to rise again. The Arms was packed, whoever had come in to see what the fuss was about had decided to stay. Nailer, eyes closed, savoured his drink.

– It was by the sounds of things an unmerciful hail of bullets.

– It was lashing them down Nailer so it was.

Nailer shook his head.

– A pure miracle is what it is.

– Pure slaughter anyhow. Lucky for me they were focused on the front. On Bernard in particular

– Ah Bernard.

– Ah Bernard my hole. As I was telling the boys it was his stammering that fucked us. Caused an awful delay so it did before they even knew they were being robbed. They'd practically the whole morning then to call the cops. We'd no chance. Kaj and the boys bore the brunt of it. You couldn't even hear their screams. Kaj collapsed right in front of me. Not a peep out of him. I thought he was dead. It was like a switch being flicked off. Thank fuck I fell over him. That's what saved me I reckon.

– But you got away.

– I did.

– A wonder that the cunts knew about it. We should go through the list, of who and all was privy to the details, the date and time of the thing in particular. Though we could probably list them here between us.

Both Handy and Gerry looked at each other. Gerry sat forward a bit.

– None of any of that'll be necessary Nailer. It's as clear as day who's to blame for this shitshow.

– Go on.

– That creature you tolerate out at your complex. Everything points in his direction. Lurking outside your window, listening to everything. He must have accumulated some state of knowledge these past number of months. Our'Fella tells me he was there when the dates and times were being finalized, lurking in the shadows, pretending to be working, hanging around by the open window.

– Sure you only have to look at the family, said Handy. What they'd done down the years. Touts the whole pile of them, right through. Not to mention that bitch of a sister of his and the lies she's been spreading about me.

– Aye, said Gerry. Dragging our family name into the muck at every opportunity.

Nailer said nothing.

– You have to give us this Nailer, said Gerry. For blood and the family name.

– For Bernard and the boys, said Handy.

Nailer focused on his glass, the play of light off the amber surface, the streak of dark in it. He didn't say anything. Those around him were listening, curious as to how he would play things, what he was going to say next.

– The problem you boys have, you see, is that we're under fierce scrutiny at the moment. The whole thing's out of my hands so it is. I've been told that in no uncertain terms. A single firearm gets discharged and we'll be cut off. . . . No, I'm serious Gerry! One bullet and they'll turn off the spout. Maybe even worse than that. Better to lie low fellas, would be my advice. We can despise those political fucks all we want but, again, and I cannot stress this enough, they do control everything, the dumps, the cash flow, everything.

One might have imagined Gerry flying into a rage but he broke instead into a wide and manic grin.

– Do you hear that Our'Fella? As the man here says, it's out of his hands.

Searching into his pockets he produced a screwdriver and put it on the table.

– And don't you worry about a thing Nailer we'll not fire a single shot so we won't, don't you worry about that! I can guarantee you now that there'll not be a single bullet shot fired.

He laughed again, as did Handy. It was the first bit of mirth anyone had heard from Gerry in years. Him and Handy grinned at each other and Nailer took up his whiskey. He may or may not have been inclined to argue the point but it was clear that the weight of argument lay on the side of blood and it would have been difficult not to conclude that a decision of some sort had been made. Nailer's silence was the wide-open space on the other side of his words and, in the face of this demand, acceptance had seeped into it and taken root.

30

A group gathered in the car park of The Arms, bantering like away supporters heading to the match. Maurice Garvey had a lock of baseball bats in the boot of his car, and the mood changed as he doled them out, still stained from the last time. Gerry in particular was lit, a second wind to him. This hadn't been his life for years and he was now in his element, his clothes patch damp with sweat, the thinning head of hair on him greased back, the white of his scalp visible. He was the man in command all right, Nailer's tacit blessing having been bestowed as the older man climbed back into his Land Rover wanting nothing more to do with things. Gerry couldn't hide his delight or his impatience, rapping on Nailer's bonnet as the senile old cunt backed out and drove off, away off with you now, go on home to your complex and count your money you doddery fuck. Gerry turned then, all action to be sure, issuing clipped commands and orders to come on the fuck. Handy wasn't with the group. Gerry ordered him to stay behind and for Pat Behind The Bar to feed him hot food and keep a general eye on him. Handy complained but acceded quick enough. He was after all a wanted man. Not only the police but the UVF too were on his trail, their blood up, even more so than usual. The group piled into Maurice's car and a van belonging to Frank McQuillan's cousin, and both then headed out, going the long way around on the forest road in the direction of Silverbridge. No other vehicles were on the road and it was almost pleasant driving across the side of Gullion with the windows open and the wind whipping through the van, a grand late-summer breeze it was, the frequency of trees increasing as we descended to the other side until we were soon beneath their canopy and within range of the Murphy farmhouse which, pulling in, we sat and observed from a distance. There was not much sign of life in it. Both vehicles then drove on through the large rusted broken gates which whined in pain when two of the lads got out and lifted them apart, then up the long drive beneath the large sycamores and sessile oaks that were everywhere, like weeds. The van and car emptied and everyone walked up to the house, following Gerry across what seemed at first to be an unkempt yard, a pure wilderness, but on closer inspection had a definite pattern to it, some intent certainly, strewn wildflowers, a corner here of fuchsia, a crop of ponytails over there and around the side of the house a glimpse of vegetable plots, a herb garden in potted rows and tomato vines pressed up the sides of an enormous greenhouse. The more you looked the more you were likely to see that the land was perhaps loved after all, despite what you might have thought, it was thick with ordered growth, a dense cultivated matting of scrub and vegetation. In front, the thick wall of ivy swooned down over the frontal aspect of the farmhouse, encasing it like a fairy tale, an impressive sight all right, barely any of the old stonework visible. All remained dark and evidently uninhabited. Jarlath went around the back while the rest of us went to the front door and knocked loudly on it. There was no answer and after giving it a minute someone broke the glass and reached in and unlocked it. It was obvious the minute we set foot in the hallway that the house was empty. At least the lights worked when someone flicked the switch on, and we went into the living room first and then the kitchen off it. The place was in immaculate condition, with no sign of the rumoured decay, the rot and damp matter of neglect, the stench of human effluent and waste that we were expecting. Pride of place on the kitchen table went to a large family photograph, framed and full of smiles all round, purposefully placed, as if staged with an eye to our arrival. In it there was a mother, in what would have been her prime, a bit of a looker actually. A long-dead father, not as stern perhaps as in our recollections he had a tendency to act and, as suggested here with the hint of a grin, some mischief hidden in it. And a young boy looking back at the world like any normal camera-shy twelve-year-old would. In addition, in the centre, staring right out at us was a young girl, wise beyond her years, wearing thick glasses, her hair up, delighted with her current situation, whatever and wherever it was. We looked at the photograph and couldn't help but notice that everyone in it was smiling back at us, specifically us and us alone, as if they had been expecting our visit to them once again after all these years and, after an eternity, finally we had come.

Nobody wanted to stay long in the house. The energy people had had not long ago was completely dissipated and most of us just wanted to get back to The Arms. As we were walking to the van Jarlath tossed something to Gerry. It was a child's toy that he had found when searching around upstairs, some sort of stuffed animal, dressed up in the colour blue.

– Congratulations Uncle Gerry! Looks like it's going to be a boy.

Gerry didn't react, nor did he make any attempt to catch the toy, allowing it to bounce off him and fall face down into a puddle. We carried on walking back to the car and the van.

31

HANDY WAS OUT in the beer garden when Francie came into the pub. The place was a mess, it had mostly emptied by this stage but the tables were still covered in empty pint glasses, with some broken on the floor. Pat Behind The Bar was over in the far corner, in bad form, sweeping. He barely acknowledged Francie, who stood and looked around a bit before heading towards the back of the pub and then out to check the beer garden. That's where he found Handy, sitting over by the fence smoking a cigarette. Handy stood up and called out to Francie in greeting before Francie even saw him, camouflaged as the younger man was by some of the greenery. There was nobody else in the small yard area. Francie, saying nothing, went over and stood across the table from Handy, who sat back down in his seat with a big grin on his face.

– Well look who it is. The big bollox himself. You missed all the excitement there Francie.

Francie looked around him.

– So it would appear.

– Here, sit, have a drink with me.

Handy poured half his own pint into an empty glass and placed it in front of Francie. He tried then to light up a cigarette, but it was awkward, Handy's arm seemed rightly hurt this time, covered in thick bandaging, and it slipped out of the light sling as he struggled with the lighter, giving Francie a chance to look at the rest of him, the bloodstained football top, the tracksuit bottoms stained with mud about the lower end. Handy seemed jittery, his fingers shaking and clumsy, still struggling with the lighter, puffing on the cigarette as if it was a cigar, trying to get it going.

– Out on the job, were you Francie?

– Not on this occasion. I had to drop some people off at the airport.

Francie looked firmly at Handy, who seemed to be barely listening to him. At least the lad had finally got his cigarette lit.

– The boys will be back soon, Handy said.

He sat forward and blew out some smoke as he broke into a smile.

– We have the tout Francie. Turns out it was that Murphy freak all along.

– Is that so?

– The boys have headed out to Silverbridge to grab him. Maybe put manners on the whole family while they're at it. I tried my part so I did.

– Well they'll not find them, said Francie. Sure they

must be halfway to Australia by now. Unless of course the young one decides to give birth to your offspring on the plane.

Handy seemed to enjoy that joke.

– You've done me a favour there then, in fairness. Saves me forking out for the ferry to Liverpool. You must be getting soft in your old age Francie. Just like Nailer.

Francie didn't say anything for a while and then patted his own pockets.

– Here, can I borrow one of those?

He caught the packet of cigarettes and then the lighter that Handy threw at him. He lit a cigarette and took a few drags of it, looking at the younger man the whole time.

– The only one to get away again Handy. What are the odds?

Handy gave a little laugh.

– Let me guess, said Francie. I bet you were wearing something distinctive.

Handy laughed some more. He seemed to think about things for a second but then couldn't resist it and, reaching down on to the bench beside him, he took up a bright orange baseball cap and put it on.

– Well, we were in the heartland after all, you know.

He took the cap off and put it on the table facing Francie.

– But I see the arm's properly injured this time though. Not like that Warrenpoint charade. You'll have to give out to your handler Handy. Orange cap or no orange cap, that was downright careless of them so it was. They could have killed one of their prime assets right there.

– Francie, Francie, Francie, Handy said. I see you're still barking up the wrong tree. You're lucky I have a thick skin so you are.

– Tell me. Is it The Branch or MI5? Or are you military intelligence? I hear the whole thing has become very territorial these days. The word is they can't get out of each other's way.

Handy shook his head but was still smiling, enjoying the chat. He took another pull from his cigarette and was about to say something but stopped and looked beyond Francie over to the door that led into the lounge. It was perhaps the confused look on his face that caused Francie to turn around quickly. The Widow Donnelly was standing there. She was holding a shotgun and had it aimed at Handy. Francie stood up. He was almost as surprised as Handy to see The Widow. She was supposed to be lying low in Kells with her sister.

– Jesus Christ Marie, Francie said to her. Put it down will you, it's all in hand so it is.

The Widow was shaking. She took a few steps forward, the barrel of the gun all over the place. She was gripping it too tightly.

– I tried Francie. I tried so I did. But I knew he'd get away. Cockroaches and rats don't die. And sure enough, right on cue, doesn't he come parading down Main Street like the Pope? As soon as I heard the news I hopped in my sister's car. Called in to get this first which I'm not afraid to use. I had to come Francie, I couldn't hack it. There's no peace with him still breathing. No peace, only oblivion. My Darren would be alive only for him.

Francie took a step towards her.

– Put it down Marie. I told you. He'll be court-martialled so he will. I'll speak directly to the army council myself. You have my word on it.

– I'm sorry Francie.

There was a brief stand-off but then Handy made a sudden movement, either towards the gun or ducking off to the side, he may not have known himself. In response Francie also made a movement, taking a step towards the noise, which was deafening. When The Widow opened her eyes there was some smoke and it seemed to be coming from the old shotgun. Everything was quiet except for her ears, which were ringing so much they allowed in no other sound, causing only an intense pain at the side of her head. The scene in front of her didn't make any sense. There was the recognizable figure of Francie, but there was something not right about him, the way he was orientated, a clump was missing out of the side of his neck and he was bent over, but comically so, strangely erect in the legs, the top half of his body collapsed over on to the table. A steady trickle of blood was falling between the slats and The

Widow stared at it trying to work out where it was coming from and to somehow put it together with the sound that she was now able to hear, which was louder than it should have been, louder than anything, this red liquid hitting the ground with surprising vigour as if Francie had knocked over his drink, spilling it, and the drink kept spilling, the red liquid coming seemingly out of nowhere. In addition to all this there was now another sound, a horrible screeching, like a crow cawing, fighting, taunting her, full of hate, only it was none of these things but rather laughter.

– You mad bitch you mad bitch you shot him you fucking shot him!

Handy was standing behind The Widow now. Somehow he was holding the gun and pointing it at her. Though she understood the words he was saying none of it made any sense. He was mouthing them at her but the words seemed to be elsewhere, disconnected. She didn't want to be listening to him. When she looked off to the side the evening sun was in her eyes and it felt glorious on her skin, the way it blinded her, enhanced by her numb and ringing ears. But the crow was still cawing at her and she turned towards it. Maybe it was something worth doing, to try and understand the words. She registered once more the gun pointed at her. Strange, it looked like a boy's toy. She recognized it as her Jim's. Probably hadn't been used in twenty years. Jim used it for rabbits. The odd pheasant too. Her shoulder was aching and she was able to suppose that it must have been from firing the gun. But why was Handy Byrne holding it? There was a sneer on his face, no not a sneer, that's just the way he looks, the way he laughs. But he'd stopped now with his crowing and was looking at The Widow, his eyes flickering over to where Francie was bent over on the table. The pour of blood had lessened to a trickle and somehow she knew both of them were listening to it. Handy Byrne was saying something to her. He seemed to be saying many things and it took a while for the words to make sense to her.

– Do you want to know the truth, do you?

She looked at him and he said it again. *Do you want to know the truth, do you?* Then again and again and again and it took her a while for the thought to form that yes, yes she did want to know it. She did want to know the truth. She was desperate to know it in fact, but she didn't say anything and once more she was aware of the strong light and she turned towards it, opening her eyes so that it would absolutely blind her. She could sense the gun being raised at her and was possibly even aware that the door to the lounge had opened and Pat Behind The Bar was standing there looking at her as well. She was aware of all this but didn't care. It was the light she wanted to focus on as she waited for the loud noise that was going to come and after that, at long last, oblivion.

The noise never came. Handy lowered the gun.

– I'm going to let you go you mad wench. Go home and lie on your son's bed.

He was laughing now, as he poked Francie's body with the butt of the gun. The Widow watched him, everything going slow as if it was a dream. Go home and lie on your son's bed. No. She pictured a small box room and she was being pushed into it, there were posters on the wall, a red bedspread with the words Liverpool F.C. She stared again at the sun in the sky. No, not the box room, anything other than that. But Handy was already on the other side of her, the shotgun bent and limp, looking in fascination at the slumped Francie. He laughed again.

– You've done me a favour there so you have. As a reward you can go home now. Go home and lie on your son's bed.

He turned and was smiling at her.

– Lie on his bed and think of me.

Pat Behind The Bar was beside her shouting at her, screaming as loud as he could into her face, some language she couldn't make sense of. Maybe he'd been standing there shouting at her for a while but she was only now hearing him. His grip on her arm was painfully tight, all bone and claw. He opened the gate in the fence. The Widow wanted to cry out but there were still no words out of her and the strong light was already ebbing away as she felt Pat's grip on her arm as he pulled her away from it, kicking and punching at her. All she could say was No, No, No as he pulled her out of the light and, shouting at her, he changed his grip to pull her and then push her out the gate and there was another kick and a punch to her head until with effort he had shunted her out on to the laneway on the other side where she flew to fall face down on the ground.

32

NAILER WAS OUT in the field when the car pulled up to the farm. He knew already that it was the politician but Christ why did the man always have to be early? People couldn't stick to the simplest of arrangements. Nailer turned back to contemplate the dregs of the evening, this fine view he had and it another glorious autumn evening. Like summer it was, an Indian one with an orange sky on one side, the lights only now coming on around the bay. To his left, volcanic black as ever against the still-light sky, the sulking loin of Gullion. Truthfully he wasn't in the mood for this fella. He rarely was, but especially not now. It seemed that every time he turned on the radio over the past few days the politician was on it spouting on and on about the recent tragedy in Cross, this murder that had happened in broad daylight that was for some inexplicable reason all over the news and which reporters were constantly questioning M.O.C. about, they simply would not let the matter drop. But he'd say this much, the politician was well able for them so he was. Yes, indeed it was a tragedy, the politician told the reporters, and that was the exact right word for it, whatever was going on in this poor grief-demented woman's mind, because let's not forget, before people rush to cast blame and judgement on her, she is a victim in all this too and though she will rightly have to pay the full price of the law, she will at the same time hopefully get the full gamut of psychiatric help available to her because by God the woman clearly needs it. And an awful case of mistaken identity it was as well, he said, if ever there was one, or such was his own personal belief despite all of these desperate allusions and vicious rumours and terrible innuendo that some of you so-called journalists have been trying to cast upon the whole thing in recent days, whatever or whoever put it into the woman's mind that it was Francis Begley of all people who was in any way responsible for her son's disappearance and death, if in fact the young man *was* dead because even that was not one hundred per cent clear. Well, M.O.C. told the reporters, he wanted to clear up the record right here and right now about Francie Begley and address all of these scurrilous rumours head-on. In his opinion they were so off the mark it was laughable so it was. The fact is he did indeed know Francie Begley, just like the reporters and his political opponents keep saying, as if it was some big dirty secret. Well it was not in any way a secret because it was one hundred per cent true. And he would say this much. Not only did he know Francie but he knew him well, very well in fact, and he would have counted him as a friend even, maybe not a close friend but definitely a friend and someone he had known for years before that by reputation alone. He was no angel, was Our Francie, that much was also true, but linking him to the drugs trade up in Dublin and that notorious gang operating out of Coolock in particular, and implying or saying outright that he was in any way responsible for the young Donnelly lad's disappearance, was well wide of the mark so it was. Or so M.O.C. reckoned anyway. Such was his own personal belief based on his knowledge of the man. Because that was not the Francie Begley that M.O.C. knew, no sirree. And he'd like to say it loud and clear, so he would, that a more decent man you simply would not come across than the likes of Our Francie. Our Francie was a community man, he said. First and foremost, pure and simple. Not from Cross originally, but sure he was one of these characters that goes to a place and takes to it like a duck to water. Everyone knew Francie and Francie knew everyone. He was at the centre of everything and he knew everything. He'd know what time the cows would be finished with their breakfast in the morning and when the corner boys were getting antsy and looking to cause mischief. He'd know rightly if you were in a spot of bother. Sure you wouldn't even have to ask him for help so you wouldn't but the man would appear right out of the blue and be standing at your front door looking to lend a helping hand. First thing in the morning or in the middle of the night, it didn't make any difference, you could expect the knock from Francie. That was the sort of chap Francie was. It was absolutely uncanny so it was. Sure he'd know you were in bother before you would even know it yourself, practically speaking, and he'd be there right away so he would, to get stuck in and involved, to lend a helping hand and deal with the situation to the best of his ability. That was Our Francie down to a tee whatever about all this other nonsense people are saying about him now. Drugs? Criminality? No, M.O.C. didn't believe one iota of it, despite all these rumours. And if there was any truth to them, well, he'd be shocked to his bones so he would, shocked to his bones. Francie knows. That's we used to say about the man, Francie knows. And a man with knowledge is a beautiful thing in this world.

No, Nailer couldn't listen to it any more, he was sick and tired of it. M.O.C. and his little games, it was simply exhausting so it was, therefore he was quick to turn off the radio the minute M.O.C.'s voice started coming out of it. Out into the fields he went then to spend the better part of this heavenly evening there. He was just up now from throwing a bit of feed into the pigs, and after that from taking a slow walk around the perimeter looking up at the sheer operatic drama that was playing out in the sky. Christ, it would nearly put religion into you so it would, hope certainly, whatever might be in store for us all. This is where he was standing, bucket in hand, when he heard the car pull up on the other side of the house, a good twenty-five minutes earlier than the agreed-upon hour. He let the couple of minutes pass and sure enough the back porch door whined open and, he knew without looking, out came Handy Byrne, arm still in the sling and accompanied as always by The Young Goss, stepping on to the backyard. The gravel crunch was getting closer and closer before coming to a stop. He took a deep breath and let it out before speaking.

– Our political friend?

There was a delay, and some laughter from The Young Goss, before Handy answered.

– The one and only.

Irritated, Nailer turned and walked past them without saying another word. He went around the side of the farmhouse and stamped his feet loudly on the mat to kick the muck off his wellingtons. God knows what the politician wanted now. There was always something with him, absolutely no end to his demands. Didn't he get everything he wanted the last time? And doesn't he always get what he wants, that fella? No matter how he goes about it and what the price might be. Just ask Bernard Brady. They don't make them like that any more, that's for sure. Poor Bernard. Needs must that your luck runs out sooner or later in this game though. Which reminded him, he must get the mason to put Bernard's name on the monument in The Square. Up near the top of it too, if there was any room left. When things died down he might even organize a bit of a do. Maybe get one of the local scribes to come up with something as well. And why wouldn't he? Wasn't this neck of the woods supposedly the home of Ireland's first great poets, Art McCooey and those lads, so wasn't it the least he could do for Bernard and his family? Voices came from the other side of the house, among them the politician's loud Donegal patter as he greeted Jarlath, seemingly in great form altogether, and then no doubt walked straight past Jarlath, unbidden. You could say it again all right. There was simply no end to the man's demands, and in many ways this was just the start of it, with more elections apparently around the corner, and all these new talks and negotiations that were happening. He'd certainly be wanting something, this politician, that's for sure, there was no rest and no end to it. Nailer sat down on the step as he took off his boots, taking a minute to look back at the lights over Forkhill and beyond, to Carlingford, and in the foreground, just before the hill crested and dived downwards, the dark shoulder of Gullion. Silhouetted against the light and open sky were the two boys, The Young Goss, who was jumping around like a ginnet, and Handy Byrne just looking at him, cigarette lit and in his mouth, throwing bits of dirt and stone into The Young Goss's face and eyes, trying to hurt him for real, his efforts becoming more vicious, hidden by the other's laughter, Handy staring at him, an angry sneer on him and getting angrier. When Nailer stood he could see M.O.C. through the glass after being brought into the kitchen by Jarlath and settling himself at the table, making himself at home. He took a deep breath and went inside. No there was no end to this thing. No end to it at all.

Acknowledgements

I want to thank the following people: my editor Bella Lacey, and everyone at Granta; Mandy Woods; Faith O'Grady; Lisa Bellamy, Peter Krass and Cynthia Weiner of The Writers Studio in New York for setting me on the road; and much earlier than this, Sydney Peck. I would like to thank my parents – Vincent and Pauline Duffy – for everything, and my sister and brother, Eleanor Ward and Garrett Duffy, for all their support; and lastly Naomi Taitz Duffy, my first reader, as well as Theo and Vered.

About the Author

AUSTIN DUFFY'S debut novel *This Living and Immortal Thing* was shortlisted for the Kerry Group Irish Novel of the Year and was runner-up for the McKitterick Prize. He is also the author of *Ten Days*, which was shortlisted for the Diverse Awards, and *The Night Interns*, which was an *Irish Times* bestseller. He is a practising medical oncologist and lives in Ireland with his wife and two children.